After You've Gone

After You've Gone

LORI HAHNEL

thistledown press

Thistledown Press Ltd.
410, 2nd Avenue North
Saskatoon, Saskatchewan, S7K 2C3
www.thistledownpress.com

Library and Archives Canada Cataloguing in Publication
Hahnel, Lori, author
After you've gone / Lori Hahnel.
Issued in print and electronic formats.
ISBN 978-1-927068-90-8 (pbk.).–ISBN 978-1-77187-012-2 (html).–
ISBN 978-1-77187-013-9 (pdf)
I. Title.
PS8615.A365A64 2014   C813.6   C2014-905345-2
C2014-905346-0

Cover and book design by Jackie Forrie
Printed and bound in Canada

Quote from "What'll I Do?" by Irving Berlin, copyright 1923 (public domain).

Quote from BOMP! Saving the World One Record at a Time. Pasadena: AMMO
Books, 2007 by Suzy Shaw and Mick Farren. Used with permission from Suzy
Shaw.

 Canada Council
for the Arts
Conseil des Arts
du Canada
 SASKATCHEWAN
ARTS BOARD
 Canadian
Heritage
Patrimoine
canadien

Thistledown Press gratefully acknowledges the financial assistance of the Canada Council for the Arts, the Saskatchewan Arts Board, and the Government
of Canada through the Canada Book Fund for its publishing program.

Acknowledgments

My sincere thanks to Diane Girard for her thoughtful feedback on this book almost since its inception, and for general support and friendship. Much gratitude to Michael Kenyon for your wise guidance and for your poetic ear. Big thanks to Suzy Shaw at BOMP Records for your generosity. I am grateful to the reference staff at Regina Public Library, especially Sharon Maier in the Prairie History Room, for assistance in helping me discover the Regina of the 1930s and beyond. Thank you to Skip Taylor for his insights on the Regina old school punk scene. To Rea Tarvydas and Jan Markley, thank you for being there. Finally, my love and thanks always to Bruce, Nick and Dan.

I am also indebted to the authors of the following books, which provided me with a wealth of invaluable detail:

Blecha, Peter. *Music in Washington: Seattle and Beyond.* Chicago: Arcadia Publishing, 2007.

Blecha, Peter. *Sonic Boom: The History of Northwest Rock.* Milwaukee: Backbeat Books, 2009.

Dregni, Michael. *Gypsy Jazz: In Search of Django Reinhardt and the Soul of Gypsy Swing.* New York: Oxford University Press, 2008.

Mitchell, Ken. *The Jazz Province: The Story of Jazz in Saskatchewan. Regina:* Regina Jazz Society, 2005.

Shaw, Suzy and Farren, Mick. *BOMP! Saving the World One Record at a Time.* Pasadena: AMMO Books, 2007.

Waiser, Bill. *All Hell Can't Stop Us: The On-to-Ottawa Trek and Regina Riot.* Markham, ON: Fitzhenry and Whiteside, 2002.

To Nick and Dan
and Django Reinhardt

Part One

One

Seattle, Washington
June 12, 2007

Mark and I sit side by side on the packed bleachers in Seattle Center's Key Arena on a dark, rainy Sunday morning. Looks like this is a sold-out show. I've been to lots of shows at Seattle Center before — Nirvana, Pearl Jam, Mudhoney, The Pretenders, Iggy Pop, Bob Dylan a couple of times — but not usually this early in the day. Then again, this isn't a concert. This morning's show is Seattle University's commencement ceremony. Our son Bill will walk across the stage any minute now to get his parchment. He's on the floor talking to the pretty, dark-haired girl beside him. I can tell he's nervous, maybe has a little stage fright, by the way he strokes his sandy beard, and the way two little patches of red stand out on his cheeks just like when he was little. I guess it's a very emotional thing for all of us, maybe more for Mark and me than for him, since neither of us ever went to university. And even though we came to the ceremony when he finished his bachelor's, and we maybe should be getting used to this kind of thing, it still amazes me.

I know what the stage fright thing is like: I've been on stage lots of times, and so has Mark. Bill's dad, I mean. It's only been in the last little while I've started calling him 'Bill's dad'. When I meet people who don't know him and just call him 'Mark' they don't know who I'm talking about. But, yeah, neither of us went to university. I just barely made it out of high school. And now here's Bill, getting his master's degree in Mechanical Engineering. Don't know where he got those genes from. It certainly wasn't from either of us. Of course, Mom taught math and Dad was an accountant, so there's math genes there, but they skipped a generation. I got my genes from Grandma Lita and Grandpa Bill. It was always music right from the start with me. Maybe that's why it seems funny to be away from it now. Funny strange, not funny ha ha.

Something else I've been away from for a while is Mark. I haven't seen him in six months or so even though we both still live in Seattle. I don't think there was as much grey in his beard the last time I saw him. We've been in touch by phone, of course, and email; there's been a lot of back and forth over our other baby, Curse Records. But seeing him in person again I can't help but think he's aged since I moved out. I'm sure he's thinking the same thing about me. Or not. When you live with someone for twenty-five years or so you think you know them. To the extent that you think you know what they're thinking, even. But since we split up I've realized that's not true. When things start to go bad you realize how little you actually know the person. And you realize that Chrissie Hynde was right — it is a thin line between love and hate.

Finally, the Engineering students file up to get their scrolls. It's quite a show, I have to say; the bright multi-coloured hoods and tassels against the sober black gowns, the ceremony, and of course the music. A nice solo piano performance of Elgar's "Pomp and Circumstance," what else? Bill looks so handsome, so grown up. He's really got it together, that kid, in spite of his parents. I'll tell him later what I've told him before, how proud I am of him. But I don't know if I can ever really express to him just how proud of him I am. I hand Mark my camera; I'm too teary to be able to take a good picture.

"Elsa," Mark says. "Are you okay?"

I wipe under my eyes quickly with the back of my hand. "I'm fine. It's just a big moment."

He puts him arm around my shoulders for a moment. "I know."

Bill's so young and he's accomplished so much. And here I am, about to sell a record label that's been on the verge of bankruptcy since Mark and I started it in the mid-eighties. So much of it I've loved — all the people we worked with, the records we put out. But my own music got put on the back burner. Way on the back burner. Sometimes I feel like I've lost it completely. The thought of being in a band again scares me, at my age. In one way. In another way, I'd love to do it, if I had the time. And maybe soon I'll have the time.

After the ceremony's over, there's a reception in the lobby. Mark and I nibble on cheese and fruit while Bill makes his way through the crowd to us.

"Congratulations, sweetie!" As I put my arms around him, I notice the background music: Django Reinhardt's "Minor Swing". And funny, I can't help thinking as Mark claps Bill's back and shakes his hand and takes some pictures, that somehow we have three generations of the family present here, not just two. It's almost as if Grandma

Lita has joined us. I'll call her tomorrow and tell her how it all went today. She's almost as proud of Bill as I am.

Bill still shoots glances now and then, probably when she's not looking, at the girl he was talking to earlier. I was that age not long ago, wasn't I? Am I really old enough to have a son with a master's degree? Again, I think of Lita. If I feel bewildered about the passing of time, I wonder how she must feel. I will have to call her.

Maybe Sandy Denny and Fairport Convention said it best: "Who Knows Where the Time Goes?"

Two

Lita
Regina, Saskatchewan
June 1935

I PUT MY GUITAR CASE DOWN and fished the little square of newspaper out of my jacket pocket. The address was right — Dewdney Avenue, not far from the C.P.R. Yards. But the building was a corrugated steel Quonset, like the ones they use to store farm equipment and such, with long, dry, yellow prairie grass all around, not far from the tar-smelling tracks. Could the Syncopation Five be a professional outfit, I wondered, if they practised in such a grubby place? Darlene had assured me that they were really good the time she'd seen them at a dance. This didn't feel right. Still, things were tough all over. Maybe it wasn't easy to find a place to rehearse. And since I'd taken the streetcar all the way from downtown I figured I might as well knock, anyway. The grass crunched like straw under my feet as I walked up to the door.

The tall man who opened it had sandy hair, no part, slicked back from his forehead. He wore suspenders, had his sleeves rolled up, and a cigarette in a yellow celluloid holder was clamped between his teeth. He smiled a little when he saw me. "Yes?"

"I came to audition. It said two o'clock in the paper." I was nervous, had half-hoped there wouldn't be any answer when I knocked, so I could go home and tell Darlene it must have been a prank, or a misprint. She'd been all excited about it, more than me, almost. About noon she came down to my room.

"You're not going looking like that," she'd said. I had taken some time to select my outfit, actually thought I looked pretty good. Before I could answer, she took the situation in hand. She Marcel-waved my unruly black hair, fixed my make-up, even loaned me her new chevron-striped skirt. The skirt did more for Darlene than it did for me, though. The blue stripes brought out the blue in her eyes, and it fit her better. I felt like a fool, wondered if the man thought I looked like one.

"Yeah, two o'clock," he said. "But we ain't looking for a singer."

I was almost ready to crawl away then, but something made me stay. Maybe the thought of what Darlene would say if I left without even playing for them. "I'm not a singer. I'm a guitarist."

"Are you, now?" He seemed amused. "Well, c'mon in. What's your name?"

"Lita."

It took a minute for my eyes to adjust from the bright Sunday afternoon outside to the dim, smoke-blue Sunday afternoon inside. A dark guy sat behind a drum kit, a round-faced blond boy lurked in the corner behind his stand-up bass. A stooped man with thin hair tuned a fiddle.

"Look who's come to audition, fellas," said the tall guy with the cigarette holder. "Lita."

"Hey, Lita, where ya been all my life?" the guy behind the drums asked. The bass and the fiddle smirked.

"Aw, c'mon, now," the tall one said. "She came here for an audition, so we're going to give her one. Besides, no one else is here yet. I was starting to think that damn *Leader-Post* didn't run our ad. We might as well see what she can do while we're waiting. So, Lita, are you ready to jam?"

I took my guitar out of its case. It was a single resonator National steel guitar, prize of my life, which lived under my bed since I'd won it in a poker game a year before. I sat on an empty stool. "Sure. Can I tune to you?" I asked the bass player.

"Do you know 'Sweet Georgia Brown'?" the tall one asked.

"Sure."

As I suspected, he was the singer. Played ukulele, too. Not much, a bit of accent here and there. He was a pretty good singer, though. I noticed that.

It was kind of strange to play with them. I'd never played with anybody else before, not real live musicians. It was a little different than playing along with my records, all right. But fun.

The tall one put down his ukulele, looked at me and nodded. "Not bad, not bad. I'm Bill, by the way, Bill MacInnes. That's George Jeworsky on bass, Henry Onespot on drums and Otto Volk plays fiddle."

"Pleased to meet you."

"So, what else do you know?"

"I know lots of stuff. How about 'On the Sunny Side of the Street'?"

We played it and a few other numbers. By the end, the men no longer smirked and smiled to themselves, and I relaxed a bit.

Bill wanted to know how long I'd been playing. I lied and told him ten years. It was actually only a little over eight, but I played a lot. I had a lot of time on my hands.

"You hardly look old enough to have been playing that long. How old are you?"

"Eighteen," I said. I could see that he didn't believe me, so I added, "On my next birthday. In the spring."

"Hmmm. So, what's your full name? Eulita?"

"Yeah. Eulita Koudelka."

George smiled. "A Gypsy. Like Django Reinhardt, eh?"

"I love Django Reinhardt," I said. "I listen to his records all the time."

Bill looked at me from this side first, then the other, like he was buying a chair, or a picture, for his parlor. It made me nervous, more nervous. I felt in those days that I bore a fair resemblance to Olive Oyl from the funnies, with my skinny legs and long nose. I was sure he'd comment on it. But he said, "Could be a good angle. Gypsy gal guitarist."

I thought of my brother Steve, who'd changed his name to look for work. He needed something more white, he said. But being Stephen Knight instead of Stefan Koudelka hadn't helped him much. "I could change my name, if it's a problem."

"There's an easy way to do that, you know. But, no, keep it. I like it. Well, listen, Gypsy gal, how about you go on outside for a minute and let us talk this over? Like a smoke to take with you?"

I went outside a little reluctantly, not sure whether I should leave my guitar alone in there with them. I smoked the cigarette, careful to grind the butt out under my foot since the locust-hissing grass was tinder dry. After what seemed like a long time, I was about ready to go in and see whether they'd made off with my guitar in search of a pawnshop. Then Bill stuck his head out the door.

"We've decided to give you a try. We're playing a wedding two weeks from Saturday, at St. Vladimir's Church hall. Can you make it?"

"Sure, I guess so. What time?"

"We'll need to be there by 6:30 I don't know how late we'll be. Probably one in the morning or so anyway. We rehearse on Tuesday and Friday nights."

"Sure. That's fine."

On the way to the bus stop I listened to my shoes clomp on the wood-plank sidewalk, wondered what to tell Gus. Not that it really mattered, it wasn't like he needed a chambermaid that much at night. But I knew it would piss him off, anyway.

And it did. He sat behind the front desk when I returned, big bear of a man, reading his paper and munching on something, as usual. He hardly bothered to look up at first, but when I told him he squinted at me. "You did what? Joined a band? Did they even hear you play?"

Darlene was ironing sheets in the office. She came out and fussed with her blonde pincurls. Her philosophy was that you never knew who you might meet, so you'd better look your best at all times, even if you were ironing sheets. "Well, of course she played, Dad. She went to an audition. That's what you *do* at an audition."

Gus ignored her. "So what's this mean? You gonna quit your job? How much they paying you?"

I'd wondered about all those things, too, on the streetcar on the way there and then on the way back. Somehow, I never got around to asking those questions. I was too nervous. "I don't know," I said. "I mean, I don't know how much they're paying. I won't be quitting my job." *Not just yet.*

He waved a big paw at me, turned back to his paper. "That's good. 'Cause I don't know where I'd ever find another chambermaid good as you, Lita."

Cheap as me, he must have meant. Lincoln freed the slaves, I told him once. Yeah, but not in Canada, he said.

I had some trouble getting to sleep that night. The songs we'd played — that my band had played — ran through my head over and over. *My band.* I wondered what playing in front of an audience would be like. That morning I'd been a hotel chambermaid who played guitar. Now I was in a real band. Funny how your life can change just like that.

ff

Darlene was my friend, as much as anybody was my friend in those days. She was glad to have me around the hotel, that much I knew. I was glad to have her around, too. Mostly. Although she never seemed happier than when she was putting me down, usually in a backhanded way, never directly. She'd say something like, "That dress looks good on you, Lita. That one doesn't make your behind look so big." Or, "Your hair looks much better up that way." She'd snipe, make cutting little remarks in front of others about my clothes or hair when I was a little ways away, but close enough that I could still hear.

We'd been pals before, too, in school. Or the last one I was in, anyway. Not the best of friends, but we ended up with each other, because the other girls stayed away from us. With me, it was because I was the new kid. I was always the new kid, moving around so much, from house to house, from school to school. When I did stay at one school long enough to make friends, my family would just move anyway, usually on the spur of the moment, and that would be that. Sometimes, they wouldn't move too far and I'd stay in the same school. That was how I had a chance to become friends with Darlene. At first I figured the other girls didn't like her because they were jealous of her, being so pretty and all. That might have been part of it, but I got to understand after a while that there was more to it. Maybe they'd heard something I hadn't, but they all seemed to know there was something wrong with her. Sometimes I could see it. Darlene looked like Jean Harlow with her blonde hair, tight skirts, no underwear, her brows plucked almost right off. She wasn't like the other girls and she wasn't interested in what they thought of her, spent most of her time with a crowd of older guys who smoked cigarettes and cut classes. In a way, I admired her courage, admired that she wasn't afraid to be herself. She didn't have many friends, and I didn't either. So it was natural, maybe inevitable, that we'd become friends.

And much as I sometimes hated it, I was mostly glad to be working at Darlene's Dad's hotel, The Belleville, downtown. I'd been there three years, since I was fourteen. I worked as a chambermaid and Gus let me board in a little room in the basement. It was okay, it had a window and all. It was a damn sight better than what I had at home, actually. There would have been no way anybody in my family could have had their very own room.

After three years I was used to being out on my own, didn't really think much of it. Things had been hard for my family for a long time, but got worse when my pop died.

Pop was a tall, lean man, dark-haired with a thin moustache and almond-shaped amber-coloured eyes. He worked as a bricklayer mostly, though he did whatever work he could get. When he wasn't working, he loved to sing, and to tell stories. And to drink, he loved that, too. He had many friends in Regina's Romanian community, and friends he'd made in the Regina Rifle Regiment when they were stationed in France during the Great War. He was hit by a truck one morning in February of 1931. It was a cold morning, but a clear one, and the sun was already up. The truck driver said Pop stepped out in front of him, didn't even look, and he tried to swerve but it was just too slippery. I remember the police coming to the front door as Steve and I got ready for school.

"Mrs. Koudelka?"

"Yes," Ma said uncertainly. Her tired, round face was a mask, but I'm sure she was thinking *What now? What's he done?*

"Your husband is Josef Koudelka?"

"Yes." She stepped past us onto the step outside and closed the door behind her, so we wouldn't hear, I guess. But in a moment her cries pierced the door. Steve and I stood on the other side of it and stared at each other, and trembled. We didn't end up going to school that day.

ff

Things were never the same for my family after that. I was almost thirteen and my sister Maria was eleven. My oldest sister Lena, at seventeen, had already been Mrs. Jurgen Koznotski for almost a year. Steve dropped out of school and went to work not long after Pop died, when he was fifteen. The first job he had was working for Gus Klein, as a matter of fact. Gus had been a drinking buddy of my Pop's. When he heard Steve was looking for work, he took him on. Steve did all kinds of things at the Belleville: general labour, cleaning, repairs, whatever Gus needed help with. It was a relief to Ma to have him steadily employed. Ma's English wasn't all that good and she would have had a tough time finding a job, especially the way things were in 1931. She was able to take in laundry, though, and did sewing sometimes when she could get the work.

Beneath all the things I felt in the weeks, months, and even years after Pop died — grief, bewilderment, anger — was a deep sense of shame. I didn't really understand it at the time, but I guess shame was my response to the way people at school, the other kids and the teachers, avoided me after it happened. Not that I was ever anything like popular before. With my family moving all the time, and changing schools all the time, I was perpetually the odd one out, anyway. But now I was the one with the dead father, and while officially it was an accident, people talked. He was drunk, they said. It was suicide, they said. Whatever the circumstances of his death were, it didn't seem to bring out sympathy in anyone. It just seemed to confirm their ideas that we were strange people, perhaps dangerous or defective, and best kept away from.

As we ate supper one night two years after Pop died, Steve mentioned that he'd run into Gus that afternoon. He'd quit working at the Belleville after six months to apprentice for a bricklayer friend of Pop's, but had been laid off a few weeks earlier. Funny, Steve looked so much like Pop as I passed him the bread that I blinked, unsure who I was seeing before me.

"I asked Gus if he might have any work for me and he said he didn't. But he did say he was looking for a chambermaid. Said I should mention it to you, Ma, before he put up a help-wanted sign, in case either of the girls were looking for work. He'll have the job filled right away if he advertises it."

Ma looked at me as she sipped a mouthful of chicken soup. For some reason I noticed right then that there was much more white in her hair than there used to be.

"What?" I asked.

"Well, Maria's too young. But you're fourteen, now."

"What about school?"

"What about it? You're in Grade Nine. How much education do you need? Your brother only went until Grade Ten. Steve, did Gus say how much the job would pay?"

"He said it wouldn't pay that much, only a dollar a day or so. But he could offer room and board."

Ma put down her spoon. "A dollar a day. And room and board. That's a pretty good offer, Lita. I don't know if we can pass it up."

I just looked back and forth from Ma to Steve, tried to think of something to say. I should have seen it coming, I suppose. Lots of kids I knew at school, and Steve, too, had quit early to go out and work, when they could find work. I guess it just never occurred to me that I'd be one of them. Maria flashed her dark eyes at me, didn't even try to hide the smirk on her face.

"I'm going to call Gus after supper and tell him you'll take it," Ma continued.

"But, Ma," I protested. "I can't quit school now."

"Yes, you can. There are all kinds of people out there with more education than you have, missy, who would love to take this job. And it's going to be a lot easier for Steve and

Maria and me to stay afloat if we don't have you to support, too. That's just the way it is, Lita."

I left the table and went into the little room Maria and I shared, slammed the door. My first thought had been to play guitar, but I was too upset, angry, shocked. I had no choice. Tomorrow, my education was ending. Tomorrow, I would be leaving home and moving into the Belleville Hotel. And I had no say in the matter. My life was changing and I had no say. I was powerless.

ff

Gus had asked Ma to send me around to the hotel after school. I went to school in the morning to tell them I was leaving, clean out my desk, get my books to give to Maria. I came home at noon and had an almost silent lunch of cold sandwiches with Ma, who told me to grow up and stop acting like a baby. After we ate, I packed. I wanted to leave before Maria got home from school. I didn't need to see her smirk at me again.

Ma gave me a stiff hug and a peck on the cheek on the front step.

"Be a good girl, Lita. I know you will," she said.

"Goodbye, Ma," I said. I picked up my suitcase and guitar and started off to the Belleville.

When I got to the hotel, Gus showed me around, gave me an idea what I'd be doing as a chambermaid. He said Darlene would train me the next day. Darlene was the same age as me, fourteen, still in school. At home I'd had my share of chores, as well as schoolwork. It had always been hard to find any time to play guitar. Sometimes, in the summer, I'd wait till everybody else was asleep and sneak out to the shed to play. Or I'd play in the back alley, out of sight. At the

Belleville, I did my job, and the time after that was my own. Gus didn't pay much, but with room and board taken care of I had a little left over for clothes, strings, sheet music, the odd book. There were always newspapers around the hotel. So I had time to read, and I played quite a bit, and nobody minded about the noise. My room was an old store-room with a bed, closet, a little window, a table, a chair, and a beat-up radio. It was right under the kitchen, so I could play late into the night, and usually did.

That first night I didn't play guitar at all. I sat alone in the kitchen and ate a sandwich after Gus told me to go get something to eat. Then he gave me the key to a room on the second floor where he said I could sleep until he had a room downstairs cleared out for me. Couldn't have a chambermaid in a room that customers might want, he said. I wasn't so sure about sleeping in the basement at first, but later figured I couldn't have played guitar in any of the upstairs rooms, anyway.

I listened to the radio in the strange, empty-feeling hotel room for a while before I got ready for bed. Jack Benny was on, and usually I thought he was pretty funny. But that night I didn't crack a smile. I wasn't even really listening, and after a few minutes decided to switch off the radio and the lights.

I got into the bed and pulled the blankets up to my chin. Outside my window the hotel's orange neon sign glowed through the thin curtains. Sleep didn't come for a long time. What had happened in the last couple of days? I kept wondering. All of a sudden here I was with a job, living away from home. Now I was an adult, or I'd have to become one pretty fast. Would all of this have happened if Pop hadn't died? But I guessed that didn't really matter. It did happen and I had to deal with it. I knew one thing, though: I'd had no choice in any of this. I'd had no control over what had happened to me. I swore to myself, as much as it was possible, I was not going to let that happen to me again. I would not be powerless again if I could help it.

But how? How could I be sure I wouldn't be powerless? I knew one thing — one way people have power over you is when you love them. I loved Pop, and when he died it hurt more than I knew anything could hurt. I loved Ma, and she pushed me away, gave me no choice. Maybe the best thing would be not to love anyone again, I decided. Maybe if you don't love people, they don't have power over you. And if they don't have power over you, they can't hurt you. That made sense, I thought as I drifted off after my first night in the Belleville. A lot of sense.

Three

Elsa
Regina, Saskatchewan
April 1983

I DECIDED TO TELL MOM THE news just after I put Bill, who was about six months old, down for a nap, in hopes it would keep her volume to a minimum. I had a feeling she'd lose her mind when I told her about Mark and I moving to Seattle. Even before she said anything, her face flushed and the roots of her sandy hair looked white. It was no accident Lita was around when I broke the news. We had talked about it the night before, had it all figured out. That made it a lot easier for me. "The winters alone are reason enough to leave this place," she'd said. "Seriously, don't get stuck here the way I did."

Mom cleaned her glasses on her sweater a couple of times, fussed with the plate of cookies and the tea cups. "You're going to take that baby to a strange city? A strange country? Have you thought this out at all?"

"Yes, of course we have. Mark's sister and her family live in Seattle. Mark's got a visa, and there's a job waiting for him — "

"What kind of job?"

"Dispatcher at his brother-in-law's courier company. Just to start with, you know. Mark's going to get a new band going, and the bassist from Speed Queen is coming with us, so we'll get a new rhythm guitarist and drummer, should be no problem."

I watched Mom's eyes dart from my bleached blonde hair to my earrings to my tattoos. We'd argued about all those things in the past, and I'd always ended up going ahead and doing what I wanted anyway, making her mad in the process. And here we were, at it again.

"And what will you do with Bill while you're out playing music at all hours?"

"Oh, Mom. Don't worry. There's Mark's sister, Bonnie, and her husband, Dave. They have two teenage daughters. Besides, Mark and I won't always be playing the same nights."

I could've cheered when Lita broke in with, "And Sarah, I left you with your father lots of nights when I was playing and it didn't seem to hurt you."

"Not when I was a baby, you didn't! You didn't go back to performing until I was in university. That's completely different."

"I suppose that's true," she said. "But I know one thing: there were a lot of times when you were young that I was itching to get out there and play and didn't because I thought as a mother I shouldn't. I didn't realize then that I could have done both, that keeping up my music wouldn't have made me a worse mother. In fact it would have been good for all of us, but I didn't know any better then. Now I can tell you there's no reason Elsa's life has to come screeching to a halt because she has a baby. Babies are pretty flexible, you know."

"But why Seattle? What's wrong with staying here, with Bill's family?"

I sighed. Anyone who knew anything about the music scene wouldn't have to ask a question like that. "We can't stay in Regina and make anything of ourselves. There are no opportunities for musicians here. There's not many opportunities for anything here. We only have 150,000 people. In Seattle, there's half a million."

I could hear the exasperation in Mom's voice. "But why move to such a big city? Think of the traffic. Think of the crime. I keep saying you should get a job with the provincial government, like your cousin Debbie did. And then you can make a good, secure living and still have lots of time for hobbies. What's wrong with that?"

I dared to share a long glance with Lita and she smiled faintly and raised her eyebrows a little when Mom wasn't looking. You'd think that my mom, both the child of musicians and the mother of one, would have a little more understanding of us than she seemed to. Or would admit to. I had had this conversation with her many times: music was not a hobby to me. It was my passion. It was what I wanted to spend my life doing. It wouldn't endanger Bill if I continued at it.

"Mom, there's nothing wrong with that kind of life. But it's not how I want to live. And besides, we've made up our minds. We're doing it. We leave next month."

Bill's sudden and insistent wailing put an end to the conversation, and I went into the bedroom to feed him. But as far as I was concerned, the conversation was over anyway. Mom wasn't happy, but she rarely seemed to be happy with anything I did. No surprises there. I would have been surprised at any other response from her.

ff

Mark and I were still in high school when we started seeing each other, not long after my band Speed Queen opened for his band Third Class Relic at the bar at The Schnitzel Haus. The Schnitz, everybody used to call it. There were only a few places in Regina that booked punk acts then, mostly The Schnitz and the Student Union Building Hall at the university. For a while it seemed like the dynamic duo of Speed Queen and Third Class Relic played one of those venues every weekend.

I walked into The Schnitz with my guitar that first night we played with Third Class Relic and he was leaning up against a wall, watching me come in. He caught my eye the minute I saw him. His smile was wide and open, his dark hair was cut close to his head, his grey eyes were set deep. We shook hands and he seemed to hold onto my hand a little longer than necessary.

"Hello. You're with the band?"

"I am. I'm Elsa. And you are . . . "

"Mark. I play bass in Third Class Relic. Are you the singer for Speed Queen?"

"Yeah. I play guitar and write the songs, too."

"Cool. Hey, you want me to carry that guitar for you?"

I laughed. "No. Thanks. I'm good. Can you just show me where we can stash our stuff?"

"Yeah, of course. Over here," he said, and showed me to a table beside the tiny stage area. We seemed to talk all night — well, all the time our bands weren't playing. He gave me and my guitar a ride home after The Schnitz shut down and we must have talked in his car for close to an hour before I actually went inside. I don't remember what time it was, but the sky was starting to get light already as I tiptoed inside. Holy shit.

I'm afraid we got serious pretty fast. Mom thought we were too young, thought I should meet some "other people outside my group of friends." I knew what she meant by that — I should meet someone besides a musician, someone with some prospects. Could be that she was right, but it seemed to me once Mark and I started talking, that was it. And then when I got pregnant with Bill, well. Really, I thought she was going to have a fit.

"Oh, Elsa," she started, after I blurted it out to her one night in my bedroom. She paused for a bit, weighed her words, took a breath. "Are you and this Mark going to get married, then?"

She had always referred to him as "this Mark" or "that Mark." I was never really sure why. He was the only Mark we knew. Somehow it seemed to denote some of her contempt for him.

"I don't know, Mom. I mean, that was his first reaction, but I don't know."

"Well, I'm glad to hear that one of you has some sense. What do you mean you don't know?"

"I just don't know. I'm having the baby, if that's what you mean. And keeping it. What I don't know is whether I want to get married or not. I don't want to ruin our lives."

"You think getting married will ruin your lives? What about trying to raise a child by yourself?"

"No, I just mean I don't want either of us to have to get a job that's going to get in the way of playing music."

I was going to say more, explain what I meant better, when she jumped in. "I think you'd better listen to Mark.

Someone is going to have to get serious, now." She got up off my bed and left the room.

Now over a year later, I had my son, and my husband. We were a family, we were pretty happy if kind of tired a lot of the time, and we were ready to start a new life in a new city, a new country. I was excited. She was acting like I was a bad child, again. But I couldn't do anything about the way my mom felt, and I couldn't let it get me down. We were looking forward to Seattle.

Four

Lita
June 1935

THE BELLEVILLE WAS NOT A HUGE hotel, but at twenty rooms, it was enough to keep us busy. The Kleins bought it in 1928, when Darlene was nine. Mrs. Klein had mostly run the place by herself, with some help in the busy season in the summer. But she'd died a couple of years before, and after that Gus and Darlene handled it themselves. In the summers, the busy season, Gus hired some part-time girls. When I started, Darlene had been after him for months to hire a chambermaid full-time so she could devote her attention to school. Well, that was her story, anyway. Put it this way, she had things on her mind other than the hotel.

I didn't mind it most of the time, but it wasn't really what you would call interesting work. A few guests were more or less permanent tenants, but in the middle of the Depression Regina wasn't exactly a hot tourist spot, so there often weren't that many guests around. And although my official title was "chambermaid," I ended up doing a lot of things at the Belleville. After a while I was helping in the kitchen, taking out the garbage, checking guests in and out;

sometimes I'd lock up at night if Gus and Darlene were both busy.

One day the phone at the front desk rang. Gus was out and Darlene was chatting with a boy out in the lobby. She turned to me. "Get that, would you?"

"Belleville Hotel . . . She's busy right now . . . Okay. Goodbye."

Later, after the boy left, she asked me who'd called.

"I don't know. He said he'd call back."

"You need some phone lessons! Next time, say 'Who's calling, please?' And take a message."

I was too embarrassed to admit that in most of the places we'd lived we'd never had a telephone, and the few times we did, I'd rarely been the one to answer it.

ff

Sometimes the messes people left in the rooms were really revolting. And sometimes they'd leave the most incredible things behind. Gus tried to contact the owners before he turned the booty over to us girls, or sold it. I got a nice green silk georgette dress and a coat that way, as well as a few pairs of shoes. Since Darlene got first dibs though, most of the things I got were clothes she didn't want or that were too big for her.

Once, I found a portable phonograph and a wooden crate full of records that a guest left behind. My hands shook as I flipped through the 78s. I knew I was supposed to turn this stuff over to Gus, but I couldn't this time. I stowed them on the bottom of my wheeled cart, under a pile of sheets, hauled them down to my room when I finished the floor I was working on, and slid them carefully under my bed, beside my guitar. When I was finished work, I went down and listened to them at whisper volume, afraid that Gus or Darlene would hear, would want to know where I got the stuff.

But it never happened. The owner must have never tried to track them down, otherwise Gus would have asked about them. So I got to play along with Duke Ellington, Billie Holiday, Bix Beiderbecke, Cab Calloway, Bessie Smith, Louis Armstrong, and Django Reinhardt. It was raunchier stuff than the Bing Crosby, Conee Boswell and The Ink Spots they tended to stick to on CKCK, and it excited me. Django, being a guitarist, especially moved me, and when I discovered that he was a Gypsy, I felt a quiet connection. Later I read that he had two useless fingers on his left hand, his fretting hand, that had been paralyzed in a fire. And still he played like no one else ever had. After hearing him, I knew my playing would never be the same.

ff

Steve came by the hotel to see me sometimes. One night that June, he said he'd been down at Exhibition Stadium to talk to some of the men camped there. There'd been a great flood of unemployed men, more than a thousand, who'd marched all the way from Vancouver and were camped out at the Grounds. The On-to-Ottawa trek, the paper called it. They demanded that the government do something to help them, and though Prime Minister Bennett threatened to call in the army, they found a lot of support in Regina. People donated food and money. Steve had gone to see what all the fuss was about, and he told me he'd decided to join them. That got me curious — I wanted to see the sea of men for myself. He came back to get me after my shift was over and we walked to the Grounds.

This side of Steve, the serious side, was something I hadn't seen before. As far as I could tell, before this his main interest in life had been girls. He was with a different girl every time I saw him. And why not? He was tall, had wavy black hair. I was glad to see him interested in something else. I'd read about the unemployment in the paper and knew my brother was having a terrible time. Men like Steve were lucky if they could find casual labour now and again, and they'd beg door-to-door for work. But the size of the problem didn't really hit me until I saw all those men, from boys my age to white-haired grandfathers, all needing work, all angry and tired and frustrated. Steve tried to convince me to join the march, too, but I just laughed at him. A girl, join the march? Besides, even though chambermaid work was far from glamorous, I didn't think my life was so bad. As it turned out, the whole march ended only a few days later in a bloody riot that saw two men killed.

I did, however, join a poker game outside the Stadium, near a roaring firepit.

I'd only played poker once before, with Darlene, for pennies. Call it beginner's luck, but I won that night at the Grounds, and my final opponent owed me big. I knew none of the men had money, and I knew they just played poker to pass the time. I really didn't expect the man to pay up, but he went into his tent and brought out the guitar.

Even as I told him no, I couldn't possibly take it from him, I salivated over it, my fingers burned to reach out and possess it. I couldn't take my eyes off it glinting in the flickering firelight. A National guitar, with a sleek polished steel body, pair of f-holes, beautiful patterned sound holes on the round resonator.

"C'mon, Lita, take it," Steve urged. "She plays, you know, and she's good, too."

Nothing would do then but that I take it. My opponent insisted I'd won it fair and square, said he'd be insulted if I didn't take it. Besides, he said, it was a pain in the ass to lug around and he sure as hell didn't want to haul it all the way to Ottawa.

I couldn't hold out anymore. I took it from him, adjusted the tuning a bit, and played, just some of my own stuff I'd fooled around with a while. I'd only ever played my grandmother Mami's little bashed-up guitar before, and playing the National for the first time was like a dream. The tone, the action, the feel of it in my hands. I hadn't known it could be like that. I could have played all night, watching the orange sparks whirl up into the velvet blackness.

But when I stopped after a while, I heard applause. Only then did I realize they'd hushed to listen to me. I'd been spellbound, someplace where I was alone with the National.

I laid my new guitar gently into its case, and Steve said he'd walk me back to the hotel. But before we left, I thanked the man.

"Are you sure you want to give it up?"

"You take it and enjoy it. The way you play, girlie, I think it was meant to be."

Five

Lita
July 1935

THE SYNCOPATION FIVE HAD A LITTLE over two weeks to practise before the wedding, and while I wasn't completely comfortable by the last rehearsal, I felt pretty good about the way it went. Our two sets ran about forty-five minutes each, and many of the songs I already knew. The ones I didn't were fairly easy to pick up.

Still, I was more nervous than I expected to be on the way over to the hall. It was one thing to play in front of the rest of the band, but there were about a hundred people at this wedding. When we got up on the stage the lights were hot and bright. I didn't know if I would last the whole show in front of all those people and under those hot lights. But once I realized that the audience was watching the bride and groom, and weren't all that interested in the band, I was able to relax a bit.

"You're doing a good job, kid. I think this is going to work out fine," Bill said when the first set was over.

At the end of the night the band was paid fifty dollars, and Bill handed out ten dollars to each of us. I tucked my money in the little section in my guitar case for picks and strings. Ten dollars was more than I made at the hotel in a week. I'd almost forgotten about the money part of it.

ff

Next rehearsal we tried to get some new numbers going. As the greenhorn, and the youngest, and the girl, I didn't feel I had much say in the matter. But if I'd felt a little more secure, I would have said something about the smarmy songs that certain people leaned towards. Bill, specifically. In fact, I happened to know I wasn't the only one who objected to his choice of material.

"Well, since old candy-ass isn't here, why don't we play some real jazz for a change?" asked Henry.

George sighed. "You drummers. Always the instigators. Let's just rehearse the stuff and get out of here. I got a date tonight."

"Aw, c'mon. You know what I mean. Bill's my pal, but the stuff he likes, man. It's so lame. Let's play something hot while we have the chance. You with me, Otto?"

Otto laughed. "The stuff we play isn't so bad. Besides, the ladies love it, don't they, Lita?"

"I don't love it so much," I said.

"I don't mean you, I mean the ladies in the audience. They absolutely swoon when he does those crooner numbers, didn't you notice at the wedding? Guess he's the closest thing they'll ever see to Rudy Vallée."

I hadn't noticed anyone swooning. I had tried not to look at the audience too much. It made me nervous. I figured establishing a rapport with the audience was part of Bill's job, while it was my job to play the guitar. But this news interested me. Bill, whom I had mostly perceived as

big and gangly, was sexy? I made a mental note to observe
the effect he had on the women in the audience at the next
opportunity, just for amusement's sake.

He made it to the next practice, and we were still trying
to decide on some new numbers. As always, Bill had loads
of suggestions.

"How about 'What'll I Do?' I've got the chords figured
out," he volunteered. He ran through them once, and the
rest of us followed along. It wasn't too taxing, a cute little
old Irving Berlin confection I'd heard on the radio before. A
waltz, a real Bill kind of tune, when you got right down to
it, with that minor seventh chord heartstring tug in there.

We ran through it again, and he began to sing: "*Do you
remember the way that we met . . .*"

I decided to watch him. Yes, I thought I saw what Otto
meant, thought I could see what the ladies might see in Bill.
He was tall, and well built. Slim, but with nicely defined
muscles, thanks to his day job stocking shelves at a hardware
store. He dressed well. Bill always dressed well, even at
rehearsal; not too flashy, not too neat. Of course, with his
build, he could wear pretty much anything. I felt bad about
my first assessment of him — I could see now that it wasn't
very accurate. And he did have a nice voice; deep and rich,
and he made it sound effortless. I'd never really watched him
sing before, but it was interesting. For instance, I noticed
that he had a certain way of establishing eye contact that
held your gaze, and also that he had very clear grey eyes. I
hadn't noticed his eyes before.

"*What'll I do with just a photograph to tell my troubles to?*"

Then the pick flew out of my fingers and instead of
carrying on like I normally would, I got it into my head that
I had to stop and look for it.

"Well," Bill said when we finished the number. "What do you think?"

"It's great," I said. Nobody else said anything, but Bill smiled at me.

Henry took off as soon as the practice was done. I started to walk over to catch the streetcar, but Bill took hold of my upper arm and stopped me.

"Hey, Lita, you shouldn't catch the streetcar out here by yourself at night. It's almost 10:30."

I shrugged. "I can't expect you to wait for the streetcar with me. Anyway, I do okay. I'm by myself most of the time. You don't have to worry about me."

He let go. "No, I guess I don't. Supposing I was to offer you a ride home?"

I laughed. "In your ukulele case?"

"No, in my new car. Come and have a look."

I was sure he was lying, but I went with him anyway. And there was a black Packard parked behind the Quonset. A little beat-up, maybe, but it looked like an okay car from what I could tell in the dark.

"You're kidding. This is yours? Where did you get it?"

He ran his hand slowly across the hood like it was velvet. "My brother Ian got a new car. Well, a newer car. So he sold me this one. Pretty slick, eh?"

I was impressed. Cars in general didn't impress me, but the fact that Bill actually had saved up enough money to buy it did. I hadn't thought he was that serious. I looked at the whitewalls, inspected the somewhat worn upholstery and the spacious trunk, tried to look like I knew something about cars.

"It's a swell car, Bill. But why didn't you tell the fellas?"

"I will later. But if I'd done that, they'd have all wanted me to drive them home. And I wanted you to be my first passenger."

How could I say no to that?

ff

We parked on the street in front of the hotel. "So this is the famous Belleville, eh?"

"Yes." What was the next thing to say? *Well, thanks, Bill. Goodnight?* I probably should have said that, probably should have got out of the car. But he switched off the ignition, turned toward me and smiled, a streetlight sidelighting him. I watched his gaze move across my face, watched him lean a little closer. Something made me turn away from him and look at the dashboard, something I didn't really understand. I wanted him to kiss me, all right. But I'd only been aware of wanting that in the last few minutes, and wasn't sure I was sure. I was also afraid.

"Lita?" He'd backed off. Now he looked unsure, maybe even hurt. I didn't want that. I took a deep breath, put my hands on his shoulders, pulled myself up and kissed him.

When I sat back he blinked at me, amazed. Before he could say anything, I got out and took the National out of the back seat.

"Goodnight, Bill. Thanks for the ride."

"Can I walk you to the door?"

"No, it's okay." I started to walk to the hotel. "Sweet dreams."

"Yeah. You, too."

I hummed a little tune as I got into bed. Something new. Something mine.

ff

At the next practice, Bill seemed different. He barely noticed I was there. When he asked if I needed a ride home, I said I'd be okay on the streetcar.

"That's good, 'cause I'm already late. See you around."

I hated to wonder what the hell he was late for and who with. I hated to feel confused, hated to run over and over and over in my mind whether I'd done something wrong last time, something to offend him or disgust him. I didn't want to waste any time, any of my life thinking these stupid things, but I couldn't help it. I stewed about him all the way home, and until I fell asleep, which turned out to be far later than usual.

ff

By the next practice, I'd decided that if he wanted to play games, that was fine, but I would have no part of it. No more would I watch him to see if he watched me, or any of that stupid stuff. I was there to do a job, by God, not to flirt with the other musicians. I did my job, and when we were done, I cleared out fast as I could and headed over to the streetcar stop.

In a couple of minutes Bill ran out. "Hey, Lita," he panted when he reached me. "You played beautifully tonight. Outdid yourself."

The streetcar approached, and I picked up my guitar. "You ran out here to tell me that?"

"Well, I wondered if you'd like to go for a drive with me."

"Where to?"

"I dunno. Just out for a drive, maybe out around the park."

He smiled at me and I knew I'd say yes, so why didn't I just hurry up and say it? But I didn't know if I wanted to risk falling in love with him, wasn't sure I liked the idea of having my feelings tangled up in someone else, someone I wasn't sure I trusted. On the other hand, something strange and powerful was going on with my body: blood pounded in my ears, my mouth felt dry, my palms were damp. It had to do with the memory of kissing him the week before, and how he smelt. How his soft, warm lips and his slightly stubbly chin felt, how his nearly white lashes opened and closed quickly after I pulled away from him.

"Sure, I guess so," I said, and waved the streetcar on.

"Let me carry your guitar."

"No, that's okay. Thanks."

ff

We drove around downtown for a while and then parked near Wascana Lake. The lake had started as a reservoir in the early 1900s and then had been deepened into a lake in 1931, as a make-work project. The legislature buildings overlooked it, and it was surrounded by a park. It was a Tuesday night, no one else was around. Dead quiet, if you didn't count the crickets and the frogs.

"Where were you off to in such a hurry the other night?" I asked.

"On Sunday? I was going to a poker game at my brother's. Why?"

"I just wondered. You seemed to be in a big hurry, that's all."

"Yeah, I guess so. I'm surprised you'd notice something like that. You're so serious."

"Am I?" He took my left hand and ran his thumb over the thick calluses years of playing had left on my fingertips.

"Sure you are. You play that guitar like a wild thing, like you've got a soul full of fire. I've never heard anybody play like that before. But then when it comes to everything else, you're very quiet, very serious. Like when you kissed me that night."

I wasn't sure what he meant. "You didn't like it?"

He smiled. "I did like it. Very much. But it was over so soon."

"That's why it *was* over so soon. I liked it, too. Maybe too much."

We didn't say anything else for a minute. But he had his arm around my waist now, and I could hear his breathing. "Lita. Look at me."

I did. He leaned over and put his lips on mine. A voice in the back of my mind tried to get my attention. Something about this being dangerous, being a mistake. I decided to switch the voice off and go with what my body told me. Kissing Bill felt too good to stop.

Six

Lita
July 1935

HOW DID THIS HAPPEN, I WONDERED? One moment Bill was a peripheral figure in my life. Suddenly, it was all different, the line between before and after razor-thin and deadly sharp. Could this be right? Wouldn't it be more reasonable to think that I'd taken notice of him in a romantic way from the beginning? I had to think that, because the idea that you could suddenly feel this way without warning was too frightening. I seemed to have no choice in it, and it scared the hell out of me.

Also, I knew it was inevitable that one day Bill would ask about my family. I had no idea what to tell him. I almost told him they were all dead. That seemed like the easiest solution. But then I realized he might meet Steve at some point. I thought about telling him I'd decided to go out and work at fourteen just for a lark, for fun. I could have been one of those madcap heiresses like you saw in the movies, like Carole Lombard or Katharine Hepburn, running around doing crazy things because I had nothing better to do. Not because my family had to skip the rent again. The thing was, leaving home and all that seemed like such a long time ago by then, almost four years later. At that age, four years is an eternity. I just didn't want to dredge it up again, especially not with him.

I didn't want Bill to find out anything about me that might drive him away. I wanted him to think I was perfect. He lived with his mother in a nice house on College Avenue. He'd lived there all his life. That alone seemed so completely foreign to me, I couldn't begin to imagine how to tell him about my family. The longest we'd ever lived anywhere was about a year. How could I tell him I'd had to leave home to work when I was fourteen? Looking back, I don't know why I should have felt ashamed about that. It's not as if it was my fault. But I was ashamed.

One night the two of us hung around the Quonset after the others left. We did that after most practices. It was Otto's uncle's workshop during the week, so it wasn't exactly a comfortable or romantic spot. But we could be alone there. We sat behind the drum kit and passed a flask of rum that he'd brought back and forth. I took small sips. It was pretty harsh stuff, and I wasn't used to it.

"So you've been working for Darlene's dad for four years, now?"

"That's right." I could see what was coming, tried to think on my feet.

"Ever since you were fourteen."

"That's right. My family was pretty hard up."

"Was? They're not anymore?"

"I just mean they were. I'm sure they still are."

"Don't you know?"

Damn. How'd that happen? "I keep in touch with my older brother, Steve. But I don't hear much from the rest of my family."

"Oh. That's too bad."

I shrugged. "That's just the way it is. Guess things are a little different in your family." I tried to change the conversation but he wouldn't fall for it.

"I'm interested, you know. Really."

"In what?" I tried to stall, scrabbled in my mind for what to say, how to say it, what to leave in and leave out.

"In your family. In you. I'm interested in you. So tell me what happened."

"I left home. We were poor, and there were four of us kids. After my Pop died my Ma had a hard time providing for us. It was just easier if I moved out."

"But at fourteen? That's kind of harsh. Did you already have this job lined up?"

"Well, I got it right away. I've known Darlene for quite a while."

"Your mom just let you go?"

God Almighty. Stop asking me all these blasted questions. "She was pretty . . . well, Ma kind of asked me to leave."

"Oh. Sorry if I was prying."

"No, no. Don't worry about it. It wasn't so much that she wanted me to leave as that she felt she couldn't support me any longer. My family is very poor."

"I'm sorry to hear that. That's a tough thing. You know I only want to know because I care."

He cared? I had no idea he cared. And now I didn't know what to think. He cared, he wanted to know about me and my family. And I had these powerful feelings about him. The whole thing was a little overwhelming, frightening, even. How could I be independent if I was completely crazy about him? How could I be sure I trusted him? The only thing I could think of at that slightly drunken moment was to try change the subject again.

"Otto tells me the ladies in the crowd think you're like Rudy Vallée."

The look of disgust on his face surprised me. Though I would have been disgusted if someone had compared me to Rudy Vallée, I thought he would be pleased by it, a little, anyway.

"Did he really say that?"

"Well, he said that you're the closest thing to him they'll ever see."

"That's just about Otto's speed. I mean, Rudy Vallée would have been hot about ten years ago. Russ Columbo would be tops with me if he hadn't accidentally offed himself. Now Bing Crosby, there's a singer for you. Don't you think so?"

"Sure. I guess so." I really didn't want to get into this discussion. Singers, well, I was more into the Billie Holiday side of things, there. Vocals only interested me to a certain degree, and then only if they were exceptional, different somehow. Billie Holiday's voice was more like an instrument. Most of the time I preferred to listen to guitarists, like Django, Lonnie Johnson, Tampa Red, or Memphis Minnie. I liked Memphis Minnie a lot, felt I could relate to her. For one thing, she ran away from home at age thirteen, even younger than I'd been. And she played a National. But Bing Crosby rubbed me the wrong way. I thought he was a smarmy little Hollywood average talent aimed at the females. I knew, though, that Bill was fond of him. The band already did "Thanks" and "Love in Bloom" and he'd said he wanted to do "If I Had You" as well. The rest of us tried to ignore him.

"I'm glad you think so," he said. "Not only is he a talented singer, he's also a really admirable person. Kind of man I'd like to be someday, you know?"

"I think you're already as good a man as Bing Crosby is. Maybe even better."

"You really think so?"

"I do."

"Gee, Lita. I don't know what to say."

Seven

Lita
July 1935

THOUGH IT MAY HAVE TAKEN ME a while to figure out that I was in love, it didn't take Darlene long, perhaps because she was such an expert in that field. She confronted me one day at work after she heard me singing as I made up the rooms.

"Hey. You never sing."

"What?"

"You're singing. What's up?"

I hadn't even really been aware that I was doing it. "I dunno. I'm just in a good mood, I guess."

"So, which one is it? The drummer, right? He's a good-looking fella. I like drummers myself. You know," she said, and elbowed me.

"Henry? No. I mean, he's nice and all, but —"

"Don't tell me it's that gawky Bill? All legs and feet, that guy. Imagine it's your wedding day, and there *he* is waiting for you." She shuddered.

What was a person supposed to say to something like that? "As a matter of fact, it *is* Bill."

"Oh. Well, listen, I'm sorry. I was kidding. I didn't mean anything."

"That's all right. I should get down to the main floor, now, though."

I was overcome with regret as soon as Darlene left. Why had I told her anything?

ff

Bill and I found some shade on a bench in Wascana Park one evening. The day had been hot and humid.

"So, I got this letter today," he said and handed me an envelope. I couldn't imagine what it might be. He sounded so grim. Bad news of some kind, I guessed. I took out a folded letter and a 3 x 5 inch photo of Bing Crosby.

I knew how he felt about Bing. "Hey, look at this," I said. "That's pretty nice."

"Ha. Look at it. It's a form letter. Not even really from him, or signed by him, either, I bet. The autograph on the picture is a stamp, you can tell."

He was right, it was a stamp. The whole letter was probably hastily slapped together by some secretary who'd probably never even met Bing Crosby, someone they hired to fend off the mountains of fan mail they dealt with every day. I looked at it, and looked at him, tried to think what to say, tried to understand why this upset him. "So how did this all come about? Did you write him a letter?"

"Yeah. I wrote and told him how I thought he was one of the finest singers around, and I told him a little bit about being a singer myself and how we did some of his songs. And this is what I get in return."

"Well, I guess he's a pretty busy guy. Imagine the mail he must get."

"Sure. But if it wasn't for individual fans like me, he'd still be a struggling nobody. Like me."

"You aren't a nobody."

"Maybe not. But do I have what it takes to be him?" He shoved the picture into his pocket. "I don't think so. I'll never get there."

"You don't want to be him. Some big-headed movie star, too big to answer his own fan mail. You're better than that."

He just looked at me and laughed, shook his head. I don't think he believed me.

♮♮

A few nights later, I was filing my nails in my room, in my slippers and nightgown and robe, after a bath. I kept my nails short, otherwise they got in the way of playing too much, you know how it is. Inwardly I scoffed a little at other women's long talons, which it seemed to me must make their hands almost useless for any tasks. I did covet the red polish many of them wore, though. I tried it once, but I looked like a six-year old who'd got into my mother's cosmetics, with my stubby red nails.

Darlene knocked on the door. She waved a bottle of wine at me and held two coffee mugs. "Can I come in?"

"Sure."

"Listen, about the other day . . . I didn't mean anything. I didn't know what I was saying. You know me, I just get carried away talking and pretty soon — "

"Never mind. Forget it."

"And Bill. Well, you know, I never really imagined him being the one-girl type."

"What do you mean?"

"Oh, he's said things. Doesn't want to tie himself to one woman, that kind of thing. But I guess he's changed."

When would he have said things like that to Darlene? I didn't want to believe her, couldn't imagine him saying things like that. On the other hand, how well did I really know him? I decided to say nothing.

We talked a bit about beauty school. Darlene had quit high school, at Gus's urging, and was now enrolled in Miss Marcelle's Beauty School down on Pasqua Street. I wondered if Gus wanted to give his daughter a career or keep her away from the boys at school. Probably both. Darlene enjoyed learning about cutting, colouring, and setting, but she missed the boys fiercely, and soon we got to talking about them.

After a while she poured us another mug of wine. "So. Has my Dad been giving you any trouble?"

"Trouble? No. He mostly ignores me."

"That's good. Can I have one of your smokes?"

I handed her the pack. "You gotta watch out for him, though," she continued. Something in me knew what she was getting at, but didn't want to know.

"So he's . . . " I began to ask and then couldn't find the words.

"Sure, he has. With me, you mean?"

I nodded, again half wished she'd kept her mouth shut.

"Yeah. Not as much lately as he used to, though. Maybe he's scared of some of the boys I bring around, I don't know. But I still don't trust him, and neither should you."

"I don't," I assured her.

She sighed. "He wasn't always like this, you know. It was when my mom died . . . that almost finished him off. He started to drink a lot. And eat a lot, too. He gained a lot

54

of weight. Grief bacon, my grandma called it. So when he started to do this to me, in a way I could understand it. He lost his mind, you know. He's not really himself anymore."

"But, still, Darlene. He can't. I mean, he shouldn't do that . . . especially to you."

"No. No, he shouldn't. But he does. And I'm just trying to understand it."

"How can you be so strong?" I asked, and shuddered.

Darlene shrugged. "I don't really have a choice."

$$ff$$

Last night of the month I was getting ready for a date with Bill. The band had planned to practise, but Henry was sick and we all decided to take the night off and meet again later in the week. So Bill and I decided to go out to the late show of *After the Thin Man*. We didn't have that many actual dates, even though we saw each other most days. The band practised two or three times a week. We were waiting for our next gig, and then we all had day jobs. It didn't leave a lot of time for romance, and Bill grumbled about it some. Anyway, when the opportunity came along, we tried to do normal couple things like going to movies and all that.

My basement window was at the front of the hotel. I could see him pull up from there, and be out the door and he wouldn't even have to get out of the Packard. That way, we didn't waste any time, and I didn't get any guff from Gus. I had a feeling he'd give me trouble over Bill.

I'd bathed upstairs, as usual, put on my makeup and was dressing when I heard a knock at the door. I didn't want to peek through the curtains to check for the Packard because I was in my slip. Why was Bill early, I wondered as I slipped my robe on. It wasn't like him. If anything, he was usually late.

I opened the door, and there stood Gus. He smiled, and I felt his eyes move up and down my body.

"Hello," he said.

"Hi, Gus. Something you wanted to talk about?"

"Yes. Yes, there is. May I come in?"

I smelled fumes on his breath, felt my insides knot up and my shoulders tense. "Well, I'm just getting ready to go out, actually. Can we talk about it later?"

He shoved past me and closed the door behind him. "Funny thing. That was what I wanted to talk about. What's this I hear about you having a boyfriend?"

My mouth went dry. "Is there something wrong with that?"

"Nothing at all. Fact, I'm glad to hear it. Always thought there was something wrong with you, like you might be frigid or something."

I backed away from him to the other side of the little table in one end of the room. Maybe I shouldn't have let him know I was afraid. Maybe I was sending out the wrong signals doing that, but I was scared. Damn it all to hell. In all the time I'd worked for him, he'd never tried anything funny. I'd wondered if Darlene hadn't made things up about him, or exaggerated.

"Aw, c'mon now. You can relax. I'm not gonna hurt you."

"Bill will be here any minute."

"Bill, eh? Darlene tells me he's the singer in your band. Good-looking fellow, is he?"

"Gus, I think you should leave now."

He moved around back of the table toward me and I edged away from him, closer to the door. With my luck,

I thought, Bill would be late. And I knew Darlene wasn't around, although I wasn't sure how much help she would have been, anyway. Then I heard knocking on the door, slipped past Gus to answer it.

"Hi, Lita," said Bill. "You aren't ready yet." He pulled me up for a kiss before I could answer. "Hey, is something wrong? You're shaking."

With his arms around me, I could breathe again. I felt like I'd forgotten to for a long time. I stood back. "Bill, this is Gus Klein, Darlene's dad. Gus, this is Bill MacInnes. Gus was just about to leave, weren't you?"

He slipped past us without saying a word.

Bill looked at me for a minute. "What was that all about?"

"Do you really want to know?"

"Of course I do."

We ended up not going to the movies and instead drove the Packard out to Wascana Park again. Only this time, we parked and talked the whole time. I was afraid, so afraid, that he might misunderstand. But he let me tell the whole story, didn't interrupt much, mostly nodded and shook his head.

"We have to get you out of there," he said after I finished. "You can't stay there anymore."

"But my job . . ."

"You don't need a job that bad."

"Well, maybe I don't. But where will I stay?"

"My mum's gone to Toronto to visit her sister for the rest of the summer. She left on the train yesterday. She won't be back until after Labour Day."

"So?"

"So, there's no reason you couldn't come and stay with me for a while."

I swallowed. No reason, eh? No, not unless you counted that we weren't married, that there were neighbours. I looked at him.

"Well, you know what I mean."

"Not really, Bill."

"I mean, this is an emergency. You can't stay at the hotel. It's too dangerous. We'll be sharing the place. Strictly. It's a big old house, lots of room for the two of us to bounce around in. You can sleep in my brother Ian's old room, on the main floor, and I'll be in my room upstairs. Nothing wrong with that, is there?"

"I guess not. But how will it look?"

"Unless we tell people, who'll know?"

I couldn't argue with him. Moving made perfect sense. And mostly I thought it sounded like a great idea. Still, I wasn't completely convinced.

"I don't know. This could lead to trouble."

"You're already in trouble."

That was true. I softened, although I began to mistrust his motives a little. A flush had spread up his face to the roots of his hair, and I guessed his thoughts at that moment were not a hundred percent innocent. Mine certainly weren't.

"Well," I said. "As long as we know that it's just temporary. I'll look for a job, and as soon as I get one, I'll find another place to live."

"Of course."

"But, I guess for now, it's the only thing to do."

"Let's go get your stuff now. It's ten o'clock. Will he be at the desk?"

"He'll be around. But I have a key. We can go through the back."

So we returned to the Belleville and crept quietly up and down the back stairs a couple of times with my belongings. I didn't have much: my guitar, the phonograph and crate of records, some clothes, a box with sheet music, books, and my makeup in it. It only took about ten minutes to clear everything out. We got in the Packard and headed for College Avenue.

ff

I look back at this time, not with regret or sadness, but with a strange feeling I can't identify. Once again, I was being uprooted suddenly. It always seemed to work that way for me. It seemed I'd never be able to plan what would happen to me. Things happened in a flash. That morning when I woke up, for instance, I'd had no idea that by nightfall I'd walk away from my job, from my little room in the basement of the Belleville, and go to live with Bill. If you'd told me that even three hours before, I wouldn't have believed it.

On the drive over to Bill's parents' house I was quiet, thought about my own family. There were five children: Lena was born in 1912, Hana in 1914, Steve in 1916, I was born in 1918, and Maria was born in 1919. Hana died of Spanish Influenza the year I was born. Lena married at sixteen, when I was nine; with that and the age difference, we were never close. Maria and I always seemed to be at each other's throats. Maybe we were too close together. I got along best with Steve. We understood each other, could be close without talking a lot. I liked to talk as well as anyone, but I also knew that it wasn't necessary or even desirable to be doing it all the time. Maria was a talker, more like Ma. Those two could talk up a storm, and that's usually what you could find them doing. I heard Pop ask them once, in sheer exasperation, what the hell it was they found to talk about all the time.

Ma said it was after Hana died that Pop started to drink in earnest. Pop was always fond of a drink before then, but after that things were never really the same. It affected his work. He wouldn't show up for jobs, and soon it was hard for him to convince anyone to take him on. Then we started to have to move all the time. Sometimes to skip the rent, sometimes to avoid other creditors. Sometimes we needed a cheaper place, or hoped we could find one that wasn't so run down. We ended up in all kinds of places: hotel rooms, one-bedroom apartments, old farmhouses on the outskirts of town with no plumbing or electricity.

Then things seemed to go better for a while. Pop drank less, worked more. For almost a year we were in a nice little house with a yard, although it was right on Albert Street, near the tracks. But in the months before Pop died things got worse again, maybe worse than they'd ever been, and we had to move again, this time into a rundown house on Pasqua Street. We'd only been there a few weeks when I went one night to see *It Happened One Night* with a boy from school, David Walsh. David was good looking, fair haired, had nice manners, and I was eager to impress him. Everything went fine until he walked me home. The house was dark when we got there, even though it was only 9:30. Then I noticed our beat-up Model A wasn't parked outside. The front door was unlocked, and I had to make a snap decision. Did I open the door, turn on the light, and let David see what had happened while we were at the movies? Or did I try to fake my way out of it?

I opened the door and flipped on the light switch. Everything was gone. I stood there and wondered what to do next. They'd done this before; I wasn't really surprised. Never before had they been in such a hurry that they'd left anybody behind, though.

"What's happened?" David asked.

"They're gone." I took a sad last look at him. I knew I'd never go out with him again, not after this. How could I ever explain? But I wasn't as sad about it as I might have been, because I realized I had other more pressing worries. Like how would I find my family and where would I sleep? Luckily, Steve showed up right then. He nodded at David.

"C'mon, Lita."

We all walked down the front steps together and started down the walk.

"Goodnight, David. Thank you for the movie."

"Is everything all right?" he asked. The poor guy had no idea.

"Fine. Thanks."

The next morning I started at a different school in another part of town. I never did see David again.

Our new place was a cramped suite on the second floor of a tiny house near the Exhibition grounds, on Connaught Street. Pop was killed after we'd only been there a couple of weeks. Ma had one bedroom, Maria and I had another, and Steve had to sleep on the battered couch in the living room.

One night I couldn't sleep, thinking about everything: Pop, how broke we were. What was going to become of us. I could see the glint of my sister's eyes across the room in the half-light of the streetlight outside our window. "Maria, are you awake?"

"Yeah."

"Sometimes I wonder about Pop. Don't you?"

She switched on the cracked yellow celluloid bedside lamp, brushed her dark hair out of her face, and looked at me hard. "What do you mean?"

"About whether it was really an accident. The driver said he stepped out in front of him without looking. It seems so strange that he would do that."

"Are you saying our dad committed suicide?"

"I don't know. I just wonder. Pop was pretty sad sometimes."

"How can you say that? Didn't you love Pop?"

"Of course I did. I always will. But I can't help wondering."

She stood up, face flushed, breathing hard. "If you loved Pop, you wouldn't even think things like that. How can you?"

"All right, Maria. Forget I said anything."

I switched the lamp back off and said no more. I didn't need Maria waking Ma and Steve up, too, though it wouldn't have surprised me if they were already awake.

And sometimes I think about Mami. Somehow Mami, my grandmother, managed to convince her son and daughter-in-law to bring her along when they came to Canada. She'd seen a lot in her lifetime, from gaining her freedom from slavery as a young girl to the birth of the Romanian state. Coming to Canada, where electric lights and automobiles were commonplace, must have amazed her.

Mami died a year before my Pop, in 1930, when I was eleven. She was eighty-nine. Ma always maintained that Mami started to go downhill when my grandfather died. She tried to teach me about all kinds of things — reading music, tarot cards, medicinal herbs — on the sly, when Ma wasn't looking. Ma tended to disregard most of that stuff — superstitious nonsense, she called it. The one thing she did listen to Mami about, though, was music.

For Mami was a deft guitarist. She also sang beautifully, something she did not pass on to anybody else in the family but Steve. One day when I was nine I sat on the front porch, picked up Mami's guitar, the one she brought over from Romania, and started to fool around on it.

Mami came out onto the porch. "I thought I heard someone playing."

"I'm sorry, Mami. I just wanted to try it."

"No, no, child. That's all right. You want to learn to play? You have good, long fingers, a great thing for a guitarist."

Her long, leathery hands, covered with age spots, held mine gently, helped my left-hand fingers find their places on the frets, helped my right hand strum the strings. Showed me how the marks on paper related to fingerings. Now, instead of making noise, I was playing music.

The first thing Mami taught me was "Malagueña," a basic Flamenco piece. Once I got that down to her satisfaction, we moved on to "Ochi Choryna" or "Dark Eyes," a traditional Gypsy melody.

"Sheet music is good, but ear is everything. For Flamenco playing, you pick and strum with your fingers. But you need to know how to use a pick, too. It gives you a different sound," she said, and gave me a little triangular piece of amber-coloured celluloid.

By the time I could play "Ochi Choryna" fairly well, the calluses on the ends of my left-hand fingers had built up. Mami taught me a lot over the next two years, and passed on some fine technique. I missed her dearly when she was gone, and kept her guitar.

Eight

Lita
August 1935

THE MACINNES HOME, A SQUARE TWO-STOREY red brick house with a huge willow on the sloping lawn of the front yard, was not one of the larger ones on College Avenue, but it wasn't the smallest either. I often looked around at the antique furniture in the parlor, the family portraits, tried to imagine what it would have been like to grow up in this house and wondered how Bill and I ended up together.

As I suspected, it was a little awkward living there without letting anybody know, or trying not to let anybody know. For one thing the neighbours would be sure to figure it out sooner or later, whether I made a habit of using the back door or not. Then there was the phone and the door.

"What am I supposed to do when the phone rings?"

"You'd better not answer it."

"Well, what if it's you?"

"I'll call and let it ring three times. Then I'll hang up for ten seconds and call again. You'll know it's me, that way."

"Uh-huh. What about when someone comes to the door?"

"Don't answer it."

ff

One Saturday afternoon, I was going downtown. I needed a new lipstick, thought I'd take a walk and keep an eye out for help-wanted signs. I just needed to get out of the house. Being there alone all week, keeping out of sight while Bill was at work in the hardware store, was lonely. The band had started regular gigs in town and out at Regina Beach. We'd worked the night before. I asked Bill if he wanted to come with me, but all he wanted to do was rest, he said. He offered to give me a ride, but I said I'd take the streetcar. At the bus stop I realized I'd left my sunglasses on the kitchen table and went back to get them. I was about to push the screen door into the kitchen open when I heard Bill laugh. Something made me stop and listen. He must have been on the phone, because I heard him talk after a silent pause.

"That's a good one. But don't worry about it . . . Sure, I'm sure it's fine . . . So, I'll see you there. Toodle-oo."

Toodle-oo? I didn't hear any more talking, so I went in. He was making himself a cup of coffee, whistling "Love in Bloom."

"Oh, hi, Lita. I didn't hear you come in. What's up?"

"Who was that on the phone?"

"Oh, just Henry."

Henry, eh? If he'd said "toodle-oo" to Henry, I thought, Henry would deck him. I looked at him for a minute, tried to decide whether to push the matter.

"I thought you were going downtown."

"I am. I just forgot my sunglasses. Here they are. See you later."

On the streetcar all the way downtown I went over in my mind what I'd heard, trying to fit Henry onto the other end of the conversation. It didn't work, no matter how hard I tried. I was sure whoever he was talking to wasn't Henry. Still, how could I mistrust him? He'd been good to me, had never given me reason to doubt him, so why start now? I put it out of my mind and went into Woolworth's.

When I came back around 5:30, he was out. The note on the table just said he'd be back later. I tried to swallow my suspicion. Big deal, he had to go out. Could have been doing any one of a million things. I made a sandwich for supper, read the newspaper. Listened to the radio for a while. Finished the book I was reading, *The Good Earth*. By that time it was 8:30. I played guitar, had a bath. Listened to the radio some more, and by 11:30 decided to go to bed. I was awake another hour or so listening for him, imagining all the horrible (and not so horrible) things that could have happened to him.

When I got up about 8:30 the next morning, it was obvious that he was home. His shoes were at the front door, his jacket lay in a heap not far from them, and the Packard was parked out front. He didn't get up for another hour, and didn't exactly look fresh.

"Hiya," he said, and kissed my forehead. "Sorry about last night. I meant to call you, but I lost track of time."

"Where were you?"

"There was a poker game on over at Ian's. You were already asleep when I got in, and I didn't want to wake you."

"Oh." I wanted to tell him how worried I was. I wanted to tell him that I didn't believe him. I wanted to reach up and shake him by the shoulders and tell him to never, ever do that again. I almost did. But I curled and uncurled my fingers once, and let a breath out. I would not be accused of possessiveness, of jealousy. I knew that if I wanted to be in complete control of myself, I had to start with my emotions. We weren't married. We were free people.

I turned from him and made myself busy, starting with sweeping the floor.

ƒƒ

Whether there was actually a poker game at Ian's house that night, I never did discover. Maybe I didn't really want to. I thought about calling Ian and asking him, but told myself I wouldn't because I trusted Bill. Still, the seeds of doubt had been planted in my mind. Every time the phone rang when he was out, I wanted to pick it up and find out who it was. And maybe it was my imagination, but it seemed that the phone rang a bit more often after that night. Finally, a week later, when he was at work one afternoon, I could stand it no longer. The phone rang and I picked it up and said hello.

"Hello," said a woman's voice, sounding uncertain. "Is Bill there?"

"No. He's not. He's at work," I said, trying as hard as I could to sound cool. "Who's calling, please?"

The voice didn't say anything for a bit, and I was about to ask again when it asked, "Lita? Is that you?"

I had to think fast. I never imagined it would be someone I knew.

"Yes, this is Lita. Who am I speaking to?"

"It's Darlene. Pop and I have been looking everywhere for you! What happened?"

"Maybe you ought to ask your pop that."

"Did he try something?"

"Yes. So I decided it was time to leave."

"You really left us in a pinch," she said, as if I were the wrongdoer. But I wouldn't let her do that. Being away from the Belleville for even the little time I'd been gone had proved that I no longer had to feel beholden to Gus Klein. For the longest time, I'd kidded myself into thinking I should somehow be grateful to him, that he was doing me some great favour by letting me work at his hotel for peanuts and allowing me to sleep in a room in the basement. And if he decided to try to attack me once in a while, who was I to complain? I was sure Darlene had been manipulated into thinking these same kinds of things, and worse. I hadn't spent a night away from the Belleville in over three years, and after being away only a little while I realized how unnatural it was. Staying at Bill's put that all into perspective for me.

"I'm sorry you were left short. Did he find someone else?"

"Yes, he had to. With me in beauty school and all, you know. But this new girl's an absolute idiot."

"That's too bad."

"But, so, what are you doing? Are you working?"

"No. I'm looking for a job, but there isn't much out there."

"And where are you staying? You didn't go back to your family, did you?"

What to tell her, what to tell her? On the other hand, what was she doing calling Bill, anyway? I decided to tell her the truth. Perhaps it would show her what was what as far as Bill went. "Well, I'm staying here, actually. Bill said he didn't want me staying at the hotel anymore."

"You're living with Bill?"

"Yes. I mean, it's just temporary, until I get a place of my own. I'll have to get a job first. His mother is away until the end of September."

"Oh, my. I had no idea. I didn't even know you and Bill were still seeing each other."

"Yes. So, anyway, what was it that you wanted to talk to Bill about?"

"Nothing very important. I wanted to get Ian's phone number for a friend of mine."

"Oh. Well, I can give it to you."

"That would be great."

I found the number in a little leather-bound book in a drawer in the phone table.

"Thanks, Lita. Well, hey, that's great about you and Bill."

"It's not what you think. It's just that I had nowhere else to go."

"Of course."

I felt very irritable as I hung up the phone. I'd checked as we were talking; Ian's number was in the city phone book.

ff

When Bill came home later I told him, casually, that Darlene had called.

"Darlene? What did she want?"

"She wanted Ian's phone number for a friend of hers. The funny thing is, Ian's number is in the phone book."

"Well, you know Darlene. Not the brightest gal. Anyway, why did you answer the phone?"

"The last few days, the phone's been ringing like crazy when you're out. Today I couldn't stand it anymore and I picked it up. You know what else? It hasn't rung once since I talked to her, and that was four hours ago."

I'd said too much, I was sure, even as the words rolled off my tongue. Yet, they suggested only half of what I felt. I wanted to yell at him: *you were on the phone with her that afternoon, weren't you? And with her that night. That's why she's phoning here.* Instead, I only cringed a little inwardly, waited for his anger. I had no right to accuse him of anything. I had no proof of anything.

"Huh," he said, and put his arm around me. Then he slid his hand to the back of my neck. "So do you feel like eating right now?"

I shrugged. "Not really."

"Me neither. Let's go upstairs."

Maybe I should have refused, should have demanded we continue the discussion. But the pull of him was too strong, my body's response to his touch was too hard to fight, I wanted him too much. I followed him and soon I forgot all about Darlene. For a while.

Nine

Elsa
Seattle, Washington
May 1983

IN SOME WAYS, MOVING TO SEATTLE was like moving to another planet. For one thing, there was the ocean, which I'd never seen before, and which I fell in love with immediately. The ocean, and the mountains. Bridges and water everywhere, and hills. In Regina we had Wascana Lake and Wascana Creek, pretty small time compared to the Pacific Ocean. And Regina was flat, oh so flat. I mean, it's well known that Saskatchewan is flat, but I didn't really realize how flat until the clear, warm day that Mark and Bill and I drove out of town on our way to our new home, and I kept looking back for one last glimpse of the Queen City. And it kept being a little speck on the horizon behind us for a long, long time.

Regina to Seattle's a long drive. We'd tried to keep our stuff down to a minimum, but still, with baby gear and guitars and amps and all that, we ended up renting a U-Haul van. Mark wanted to barrel through, take turns driving, do it all at once. I would have been okay with that except for having Bill along with us. I was nursing him and if I wanted to keep my milk up I had to have some rest. I'd learned that pretty quickly. A non-stop thousand-mile road trip was not my idea of resting, even if we did share the driving.

"I'll take care of the driving," he'd said. "You can just take care of Bill."

"No way. That's got to be a good twenty hours or more driving, even with no stops. Forget it. We are going to stop and sleep in hotels or we'll get into an accident. We can afford two nights in hotels. And anyway, what's the big rush?"

"No rush. I just can't wait to get out there and get started, is all."

Sure, I knew what he meant. I couldn't wait, either. Getting out of town with my new family, starting a new life. I couldn't sleep much thinking about it — well, that and Bill seemed to want to eat every couple of hours right then.

So we ended up stopping in Lethbridge the first night, which is a pretty city, if a bit windy, with lots of old houses and winding streets and the coulees. We must all have been pretty tired because Bill was down from about nine that night until almost six the next morning — first time he'd slept through the night. Mark and I were almost delirious with joy from having almost eight consecutive hours of sleep for the first time since Bill was born. It felt like we were new people.

Good thing, too, because the next day was long. We drove through the mountains in the southeastern tip of B.C. and crossed the border at Eastport, Idaho, which seemed to me to take longer than it needed to. Probably because the customs guy took a dim view of our hair and tattoos and such. But we did have all our paperwork in order and we did have a screaming infant with us — nice timing, son — so they processed us. Then we drove through to Spokane before stopping. That night wasn't quite so peaceful as the one before had been. The hotel room was hot, but if we turned the air conditioning on it got too cold. So sleep was spotty, uncomfortable. Bill fussed a lot. He'd start nursing, fall asleep before he'd had much, and then wake up hungry a little while later.

But the next day we made it to Seattle. If I hadn't been so tired, I would have been more impressed by the beauty of the city. As it was that day, I just felt overwhelmed by the sheer size of it. It took us forever to get to Bonnie and Dave's place in Fremont, and we got lost because we were so tired. Still, we made it.

Bonnie and Dave put us up for a week before we found an apartment that worked for us. It was a walk-up in an old brick building not far from them. The building wasn't in the greatest location; the street was kind of busy. But there was a little yard out in the back, and a playground for Bill about a block away. The neighbours seemed nice and I loved the dark wood mouldings and glass doorknobs everywhere.

The first night there, after we got Bill to sleep, we stood and looked round at the mess. Boxes everywhere, almost nothing unpacked.

"The hell with it," said Mark. "We'll unpack tomorrow. Bill's asleep, it's been a long day. Let's have a beer."

"Sounds good to me."

We sat, backs against the wall on the futon in our bedroom, surrounded by our stuff. I stroked the stubble on his chin.

"How you liking Seattle so far?" he asked.

"I love it. It's so beautiful. I had no idea how much I'd love just looking at the ocean."

"Pretty cool, isn't it? We're not in Saskatchewan anymore, that's for sure. What about the apartment?"

"It's great, too. I think we're going to like it here. And did you know we have an ocean view?"

He laughed. "I didn't notice. Where?"

I stood on tiptoe in front of our bedroom window. "Get up here. See? You can just see a little glimmer around the corner there. Hey — "

He had grabbed me and was pulling me down onto the futon.

"You're right. I do love the view in here."

Sometimes I think those early days after we moved to Seattle were about the happiest we ever had.

Ten

Lita
September 1935

THE SYNCOPATION FIVE PLAYED A GIG at The Terrace at the Regina Beach Hotel on the Labour Day weekend. Working people would take an excursion train from Regina out to the beach for the day, and The Terrace had acts booked to entertain them all summer. We'd been regulars since the start of August. That afternoon we drove out was hot and still, glimmering pools of sky disappearing on the road ahead during the hour in Bill's Packard, all five of us, with George's bass roped up on the roof. Bill wanted me to put the National up there, too, but I refused. It sat on my lap the whole way.

Maybe if I'd been in a better mood I would have considered it, but Bill confused the hell out of me. I wasn't at all sure I liked what was going on between us. He had the car radio on CKCK, and sang along with everything. I tried not to listen to him, tried to tune him out and concentrate on the steady *thuk* of locusts against the windshield. He'd been out a lot lately and I was still suspicious about Darlene. And his mother would return from Ontario in a few weeks and I had no idea where I'd live yet. It made me feel like those locusts had it pretty easy, dumb things. They'd hatch, eat their faces off, procreate, and then end it all in a numb second by becoming a green smear on the front of the Packard. Not so bad, I thought. At least they didn't have to watch the man they loved eyeing all the women in the audience every time the band played. Or watch him talk through entire set breaks to Darlene, who was supposed to be going out with Otto. I almost talked to Otto about it once, but decided in the end to keep my mouth shut. I didn't want to start any trouble. Any more trouble, that is.

Anyway, since the weather was good the band decided to stay at Regina Beach overnight. Henry's brother, Jimmy, lived in Lumsden, only a few miles from the beach, and we stayed with him, all five of us sleeping in the living room. One good thing about being the only girl was that I tended to get the little niceties, like the couch. The rest of them had to sleep on the floor in front of me. In spite of the mournful look Bill sent me as he turned out the lamp, I couldn't help smiling broadly at him. The arrangement suited me at that moment.

ff

The sand blistered my feet the next day as I wove between sweaty bodies and blankets. It looked like everybody in Regina wanted one last summer day on the beach. No wonder, with the winters. In less than a month no one would think of being near the beach and in two there'd likely be a foot of snow on the ground. That particular day, I wasn't thinking about that, though. I was thinking what a shit Bill was. I wondered why he treated me like he did. I couldn't think why, I only knew I loved him. He'd become necessary to me in some way I couldn't explain.

I watched him get into the water, wave at me, flash a smile. I did not wave back. I jammed my wide-brimmed straw hat further over my face, kept my eyes on his dark blue suit as he swam way out, past the buoys. Why did he do things like that? He could be hit by a motorboat. Why didn't the lifeguard say something? How could I be in love with such a damned fool? Eventually, he turned around, started back, and I relaxed once he got back into the swimming area. I opened my book and started to read when he got closer in, when I could relax. When he might be able to see me.

He came and lay on his side on the blanket, and I watched him towel off when I was sure he wasn't looking my way. He'd be all red and freckled when we got back home. Maybe Darlene wouldn't talk to him so much then.

"Got a cigarette?" he asked.

I tossed him my case, after lighting one for myself.

"Good book?" he asked after a minute.

"Yes."

"*Lost Horizon*, eh? I don't know, it looks pretty long. Say, are you going to sit under that hat and read all day?"

"I guess I might."

I started to read again, kind of. I wasn't really reading, I just looked at a spot in the middle of a page. But he didn't know that. He couldn't see through my sunglasses that my eyes didn't move back and forth across the page. He probably wasn't even looking at me anymore, anyway. His attention had probably been long ago caught by some girl down the beach, some fat little blonde. He probably wondered what Darlene was doing, maybe thinking about calling her.

"Hey, you're not sore or something, are you?"

I couldn't help laughing. "What makes you think that?"

"I don't know. You haven't been talking much."

"I didn't think you'd notice a little thing like that."

He flicked some pebbles around on the sand a minute before he said anything else. "What's that supposed to mean?"

"Well, you just seem to be so busy talking to other women."

"Oh, so that's what this is about. Listen, can't a guy talk to people anymore?"

"Sure. Talk to whoever you want. Only if you spend entire set breaks talking to Darlene, don't expect me to be happy about it."

"Darlene? That girl would talk you to death if you gave her half a chance. She just starts. What am I supposed to do?"

"You could say, 'Excuse me,' and come over and talk to me."

"Well, I had no idea it bothered you. Really. Otherwise, I'd never even . . . I mean, how could you even think I'd be interested in her?"

I shrugged. "You're not the only one. Ask Otto."

"Exactly. Otto. That's who she's interested in. I'm just a target for her mouth. But listen, no more. I promise."

I shrugged again, turned back to my book. After a minute or so, I felt his finger run gently along my shin. He smiled when I looked at him, squinted a little for the sun in his eyes. He'd never think, all on his own, to bring sunglasses with him to the beach. Little patches of sand clung to his arms, and I thought how easy it would be to reach over and brush it off his warm skin. I turned a page, still feeling his finger run up and down my leg.

"Want to go for a walk?" he asked.

I considered for a moment, a little distressed at the reaction of my entire body to the small movement of his finger. "Where to?"

"I don't know. There's some trees over there. Or over there."

We walked down the beach to where the sand stopped, then on the grass on the rocky shore of the lake. The noise of the crowd got smaller. We paused briefly in the cool shade of a stand of trembling aspen, then he held back some branches and I made my way in, careful not to trip on roots and branches. Some ways into the knot of trees we found a little clearing. The light softened, the damp ground gave under our feet a little. I breathed in the smell of earth and trees, and when we stopped and Bill stood close to me, I breathed in the smell of him. "Aren't you going to take that hat off now?"

"I guess I don't really need it in here."

He took it off and hung it up on a nearby branch. He looked me in the eyes for a minute, then found my mouth. After a while I noticed faint music coming from somewhere, a piano.

He slid the black straps of my swimsuit down my shoulders.

"Listen," I said. "What's that music?"

"I don't know. Beethoven, I think."

"It's beautiful."

"It is. Beautiful."

He wasn't really interested in the music right then. I was, but then women have this ability to do two things at once. Faint dapples of shade and light flickered through my closed eyelids, and I listened with awe while we sank slowly to the ground and a little awkwardly rocked on the earth and grass and leaves. A gnarled tree root stuck into my lower back, I noticed after a while. It didn't really matter. Eventually, I must have lost track of the music, too, because afterward all I heard was his breathing, and the pounding of my own pulse. We'd gained a little skill at making love. It seemed to me that it had taken a long time, though I really had no idea how long these things usually took. It used to be that people didn't talk about things like that. Well, most people didn't. Darlene did.

"Did you bring your cigarettes?" he asked.

I pulled them from my bag. "So how are you?" I asked.

"Fine. I have mosquito bites in some pretty strange places, though."

We leaned back against a tree, tangled in each other, and smoked. He ran his fingers through my hair and buried his face in a handful. We stayed there a long time, talked and smoked until it started to get dark.

"I guess we'd better get back," I said, and slid into my swimsuit.

"Yeah. I could eat a horse. But before we go, I've been thinking about how Mum will be home soon, and what we're going to do."

"I've been thinking about it, too, Bill. I guess I'll have to find a place. And I'll have to get a job. I've been keeping my eye out for something, but there isn't much around. I might have to go back to the Belleville."

"You can't do that. Besides, I couldn't let you go now. So I was wondering if you'd want to marry me?"

Maybe I should have expected it. But I'd had no idea that was on his mind right then, or ever, for that matter. When I thought of how mad I'd been at him earlier in the day,

I was pretty amazed that we were even talking, astounded that we'd had sex. Or maybe not, maybe sex was a whole lot easier than talking. Right before he asked me if I wanted to marry him, I'd thought he was going to ask me for yet another cigarette. And I actually wasn't so sure I wanted to give him one.

Marry him? Not that I didn't want to. I did, badly, wanted to be with him always. But it scared me to feel like that, scared me to think that I could feel about anybody with that kind of intensity. It made me feel weak, vulnerable. That there was something wrong with me to feel like that about anyone, that it would be stupid and possibly dangerous to let him know the extent of my affections.

"Lita?"

I had to smile at the expression on his face. He looked worried, must have wondered what was taking me so long to answer. Even worried, though, even in the dusk in a stand of aspen trees, his grey eyes glowed as if lit from within. I couldn't have said no to him if I'd wanted to.

Being in love, I was discovering, was like standing at the edge of a huge canyon. It was beautiful, awe-inspiring and all that stuff. It was also scary, made you feel dizzy and nauseous, like your stomach and lungs were fighting to see who'd get out your throat first. The worst part was the vulnerability. Being in love seemed to mean you were prone to injuries of all kinds at the hands of your beloved: purposeful, accidental, what have you. It seemed like the kind of thing reasonable people would want to avoid. Unfortunately, it also seemed like the kind of thing you didn't have a choice about.

Then again, I thought as we strolled back down the empty beach hand in hand, love had its good points, too. Make no mistake.

Eleven

Lita
Regina
Fall 1935

AT THE END OF SEPTEMBER, JUST before Bill's mother was due to return, we moved our things from the MacInnes house to a suite in the upstairs of a house we rented on Scarth Street. Then we got in the Packard one Friday morning with the marriage license we'd applied for a few weeks earlier, and took it to the justice of the peace at City Hall. Then we drove down to Minot, North Dakota for a brief honeymoon. Being a guest in a hotel, being on the other side of things, seemed strange. In a nice way.

There weren't too many other guests in the hotel dining room that evening, though I would hardly have noticed if the place had been packed. The whole day had seemed unreal and now sitting in this fancy dining room, eating steak with my husband — it was still hard to comprehend. Bill wore his suit and I wore a new pale green and cream print silk chiffon dress, the clothes we'd been married in that morning.

"I don't know, Bill. Do we really have the money for champagne?"

"Aw, relax. I've been squirreling away a little for this. Besides, how often do you get married?"

I smiled. "Not too often, I hope."

"When the Syncopation Five starts to make some real dough, I think we ought to move." Bill was perpetually convinced that we were on the verge of success, about to become the next big thing. I preferred to take it one day at a time and see what happened.

"Where to? Toronto? Montreal?"

"No, somewhere warm. A guy could freeze to death in Regina. Maybe we could go down to California. I'll bet there's lots of work in pictures there."

"I think we'd have to be making a lot more than we are now before we could move to California."

He reached across the table and took my hand. "Aw, c'mon, Lita. Have some fun with me, here. We could get a brand new Packard. And I'd buy you one of those guitars like Django plays. That fourteen-hole, oval fret job you were talking about."

There we were, on our wedding night, a seventeen-year-old and a twenty-one-year-old, drinking champagne for the first time, dreaming of what might lie ahead. I giggled. "That's an oval hole, fourteen-fret Selmer. Sure, buy me a few of them. I'm looking forward to playing them."

"I'm looking forward to getting back to our room," he said, running his chin back and forth over my knuckles.

I was anxious, too, but glad to hear that he was. Sometimes I thought it was just me. "What's the rush? We won't be doing anything we haven't already done before, will we?"

"Maybe not. But I'm still looking forward to it."

ff

On a cool October evening a couple of weeks later Mary MacInnes had us over for dinner. Bill had finally decided that it was time his mother met his wife. Although she was obviously aware that he'd moved out, he hadn't got around to mentioning we were married yet, and had sworn Ian to secrecy.

I was nervous, felt like I'd be under a magnifying glass. I tried to find out a little bit from Bill what his mother was like, so I'd have an idea what to expect. He was kind of vague, said she was sweet, old-fashioned, very traditional. Looking back, I'm not sure whether I should have read between the lines, or if that really was Bill's assessment of her. Then again, how objective could he be about his own mother?

"You know, for some reason I'm not afraid of what your mother will say," I said on the drive over.

"Why would you be afraid?"

"Why wouldn't I be? I'll bet she'll be furious with us."

"You need to get some courage."

"What do you mean?"

"Well, you're afraid of so much, aren't you? You've got stage fright. You're afraid to stand up to people, like your mother, and Gus. You always worry about money, too, you're afraid we won't have enough. That's a bad way to be."

"And I suppose you have courage."

"Sure. I mean, I'm not the bravest guy you'll ever meet, but I don't let little things scare me. I just don't think about them. I think about something else, that's all. You ought to try it sometime."

I was annoyed with him at first. What he said didn't even make sense. What was brave about thinking about something else? Wasn't that pretending? But on reflection, I couldn't think of any situation in my life where I'd been particularly brave. Then I thought maybe he was right. Only I couldn't see how I could do it, how I could change from a coward to being brave. Maybe I'd have to watch him and find out. Somehow, though, I didn't really think that was the solution. We got up to the front steps of his mother's house, and that was the end of that discussion.

Bill unlocked the front door. "Mum? We're here," he called, as we took off our boots and coats.

Mrs. MacInnes emerged from the kitchen, a small, square woman with faintly blue-tinged white hair and the same fair complexion as Bill. Her tiny, round, close-set eyes were pale blue, and deep wrinkles criss-crossed her skin. "You're right on time. The roast's just out of the oven."

"It smells wonderful. Mum, this is Lita."

"Pleased to meet you," she said, and shook my hand.

"It's a pleasure, Mrs. MacInnes. You have a lovely home." I wondered whether I'd be able to conceal my familiarity with it. It was impossible to look at it with new eyes, after spending half the summer there.

ff

Bill was right about his mother being old-fashioned and traditional. That was certainly the impression she wanted to give you, anyway. But even that first night, I sensed a phoniness about the woman. While we washed the dishes, she said, "When I was a girl, life was so much simpler. Back then we weren't brought up to be working girls. And we never wore any makeup, didn't need it in the slightest. We had chores and fresh air and sunshine to keep us lovely, and the boys didn't mind one bit."

"How nice," I replied through a full face of Max Factor. I could see how the sun had been a definite contributor to

Mary MacInnes' current looks. Hey, I thought, if people don't want to wear makeup, that's fine with me. But personally, I knew makeup was simply an enhancement of my good features on good days and the only thing that saved me from looking half-dead on bad ones.

My new mother-in-law talked through the entire dinner about how her family, the Fletchers, came to Saskatchewan in the 1880s. Her parents were among the original settlers, she said. I was sure Henry Onespot's family might have a bit of an argument with her on that. Then she said she didn't know what the government had been thinking the last thirty or so years, didn't they have any kind of immigration policies and did they let just anybody in?

"Used to be, in my father's day, they'd make sure the people they let in were hard-working, would be a credit to the country and contribute to the economy. Now I look at all these loafers they've let in and I just have to shake my head. They won't work an honest day, but they expect the rest of us to provide for them. Put them to work, I say, let them sweep the streets if we have to feed them. Let them find out that a day's work doesn't hurt anyone. Those Bohunks they let in are no better than the Redskins."

Bohunks? Redskins? This was a sweet little old lady? I looked over at Bill for some kind of clue. Was she always like this, did the sherry bring out something mean in her? Unperturbed, he shoveled forkfuls of the bland meat and potatoes into his mouth like he hadn't eaten all day. He probably hadn't, either.

Years later, I would have given the old bird a piece of my mind, would have asked her why she thought she and her kind were the only ones entitled to live like human beings. Back then, I was foolish and uncertain enough to say nothing. I didn't want to offend her or Bill, so I sat there in silence. Then I nudged Bill, again, and finally he told his mother the news.

Mary MacInnes came from a time and a place where ladies didn't show their anger, or at least that's what I'm sure she told herself was proper. My mother would have laughed at this notion; anger was her verse and chorus. But Bill's mum saw herself as a Lady, and Ladies did not yell, scream, or fly off the handle in her version of the universe. Although they could pout, make catty remarks, and attempt to manipulate others. I wasn't sure which mother's approach was the better. Mrs. MacInnes was angry, no two ways about it. All the colour drained out of her pink face, and her already tiny mouth pursed into such a small line that I thought, or maybe hoped, it might disappear altogether. She looked from one to the other of us and then her eyes rested on me for a long while.

"You've gone and done it, then. Nothing can be done."

Bill was annoyed. "I thought you might congratulate us."

"I'm away for a month and . . . You might have told your own mother you were planning to get married."

"That didn't go over too well," Bill said later as he started the Packard.

I shrugged. "She'll get used to it, I guess. Is she always like that?"

"Like what?"

"So opinionated. You know, about other people?"

"I didn't notice anything in particular." No doubt. He'd probably been listening to her rant for so long that he'd learned to tune her right out.

"Didn't you hear her talking about Bohunks and Redskins?"

"Oh, that." As if that could offend anybody. "Well, I'm sure she didn't mean anything by it. Don't take it personally."

ƒƒ

Mary MacInnes' attitude wouldn't have gone over very well with my brother, especially not lately. He'd dropped the whole Stephen Knight business and gone back to being Stefan Koudelka. It wasn't only that being Stephen Knight hadn't got him anywhere, he said it felt fake, like it wasn't really him. He told me all this during a set break when he came out to see the band one night when we had a week-long gig at the La Salle Hotel.

"I'm starting up a Regina chapter of the Gypsy Lore Society. You want to join?" The redhead he was with rolled her eyes and lit a cigarette. I wondered how long she'd been around. Steve's romantic attachments still never seemed to last long.

"What is the Gypsy Lore Society?"

"It's an organization concerned with the preservation of the culture and traditions of the Roma people, the Gypsies. I've been doing a little research at the library and it's very interesting. I tried to get some information about our background from Ma, but she wasn't much help. She said we should try to forget our background, it's mostly been the cause of a lot of trouble. I disagree. How can you know what you are if you don't even know who you are?"

"Well, maybe later. I'm kind of busy right now. But it does sound interesting."

"It is. I feel like I'm finding my place in the universe. I'd like to become a *chovihano*, eventually."

"A what?"

"A shaman."

"Hey, no kidding." Henry gave a drum roll. He smiled. "My great uncle was supposed to be a shaman. Can anybody join this Gypsy Lore Society?"

"Sure."

"Being a shaman could be handy."

Steve and Henry became fast friends almost instantly.

$$ff$$

One night The Syncopation Five played a gig in one of the lounges in the Hotel Saskatchewan. We'd played there about a month earlier and the hotel manager had telephoned Bill to say he wanted us to come back.

Jacob Stone had dark hair, warm hazel eyes, and always wore suits you could tell he didn't buy off the rack. You could see from the way they fit. He was not quite as tall as Bill was, and a little more sturdily built.

"How'd you like a regular gig here?" he asked between numbers.

Bill was the spokesman for the band. He had the professional persona, the gift of the gab. But even he was a little thrown by the offer, after slogging along for such a long time, picking up weddings, parties, one night gigs in little dives like Indian Head and Melville. "We'd want to think about it for a while."

Jacob smiled. "Sure. I saw you last year at the Trianon Ball Room, when you opened for The Guy Watkins Band. You're much better now, much tighter. And that was a great move getting rid of your old guitarist and picking up Lita. She's very talented."

"She is good. And she's my wife," Bill said.

"Ah, well. Congratulations. Anyway, if you're interested, let me know and we can draw up a contract."

"Oh, we are. Well, I think we are, aren't we guys? And Lita?"

It took us about a second to think about it. As if there could be any question.

ff

It took a long while for my mother-in-law to thaw out. This bothered Bill quite a bit, but I didn't care. I was used to being estranged from my own mother. When I told my older sister Lena and her husband Jurgen we were married, they had us over for dinner one night and gave us a nice Hudson's Bay blanket. I thought Lena must have told Ma, but I didn't hear anything from her. It was several weeks before we heard from Bill's mother again. She had us over for tea one afternoon and said she'd forgiven us.

"That doesn't mean I've forgotten, mind you. But I will let bygones be bygones. Anyway, I thought it was time to give you this," she said, and gave Bill an envelope. "In your father's will," she continued, "he made provision for when you boys married. It's money to help you buy a house with. I'm afraid the amount suffered a little from the stock market crash, but there's still a respectable sum there. With real estate prices where they are, I'm sure you'll have enough for a good-sized downpayment on a nice house on a good street. Of course, Bill, you'll want to wait until you have a real job before you look for a place, so that the bank will lend you the money for the rest, but this will help."

We did no such thing. We took the money and bought a tiny house on Dewdney Avenue, around the corner from Queen Street. The agent called it a fixer-upper, but we had no intention of fixing it up. It needed paint, sure. It needed new windows. The kitchen was dark and small and dirty. The roof needed new shingles. It was structurally sound, though, and that was all that mattered. A little one-bedroom bungalow with a verandah and a few trees in the yard. We had enough money to pay for the whole thing, and to buy a few pieces of second-hand furniture besides: a couch, a bed, a little red Formica table, and two chairs for the kitchen. That ate up all the money. But we owned the house outright, and no matter what happened, we'd have a roof over our heads. Compared to what life with my family had been like, it seemed like solidity and security. To use the money to get into debt for a house we didn't want, which would force Bill to take a job he didn't want, seemed crazy. Bill's mother probably thought that giving us the money would have the opposite effect, that we'd be forced to drop music and get what she considered to be a real life. I'm sure she wouldn't have let Bill know about the inheritance if she'd known we'd buy a little hovel on a busy street. She might have put off telling him as long as she could get away with it.

When she came over to see the place, she was disappointed. But later she tried to make the best of it, said it was a good starter house, close to the downtown office buildings. Neither of us told her that this was it, that not having to worry about rent would help us pursue our musical careers. I don't think Bill's Mum could have stood that, even though the thought of it helped me smile many times when I would have rather throttled her.

Part Two

Twelve

Elsa
Seattle, Washington
1984

DROPPING INTO THE SEATTLE MUSIC SCENE after living in
Regina was amazing, really. I know now when people think
of Seattle music, they think of grunge, of Nirvana and Pearl
Jam and bands like that. What most people don't know is
there's been a strong music scene in the Northwest, Seattle
in particular, for a very long time. In 1920, Jelly Roll Morton,
the man who claimed to have invented jazz, brought his
influential stride piano here on his way up and down the
West Coast — the whole West Coast, from Alaska to
Mexico. Bing Crosby was originally from Tacoma. Field
agents for major labels were recording local acts here as early
as the late 20s. In the early 60s, local label Dolton Records
brought out music by local bands like The Ventures. Who
can forget "Walk, Don't Run"? Speed Queen even took a
crack at that one when we were still in the Queen City. And
arguably the whole garage rock movement of the 60s started
here, too, with The Kingsmen's version of "Louie, Louie".

Seattle's fringe music scene was huge, and had been for a long time. Yet just like in Regina, and every other North American city in the late 70s and early 80s, no matter how strong and vibrant the scene was, the people involved in it were still on the fringe. The little mainstream media attention we got was negative — about underage drinking or fights at shows — and suddenly a Teen Dance Ordinance (what a great band name that would have been) was passed by the city council. This ordinance outlawed public postering, which was pretty much all most bands did for advertising, as well as stipulating that anyone holding a dance had to post a million dollar insurance bond. The ordinance didn't really have much effect on posters. I think if anything there were more posters around. But the insurance thing cut down on the number of shows people gave outside of the bar circuit, for sure. Too risky.

Crystal Dunn, Speed Queen's bassist, had moved to Seattle the same time we did. We found a drummer and another guitarist in pretty short order and after we'd practised for a few weeks we had a regular stream of shows. The usual thing: a few hall gigs at first, then we opened for the headlining acts at bars and clubs like The Bird. And it wasn't long before we were the headliners ourselves. Mark had been busy getting a new band together, too. A slightly different feel than Third Class Relic, this one had a less punky, a more garagey, mid-60s sound. Mark was still lead guitar, did lead vocals, all the songwriting. He found a bassist, a keyboard player with a funky Hammond B-3, and a drummer, and they called themselves The Green Lanterns after the comic book superhero.

Neither of our bands had trouble getting exposure. When we came to town, there were bands playing all kinds of what was termed "new" music — for those who enjoy pigeonholing, that could mean punk, new wave, electronica, straight ahead rock 'n' roll — in all kinds of venues. Bars, clubs, community halls, the usual schtick, but there were just so many more of them than there were in Regina. There were quite a few hair bands, too, like Queensrÿche, Iron Maiden, and Alice in Chains. This is what I mean about labelling — was Alice in Chains a hair band or a grunge band? A hairy grunge band? I always resisted calling Speed Queen "punk" or "new wave." I just said we were a rock band. The way I see it, as soon as you're labelled, you're limited: if you're *this*, you by definition can't be *that*. Anyway. The point is, we found ourselves in the midst of a strong, diverse live music scene. It was exciting and stimulating to be around so many people playing so much music. We couldn't help but get ideas.

Mark in particular. One night after we'd got Bill off to sleep, we decided to sit and have a beer together, which I'd just recently realized had become an unusual thing for us. Often one or the other of our bands worked evenings. When it was both of us, one of Bonnie's girls would babysit Bill. More often, though, it was Mark or I staying home while the other was out playing. Don't get me wrong, I wouldn't have had it any other way. But it got to the point where Mark and I hardly saw each other except in passing, between all that music and his day job at the courier company. This particular night, I don't know what it was, but we were both at home. The baby was asleep. The stars were out. So we did what any young couple would do — took some chairs out into the backyard and cracked a couple of beers.

"How's this for weird?" he asked. "Sitting here with the old lady."

"Weird, all right. Sitting here, and neither of us has to rush out to a show. So how are you doing? It seems like I hardly ever get to talk to you anymore. You know what I mean — really talk."

"You talked to me on the phone this morning. Remember?"

"Yeah. I asked you to pick up some diapers."

"See?" he answered, and laughed.

"Seriously. So how are you, anyway?"

"I'm good. I'm busy as all fucking get out, but I'm pretty good. What about you?"

"Ditto. Busy. Getting used to things. Meeting tons of new people. Regina already seems like a long time ago, doesn't it?"

"Oh, shit, yeah. But listen, now that we finally have a chance to talk, I got an idea I want to run by you."

"Yeah, sure. What's on your mind?"

He tilted his chair back a bit, stretched out his long legs, looked up at the stars. "Well, I don't know if you remember, but a while ago I was talking about The Green Lanterns maybe doing a record. A 45 or an EP."

"I remember. I think it's a good idea. I'm thinking Speed Queen should get one out there pretty soon, too. So are you guys going to work on a demo tape that you can shop around?"

"Well, that's where my idea comes in. See, I started thinking, where will we do the demo tape, what will we put on it? That part is already going to take some time and some money, to do a decent demo. And once we have it done, then where do we take it? We can send it off to BOMP or Beserkley, and we can shop it around to some of the little labels here. And then what happens? Maybe one of them pick it up. And then we have a record that we can sell at our shows and hope the right bigwig somewhere hears it."

"Yeah, well, that's pretty much what you put out a record for. So someone somewhere hears it."

"Well, yeah. We could do all that, jump through all those hoops. Or . . . Or we could bypass all the middlemen and just do it all ourselves."

I raised an eyebrow, looked hard at him. First beer, eh? "And how would you do that?"

"Well. What would you think if I — if we, if you wanted to — started up a record label?"

I had to think for a minute before I answered. "Have you been thinking about this a long time?"

"Yes and no. It's something I've always wanted to do. Or more, I always kind of pictured myself doing it someday. So then it just seemed logical that if it's something I always wanted to do, and if my band is at the point where we want to make a record . . . "

I had to smile. "It's not enough for you that you play lead guitar, you sing, you write all the songs. Now you want to have complete control over making a record, too."

"Sure, there's some truth in all that. I mean, hey, it's my band. It's my work. Why wouldn't I want to have as much control over it as I possibly could?"

"Because there's only so much time in a day. Because you're already stretched so thin between The Green Lanterns, and your job, and me and Bill, that it's been how long, how long since we've been able to sit and have a beer together? It might be a bit much to take on right now. It might be better to hand over some of the control to someone else so that you don't drive yourself crazy."

"I'm not driving myself crazy."

"No, not yet. But what about when you're trying to run your record label and do your job and play in your band and be a dad?"

"Look. At first it could be hectic, I'll give you that. But what I'm hoping is that maybe the label will eventually make some money. Maybe I'll be able to give up my day job at some point."

"Maybe," I conceded.

"Remember how nervous you were when we first started talking about moving here?"

"I'd just had a baby; I wasn't getting much sleep then."

"Neither was I. But I had a gut feeling that coming here would be a smart move. And look how it's turned out. It's great, isn't it?"

"Yes. Absolutely. But talking about starting a record label is different."

"How is it different? You know what, I have the same kind of gut feeling about this as I did about moving here. Except stronger. This is something I have seen myself doing for a long time."

"Sure, I hear you. But now? Why now?"

"Why not now? Why wait? It's not as if I don't know this business. I've made lots of contacts in the time we've been here. I feel like this opportunity is calling me now. This is the logical time to do it, instead of getting all caught up in, first, recording a demo, and then spending time and effort shopping it around. And if we get a recording contract, then having to go with the company's idea of what we should sound like, maybe getting watered down, sold out. If we even get a contract. Maybe it would all come to nothing."

I shook my head, sighed. "Mark. It sounds to me like you've pretty much made up your mind. I don't want to discourage you. But I also don't want to see you crash and burn. I don't want to see you taking on too much. And what about the money to do all this? Where's that going to come from?"

"It's not like I haven't thought of that. I already talked to Dave about it and he's willing to put up some money. And I know it's a risky thing. But isn't anything worthwhile risky? Wouldn't it be worth it to know that we are putting out exactly the record we envision without having to spend all that time convincing someone to record us? And we could help other bands put out records, too. We could start a whole little roster of local bands. It would be so cool. But of course, you know, I can't do it without knowing you're behind me."

I watched the lights of a plane high above us, took a deep breath and let it out. "Well, I have some reservations. But of course I'm behind you. You've never steered me wrong yet, and it sounds like a great idea."

He jumped out of his chair and knocked it over, pulled me to my feet and hugged me, spun us around a few turns in celebration.

"Hey, careful," I said. "You're gonna knock over my beer."

"Sorry. I'm just kind of excited. Listen, you won't regret this. I think it's going to work out really well. I give you my word that I'll do everything I can to make this work."

"I know you will."

He poked me in the ribs. "Plus, I promise you Speed Queen will get preferential treatment when it comes to considering a demo."

"Oh, thanks!"

Later, after we were in bed and had turned the lights off, it took me a while, quite a while, to drift off to sleep. What had I done? This could end up being a huge disaster. But the wheels were in motion now. It was already too late to look back.

Thirteen

Lita
Spring 1936

DARLENE CAME OUT TO SEE THE band when we were booked at The Trianon Ballroom, opening for The Bell Family. She came out to see us a lot, all by herself, and sat right in the front and talked to us all through the set breaks. Well, she talked to some of us. She usually didn't have much to say to me, except that she'd seen a blouse just like mine on the sale rack at Woolworth's, or to tell me I should go and get my hair done one of these days, she knew a girl who could do it up really cheap. She flirted a bit with Henry and George, and ribbed Otto. The rest of the time she'd babble away to Bill. But one particular night she actually had something to say to all of us.

"You need a manager."

"Huh," Henry scoffed. "What do we need a manager for? Just someone to take our money."

"Sure, you'd pay a manager. But a manager could line up jobs for you, do some promotion for you. Find you better places to play, get you more money. A manager could do all that and let you guys concentrate on the music. A good manager would be worth it."

"So, what — do you know a good manager or something?"

"I've been thinking about it a little while. I think I could do it."

"You? What would you know about managing a band?"

"Well, I've run the Belleville with my dad the last few years. I guess if I can run a hotel, I can find you guys a few gigs. For one thing, I have some connections in the hotel business."

George wasn't convinced. "I don't know. A girl. I mean, you'll pardon me, but will they take you seriously?"

"Now, hold on, George," said Bill. "I recall a little skepticism about our girl guitarist, too, at first. And look how that's turned out."

"That's different," said Henry. "Lita has talent."

"Well, maybe Darlene's a talented manager. Why don't we give her a try?"

The way he smiled at Darlene, I had no doubt that he wanted to give her a try. He acted as if I wasn't there. To a certain degree I felt that was part of Bill's schtick, part of the act, to smile at the ladies, to make them feel like they were the ones he was singing to. It was part of Bill's nature, I knew that, part of why he was a singer. Bill could take up with any old stranger. He could yak away to someone in the street or at a bus stop, in a lineup at the bank, and they'd be like old pals for the ten minutes or whatever. I wasn't like that at all. I was the opposite. I could hide away in a cave somewhere, just me and the National, and if someone would bring food and new strings once in a while I could stay there forever. But Bill loved to be on stage, loved to be the centre of attention. Since we married he'd toned it down considerably with women. But there he was, getting lost in Darlene's eyes, and I sat and watched it happen and had no idea what to do or say.

Something else was going on as well. The owner of the Zenith Café in Saskatoon had made a gaffe a couple of weeks earlier. He'd introduced us as Lita MacInnes and Her Syncopation Five. I don't know where he got that idea. I hadn't suggested it, and the others swore up and down that they'd had nothing to do with it. But we got a laugh out of it. Bill laughed at the time, too. Later, though, he accused me of putting the owner up to it. I thought he was joking at first. But he wasn't.

The guy had hit a nerve. It took me a while to understand it, but I began to see that Bill had been the centre of attention in the band until I came along. I hated to be the centre of attention, but from early on, it just developed that way. Everywhere we went, people raved about my playing. I was glad they liked it, but I hated performing. Bill was the performer, not me. But I was the girl. Years later, Elsa told me something Grace Slick of Jefferson Airplane once said, something to the effect of if you put four rats and a duck on stage, the duck's going to stand out. It was true. The trouble was, some rats really resented it.

"Why do we need a manager? What about the regular gig we've got at the Saskatchewan?" I asked.

"Every Saturday night? Big deal," Bill said. "Tell your friend Jacob Stone that we need to eat every night. Darlene's right. We need a manager. Don't you think it's time we took ourselves a little more seriously?"

"Jacob Stone is not my friend."

But he wasn't listening anymore.

Otto suggested we put it to a vote. Oh, hell. Great. How was I supposed to vote, against my husband? Henry and George voted against it, the rest of us were for.

ff

After a while I understood that it wasn't just about Darlene. Bill really thought a manager was the answer to the Syncopation Five's problems. As far as I was concerned, we didn't have any problems. The way I saw it, we had a great time playing music and more often than not got paid for it. We didn't make a lot of money, never had any to save, but between the band and day jobs we made out okay. We all had enough to eat, and roofs over our heads, which was more than a lot of other people could say. And we had fun doing it.

But I'd noticed a change come over Bill during the winter. He'd struck me at first as very carefree, happy go-lucky. After a while, though, I realized that he was actually quite frustrated with what he saw as the Syncopation Five's stalled career. So, Bill was frustrated by me taking the spotlight, frustrated by the band's going nowhere, just plain frustrated.

"This shouldn't be happening," he said one night as we drove home after another wedding gig at a church hall.

"What shouldn't be happening?" I thought there was something wrong with the Packard again.

"This band has been together since I was seventeen. We shouldn't still be playing weddings and parties and two-bit hotels is what I mean. We're good. We should play real gigs, and get paid every time." His jaw was set and the muscles in his cheek rippled. I stifled the urge to laugh and point out that there was little work for all kinds of people, let alone jazz musicians, in Regina.

"It'll come. Be patient. And anyway, I started with you guys when I was seventeen."

"That's different. You've only been with us a little while. But this band is my baby. This is it. And I feel like after five years we're hardly any further ahead than when we started."

"Things are hard for everyone right now. And I don't think we're doing so bad. We've got a house."

"That my mom paid for. When will I start to make some money of my own? The harder I try, the less it happens. It's like grabbing for water. Everything slips through my fingers."

"You'll make money, don't worry. You're a young guy. Anyway, is that all you're in this for?"

"No. But I wonder how much longer we'll have to pay dues, how much longer we'll be a bunch of nobodies. Bing got his break when he was twenty-three. That means I got a year."

I hated to hear him talk that way. "We're not nobodies. We work hard and we're getting better all the time. We've got one regular gig." I looked at him to make sure he had his eyes on the road and wouldn't be able to see me cringe in the dark before I added, "And now that we've got our manager, maybe we'll get more."

"I hope you're right."

I thought our differences in opinion about the band's fortunes were because Bill was older and had played in front of audiences much longer than I had. After all, I'd had nothing but my guitar and my chambermaid job before the band. Now I was a working musician, married to the man I loved. We had our own house that no landlord could kick us out of. We'd never have to skip out in the middle of the night. I didn't fixate on success the way he did because I already felt successful. But it was more than that. Bill came from a comfortable middle-class home. His mum always asked him when he would get a real job, made little remarks that let him know how she felt about what he was doing with his life. The fact that he even played music annoyed her, never mind that he dreamed of making a living at it. The way she saw it, a respectable man might play music as a hobby, though that might even be a problem depending on how much he did it. That he now had a wife and would presumably soon have a family to support only strengthened her argument.

Her attitude reminded me of the story of Bix Beiderbecke's disapproving family. That young genius coronet player, whom many compared to Louis Armstrong, sent copies of his early records to his folks back in Iowa only to discover them later in a closet, unopened, unplayed. I think that his family's callousness played a part in his death from drink in 1931. He was only twenty-eight. I didn't want to see the same thing happen to Bill. I urged him to ignore his mother, and he said he did, but her words had to have an affect on him. How could they not? To people like Bill's mum, the world was black and white: either you were a success or you were a failure. And he would not fail. So he was driven, under a lot of pressure to succeed.

I think marriage caused a shift in his attitude, too. Before we were married the band meant something different than it did to him afterward. Before, it was something he did because he enjoyed it, a means of artistic expression. Afterward it became this thing, this career that didn't move along the way he wanted it to. Of course, he knew that the economy, particularly bad in Saskatchewan, was partly to blame. And we were young and working our way up. Although he already did everything he could, he was always trying to find ways to do more. And he was enormously frustrated.

At the time, I couldn't really understand all that. I only saw Bill's frustration about all the things he didn't have. Compared to so many others, we were doing well. I saw men who stood in line outside the unemployment office and I didn't feel so sorry for my husband. Spoiled rich kid, I sometimes thought, doesn't know when he's got it good. Later I realized I was as bad as Bill's mum, in my way, passing judgment on him.

ff

Darlene got on the job straight away and lined up gigs at hotel lounges in Regina, Saskatoon, and Moose Jaw, as well as at the beach resorts at Waskesiu and Little Manitou Lakes. Big deal, I thought. That took no particular managerial skill. Lots of these venues we'd played before. But now we were working five nights a week, which was new. And Darlene came out to see the band every night.

I knew it was coming, saw it coming, but had no idea what to do about it. By the time Darlene had been managing us for about three months, no one could deny it made a difference. She did all the non-musical things that Bill mostly used to do, and did them better. Now we had lots of work and didn't have to spend any time with self-promotion. We were certainly in a position to be grateful to her, no question. And so the day finally came when she asked us during a rehearsal if she could join us onstage for a number. Well, Bill, actually. She asked Bill.

"What did you have in mind?" he asked.

"I thought I could join you for 'What'll I Do?' You know, a duet. I think it'd be cute."

I looked over at Henry. He could be counted on to go a long way to avoid things that were cute. He made a face like Harpo Marx, and I had to smile.

"Well," Bill turned to me for assistance. He was red-faced, grinning. He had the hots for Darlene. Of course, that much had been obvious to me for a long time. Right then I wanted to slap him. Darlene, too, while I was at it. I knew he was waiting for me to take action, to lay down the law. For me to say, "Bill MacInnes, don't you dare sing a duet with that brazen hussy! You come home this instant!" But I did nothing of the sort. I smiled sweetly and turned away to work on a tricky little riff I'd picked up from the latest Hot Club of France record. I refused to come to his aid.

"Well, I guess that'd be all right," he finally said. "Right, fellas?"

Fellas, indeed, I thought. Nobody said much of anything. We ran through the number and I grimaced at the sound of Darlene's voice. Maybe she didn't really sound as awful as I thought she did, but how could I be objective? Her voice was thin, a little reedy. Someone charitable might have called it untrained, weak. She did stay on key, mostly. But the sound of her voice against Bill's was like listening to nails on a blackboard for me. Because his voice could still make the hairs on the back of my neck stand up, make me wish that I was all alone with him, even in a crowded barroom, even when he crooned some smelly Rudy Vallée number. He knew it, too. You could say many things about Bill, but he was no fool, not when it came to women. We'd get home after a gig, and he'd start to croon "After You've Gone," the old Tin Pan Alley standard, while he washed up, sang it while he lay in wait for me, and by the time I got into bed

I was putty in his hands. That song always did it to me for some reason, and he knew it.

And at home later that night he sang "After You've Gone" again all right, but to no avail. It wouldn't have mattered what Bill sang right then — nothing would have worked on me. I had half a mind to go and sleep on the Winnipeg couch his mum gave us after she came over and discovered we owned almost no furniture. But then I decided there was no reason I should sleep on the couch when I was the innocent bystander. I slipped into bed, back to him, extra careful not to touch him, and turned off the light. Still singing quietly, he ran his hand up and down my side. I made no move, clenched my teeth.

"Lita?" he finally asked.

"Yes?"

"Something wrong?"

"Whatever would make you think something was wrong?" *You big dope.*

"You don't seem very interested. It can't be that time again already, can it?"

As if there could be no other reason. "No, it isn't that time. I just don't want to stand in for Darlene, that's all."

"What's that supposed to mean?"

"Do you think I haven't noticed?"

"That's your imagination."

"Is it? First, she's our manager, now all of a sudden she sings a duet with you. I thought when we ran through it once, that that would be it, she'd have had her fun, and we'd get back to work. We ran through the goddamn song five times. Five times. And she can't sing worth shit — "

"Aw, c'mon," he interrupted. "Be nice."

"This is not an amateur hour, Bill. We are professionals. She can't sing and you know it. So what is this all about? I'm afraid from where I see things, the answer looks pretty obvious."

"I know she can't sing. But what am I gonna do? After all she's done for us, we owe her something."

"She doesn't do all this stuff for free, you know. She gets her ten percent. She gets paid because she does her job, that's all. We let her sing with us and it'll finish us off."

"Oh, come on now. One little song is going to finish us off, when we have three hours worth of other material?"

"I don't mean it'll finish off the band."

"Lita. Is that what you're afraid of?"

"Seems like a pretty reasonable fear to me. The way you look into her eyes, laugh at her jokes. You talk to her all through our set breaks."

"Well, I've got to talk to somebody during our set breaks. All *you* do is sulk in a corner and play your guitar. You never put it down. And can I help it if I have to talk to her? I've always been the one who takes care of all those little details like bookings and money. So it's only natural that I'd talk to her about stuff like that." Bill was a master at turning the tables, I had to give him that.

"You sure seem to have a gay old time doing it. I never saw you laugh and chatter away like that with any of the bar managers you dealt with before."

"That's ridiculous."

"Is it?"

He rolled over. "Yes, it is. Just put Darlene out of your mind. There's nothing to worry about."

His words and subsequent behaviour put me at ease for a time. He seemed to understand that whether my fears were unfounded or not, I saw Darlene as a threat, and he backed away from her accordingly. Then Darlene came up with the idea of the record.

It was the next logical step for the Syncopation Five to take, she said. We could record a couple of our best songs, and give out copies to radio stations and sell them at gigs. It sounded like a great idea, until we got into the studio. We'd agreed to record a couple of show tunes, a certain person's favourites: "Isn't It Romantic?" by Rodgers and Hart, and Gershwin's "So Am I." I wouldn't have picked them as our best songs. Had it been up to me, we would have recorded something a little more "hot," as Henry would have put it. We did a good job with "I'll Be Glad When You're Dead, You Rascal, You," for instance. But Bill finally convinced us that these two show tunes had the most appeal with audiences, so that settled it.

We were all excited about the record. Otto wanted to mail them to all his relatives for Christmas, and George was sure he could sell copies at the garage where he worked days. We were about to begin "Isn't It Romantic?" when Darlene joined Bill at the microphone, all smiles. Bill and I stood closest to the mike, so that it would pick up his voice and my solos — that was how recording sessions went in those days, one microphone that we all played around. Otto and his fiddle were in the middle, and George on bass and Henry on drums were the farthest away so they wouldn't drown the rest of us out. I looked at Darlene, then at my husband. He tried to pretend he didn't notice. I tried to think what to say, when Henry said it for me. Good old Henry.

"Since when is this outfit the Syncopation Six?"

Darlene laughed. "Why, Henry, don't get all excited. Just a little back-up vocal, that's all."

"If we'd wanted back-up vocals, we'd have hired a singer. And we would have rehearsed with her."

"Listen here, I'm doing you guys a favour. I won't charge you for this."

"You won't charge us? I'll say. Nobody in their right mind would pay you to sing."

It went on back and forth between them for a few minutes. Then the recording technician reminded us that we were being charged by the hour for studio time. That brought things to a close. Good thing, too, because it was getting a little ugly.

"We should have worked this all out before we got here. This is a waste of time," Bill complained.

The nerve. I couldn't stay quiet any longer. "We *did* have it all worked out. All those times we rehearsed, there were five of us. No one said anything about this."

"Listen," the technician suggested. "Why don't you run through the numbers once with the backing vocals? We'll cut a wax test, and if you don't like it, we can leave them out on the final version. We should have time for that."

Finally, a reasonable idea. We did just that. We listened to the first song: it began with a twelve bar intro and then Bill started. When Darlene's voice came in, I shot Henry a little glance and he made the Harpo Marx face again. I had to look at the floor. I couldn't look at anyone else because I was afraid I'd start to laugh. Not only is love blind, it's also tone-deaf.

"I don't think that'll do," Henry said decisively after it was finished.

"Fine," said Darlene. She marched out, pulled up a chair behind the technician and sulked as we rerecorded the numbers. What a relief, I thought.

ff

After that, The Syncopation Five spent a month on a tour of southern Saskatchewan that Darlene had lined up, played bars and dances. I found that very pleasant, a month away from our manager. As soon as we got back to town Bill took the Packard over to the studio to pick up the records. He had a big box full of them. It probably wouldn't seem like much now, but then, 250 records was an impressive number. Of course, 78s were heavy; maybe that's why they seemed so impressive. They were something to see, all right, with their royal blue labels and silver inscription: THE SYNCOPATION FIVE. That made it seem like we'd arrived, like we were big time, now. Side A was "Isn't It Romantic?" and Side B was "So Am I." I was about to slip one onto the record player when Bill stopped me. He went out for some beer and I got on the phone to get the others over so we could all listen to it together for the first time.

We cracked our beers and Bill dropped the needle onto the wax. As the twelve bar lead-in started we clinked our bottles in salute. But soon our faces fell. Darlene's voice was like nails on a chalkboard to all of us this time.

"Oh, God," gasped Otto.

"That idiot screwed up! How could this have happened?" Bill was furious. I was glad to see he wasn't in on it, or at least didn't appear to be. I didn't believe for a second that that version of the song ended up on the record by accident. Nor was I alone.

"You don't really think this was a mistake, do you?" Henry demanded.

Before Bill could answer, I jumped in. "Some mistake. She was up there in the booth with him when we left the studio, you all saw that. She obviously switched the masters on him, or sweet-talked him into doing it. Sweet-talked him, or something."

"Probably the something, if you ask me," George said. "I wonder if there's any way we can get them to cut us another batch?"

Worse, the wrong recordings got on to both sides. Bill and Henry went down to the studio to see what they could do. And it wasn't much. The technician apologized, but he swore that he was sure he'd picked up the right master. If Darlene had convinced him to switch them somehow, he wasn't telling. The other masters, the right ones, were already gone and if we wanted to rerecord it, we'd have to book and pay for more studio time and pay for more records to be pressed. They might be able to cut us a bit of a deal because of the mistake, but they couldn't just give it to us. The other option was to live with it.

Which is what we had to do. There wasn't enough money to do it all again, even at a cut rate. As it was, the first time had stretched our resources as far as they would go. Bill talked briefly about borrowing some money from his mum to do it. But he didn't. Probably wouldn't have been able to tell her the story. As for Darlene, she denied any part in the mix-up, though not even Bill believed her. We still sold the records at our shows and gave them away to the radio stations, but they didn't sell the way we'd hoped.

Strangely enough, though, the net effect of the whole thing for me was good. Bill was so angry with Darlene he threatened to fire her. She insisted she had nothing to do with it. We couldn't prove it, so she kept her job, but she no longer came to every practice, and she didn't sing anymore. That was a blessed relief. After a while I was even glad she mixed the masters up or convinced the technician to do it.

I was glad because Bill couldn't stand the sight of her after that, at least for a while. And, I reasoned, there would be plenty of opportunities to do more records later. This was not a big deal, the way I saw it. My eighteenth birthday came and went and I relaxed for the first time that year.

Fourteen

Lita
November 1936

FIRST REALLY COLD MORNING I WENT out and got some groceries. The week before I had spotted a headline on *Good Housekeeping* magazine (*Win His Heart With This Easy Pot Roast*) while waiting to pay for some cigarettes. I had suddenly got the idea that what my domestic skills lacked, and what our marriage really needed was some baking and some dusting. Desperate for advice, I took the magazine home and devoured it, amazed. I'd never read such a magazine before and this one seemed to have all the answers. Not only about what was wrong with my marriage; it contained the answer to everything that was wrong with me. My body, my personality, my clothes, my interests, my abilities. All these things left something to be desired, I was led to believe by the glossy pages, the eye-catching ads and the article (continued on page 62), written in such a friendly but no-nonsense fashion. All these things needed improvement, would you believe it?

So I decided to change, decided that that freezing Monday morning would mark the start of a new chapter in our lives, that 1937 would be a landmark year. I woke before Bill. The sun peeked in through a hole in the blind, shone on his hair and made it glow dark gold. Much as I wanted to reach for him, I got up and got started. I had a mission. If I was about to make pot roast for dinner, cherry tarts for dessert, and have the place cleaned from top to bottom, I had to get started.

When I returned from the store I could see Bill had had coffee, read the paper, and I thought he was out. So I put the groceries away. When I walked by the bedroom, I was surprised to see him packing his clothes into the open suitcase. He looked at me a minute, expressionless, before he spoke.

"I'm moving out."

I hadn't known how fast things could go. I knew our marriage was in trouble, sure. I was eighteen years old, maybe too young to be married. Still, it was the usual thing then for people that age to be married. I had no idea what to do, and nobody to turn to for help. I didn't even get a chance to try *Good Housekeeping's* advice, as it turned out.

"Where to?"

"I'm moving in with Darlene."

I didn't know what to say. He'd always denied seeing Darlene, of course, but I knew. Everybody knew. More and more nights through the summer he'd come in late, later. Sometimes he wouldn't come home until morning. I fought a sudden urge to walk out the door, to walk until I couldn't walk anymore. What good being exhausted on the highway halfway to Moose Jaw would do, though, I couldn't tell.

"You fucking liar. I knew right from the start that she wanted to take you away from me. Why did you lie to me?"

"If you're going to get hysterical, how can I even explain?"

"So explain."

"It's not that I'm not in love with you. I am. I'll always love you. Things just aren't working out the way I thought they would."

He closed the suitcase, took it into the front porch and got his coat and hat off the rack. My mind raced: *Now, now, Lita. Say it now. You've got to think of something right now.* That was what ran through my mind instead of what I should actually say. His hand went to the doorknob and then I felt like I couldn't get enough air, not enough to talk. I finally gasped, "We can find out what's wrong. We can try. We have to."

I am sure I said it but wonder now if maybe I didn't. Maybe I just thought I did, because he didn't seem to hear me. The only thing that made me think he might have heard was a brief grimace that flickered over his face. "Goodbye, Lita," he said, and then he was on the other side of the doorway. And I stood and watched him and still wondering what to say, didn't really believe what I saw.

ff

Not only did Bill walk out on me, he also didn't come to rehearsals. Otto sang some and so did George, but neither of them sang all that well. That first Saturday at the Hotel Saskatchewan, Jacob Stone innocently asked me where Bill was, probably thought he was sick or something.

"He's gone," I said. I saw Henry wince in the background. It probably would have been more kind, or easier for me maybe, if Jacob had happened to ask one of the fellas. But he asked me.

"Gone?"

"Gone. He left me. And the band."

"Oh. I'm so sorry."

I shrugged. I had no idea what else to say, because almost anything else would have made tears sting my eyes. Worse than they already were.

ƒƒ

After the show that night, Jacob convinced me to stay and talk. The rest of the band left, Jacob sent the bartender home and tended bar himself, mixed me a series of gin and tonics. I told him everything. I did cry, but not for as long or as hard as I'd expected. Perhaps Jacob's quiet manner put me at ease, but I felt a certain degree of detachment as I told him, as if all of this had happened to someone else.

"So he's gone for good?" he asked.

"I'm not sure. You know, we were just on the verge of going on a road trip to Seattle. Darlene was in touch with someone who booked acts for a bunch of nightclubs down there, and we were talking about going for a month."

Jacob shook his head. "So Darlene's gone too?"

"Yes."

"Too bad. That would have been a very good opportunity."

"It would have been the biggest thing we ever did. I'm wondering if Darlene was putting pressure on him or something. I don't know."

"Well, maybe he'll change his mind. But in the meantime, what are the rest of you going to do?"

"I don't know. The others want to get a new singer. Well, Otto and George do. You heard them singing tonight. It doesn't work. I think Henry's about ready to fly. He's got a cousin in Edmonton who wants to get a combo together. And me, I just don't think I have the heart for it anymore."

"What do you mean? You're fantastic. You get a new band together, your own band."

"Well, I know it's no good to stay in Bill's old band and play all the songs he used to sing. But I don't think I could do it myself. I'm a musician, not a performer, you know what I mean? I could always hide behind him. Not hide behind him, exactly, but I liked how he'd deflect the attention away. But the last few nights, to be up there without him — I hated it. I have to give it a rest for a while."

"What will you do, then?"

"Look for a job, I guess. The only other thing I have experience at is being a chambermaid."

"You don't need to do that. How'd you like to be a bartender?"

The next week, we cancelled all our dates. Jacob showed me the ropes behind the bar. It was not a bad job, the tips were decent. I also got to check out some of the other acts that played the Saskatchewan. Until then, I hadn't realized how good we were. That part of it was a little depressing. I missed the band, missed the guys, missed playing. But the rest of it was okay. I didn't mind the hours, since I was used to musicians' hours. It also meant that I got to see a lot of Jacob.

ff

The street lights through the snowy night outside gave a soft glow to the things inside Jake's bedroom. It smelled faintly of bay rum and shoe leather. His clothes for the next day, I noticed, were already neatly hung on his valet stand. I lay exhausted in his arms, under a thick down quilt.

"This is so nice. But I feel awful about it in some ways," I said.

"I know you do. But you need someone right now. And I've wanted you for a long time."

"Yes, but I'm married. And you know I love you, but I still love Bill."

"It's all right. I understand."

"I barely understand it myself."

Jacob was an easy man to love. He was kind, handsome, considerate. With Bill, love felt like an overwhelming force. It was quieter with Jacob, not as scary. Sometimes, I wondered if I was seeing him to get back at Bill. Or to hurt him. I didn't know, and the more I thought about it the more confused I got.

There was something else too, that I couldn't tell Jacob. I was afraid of going from depending on one man to depending on another. And how did I know I could trust him? I'd trusted Bill, and look what happened. Maybe I didn't know how to tell who was trustworthy and who wasn't. How do you tell, anyway? Seems like I trusted people, like Bill, like Ma, and they turned on me. Back then I thought maybe nobody was trustworthy.

"Jake?"

He was asleep. I watched the snowflakes pile up on the windowsill until eventually I fell asleep, too.

Fifteen

Lita
December 1936

I woke from a dream in the black of a night just before Christmas, mouth dry, heart racing. It played through my mind, over and over, as I stood at the sink and got a drink of water. I was alone in Bill's parents' house. It was cold and dark and I sat on a couch, nervous and afraid. I coughed hard and when I took my hand away from my mouth, three molars lay bloody in my palm. I ran my tongue over the empty sockets, stared at the teeth in my hand, tasted metallic blood. Then a cold wind screaming through the empty house felt like it would blast right through me.

For a long time, I'd been troubled by vivid dreams like this one. I didn't know what they meant, but it didn't feel like anything good. I mentioned it to Steve once and he said it might be an idea to write the dreams down. As soon as possible after waking, he said, in as much detail as possible, and eventually a pattern might emerge. At first I thought, oh, yeah, Steve and his flaky ideas. He believed that dreams were sent to tell you something you needed to know. I wasn't so sure about that. But as the dreams became more frequent

I decided to try it. I kept a pad of paper beside the bed and when I had a vivid dream, jotted down the details on waking.

Bill wanted to see what I'd written once. I refused at first. I often wonder why it should have been so, but I always felt so damned inadequate beside him, so embarrassed, so ashamed of myself, never more than when he tried to get into personal things like that. He pestered me, though, promised he wouldn't tell anyone, and I finally gave in. My ears burned as I watched him read it, but he didn't laugh like I thought he might. He handed the pad back to me.

"You really dreamt all this stuff? You didn't just make it up?"

"Why would I make it up?"

"I don't know. They're crazy dreams."

"Don't you ever have crazy dreams?"

"Sure I do, lots. But not like these. They're so violent and dramatic. You'd never know it."

"What do you mean?"

"Well, you've got that icy exterior. Sometimes you can freeze a guy right out. But then all this stuff goes on inside, like these dreams. And the way you play."

I took it as an insult at the time. But now I realize he had insight I didn't give him credit for. Sometimes I wondered what else I hadn't given him credit for.

$$ff$$

Soon after my dream of the teeth, I was up late one Saturday night after my shift, reading in bed. It was sometime between Christmas and New Year's. I was trying not to see Jacob all the time. It was a particularly dismal holiday season. I'd read a lot since Bill left. At this point I wasn't actually still reading. I knew I'd have to wake up enough to put the book down and turn off the light, but for right then I was content to try a sentence, doze, wake, try the same sentence, in an endless loop.

I began to dream the kind of vivid, odd dream you have sometimes when you're dozing off. I was walking along a dock on a warm, sunny day, talking to a man. He was tall, his face indistinct, but the red, gold, and brown hues in his wavy hair glowed, shifted. I longed to touch it, could not take my eyes off him as we walked to the end of the dock and sat beside each other at the end, feet dangling. I don't know what we were talking about, but I felt happy, calm, safe. Then a voice shattered me out of sleep.

"Lita?"

I caught my breath, sat up and stared at Bill, too confused to speak.

"I let myself in. I hope you don't mind."

"What are you doing here?"

He was drunk. "S'my house, isn't it?"

"Our house, you mean. For now."

"What's that supposed to mean?" He'd already taken off his shoes and socks, started to unbutton his shirt.

"You tell me. You're the one who's run off. Where is Darlene tonight, anyway?"

"Never mind about her. I didn't come here to talk about her." He got under the covers and put his cold feet on mine. In days of old I used to like to warm his big feet up, he knew that. This time I pulled my feet away.

"Well, I'd like to talk about her, talk about what you're doing. I mean, are we getting a divorce or what?"

He ran his hand over my back, under my pajama top. "I told you, I didn't come here to talk about that."

Oh, the way things turn out sometimes. Wasn't it only the night before that I had fantasized about this exact thing? Well, no, not this exact thing. But something like it. The night before, in my mind's ear, he'd whispered sweet nothings, thrilled me with his imaginary presence. But when it came to reality, this reality, I was so mad at him I could scream, felt about as receptive as a bucket of nails. Of course, in my fantasy, he wasn't drunk, either.

"You're welcome to sleep here tonight. But please don't do this."

"It's my goddamn house and you're my goddamn wife."

ff

The next morning, I thought about that passage in *Gone With the Wind* where Rhett rapes Scarlett. The next morning Scarlett sits up in bed, stretches sensuously, sings, and giggles at memories of the night before, as if a good rape was just what she needed. I thought about that passage and what a load of shit it was. Normally on a Sunday morning I would have slept longer, but I didn't want to stay in bed and listen to that great oaf sleep it off. I got into the bath to have a nice long soak and maybe forget it. It didn't do any good; rage consumed me.

Rage and sadness. What happened to my Bill, I wondered. What had Darlene done with him? The Bill I used to know would never have done this. Sure, he might flirt with other women, he probably even slept with a few. Leaving me was something incomprehensible, and last night he'd been someone I didn't know.

But what could I do? Go to the police? Right. Wife raped by her own husband. Yeah, that would stand up in court. I would have really liked to tell his mother. Tell her, and be believed. If she heard something like this about her dear, sweet William, I was sure she'd blame me — I must have been asking for it. Or she'd stick her fingers in her ears and hum, the old dear. Even as I listened to his long, probably still-drunken snores rip the air in the bedroom, I thought how different last night could have been, how nice it could have been. If only he wasn't such a rotten, cruel, drunken, selfish bastard.

I dressed, made myself some coffee and toast, sat in the kitchen and listened to the radio. The snores stopped after a while and I heard him stir around, go to the bathroom. I listened and tried to think what to say to him. I'd thought about that on and off since I woke, but really had no idea what to say. So when he came out and stood beside me, I only looked up at him. I didn't smile, didn't say a word.

"Mind if I have some of that coffee?" he asked.

"Go ahead."

He poured a cup, sat down across from me at the little red Formica table, and drank it almost in one gulp. Then he lit a cigarette for himself, and one for me, as an afterthought.

"When I came here last night, I didn't mean for things to turn out they way did. I wanted to come over here and tell you how I missed you and such. But it took me longer than I thought it would to get up the courage. And by the time I got up the courage, well . . . my original intentions were kind of forgotten by then."

I thought I'd let him continue, in case he wanted to apologize or anything like that. He was going in the right direction.

He finished his cigarette. "I can see now that I've just made a huge mess of things," he said, and got his coat from the tree by the door. "I don't expect you to ever forgive me. I'm sorry I hurt you, but I don't expect you to forgive me."

"Bill, it's not too late to talk."

He shook his head. "No, you're wrong. It is too late. You'll never respect me again. And what kind of a marriage would that be?"

"You're wrong. We can still make it work."

"I don't think so. Darlene and me, maybe it's not the same as it was with us, Lita. But we've got a lot in common. We're two of a kind. No-talent, faithless, selfish bastards. We understand each other."

"That's not true, not about you. You have talent. You're a great singer. We could start again, get the band back together, get a new band started. And I need you to come back to me. I love you."

He smiled. "You don't need me. You're the one with all the talent. You and that guitar, I swear, sometimes it's like there's nothing else in the world but you and that guitar. I hate to come between you." He buttoned up his coat and put on his hat.

He was here, but he was getting ready to go, slipping out of my grasp again. How could I stop him?

"Don't do this, Bill. I love you. Doesn't that count for anything?"

"It counts for a lot. Enough that I'd almost be ready to come back, if I thought it could work. But it's too late now. Every time I'd look in your eyes and think of what a rotten bastard I've been, how could I stand myself? No, I've got to go. Goodbye, Lita. I love you."

He kissed me, and before I knew what happened, he was gone.

Sixteen

Lita
February 1937

WHAT I FELT ABOUT DARLENE RIGHT then was something
I've never felt about another human being before or since. It
was a horrible, consuming hatred. I didn't really know what
went on between her and Bill to restart their relationship,
whether it was a restart, whether he made the first move
or she. Not that it really mattered. I couldn't help but see
Darlene as an evil temptress. Had I been at all rational, I
would have known that Bill acted out of his free will. But
my anger demanded a sacrifice, and Darlene had to be it. It
couldn't be Bill, because I wanted him back.

I hated Darlene enough that I wished she was dead. Not
that I wanted to kill her, I just wanted her to be dead. I found
some twisted consolation in the idea of Darlene being hit by a
streetcar, of her crashing down a flight of stairs and breaking
her neck. I imagined Bill coming back to me, distraught, in
need of solace and apologetic all at once. That part of the
fantasy wasn't all that satisfying. I would have preferred if
he'd rushed back to me, horrified with himself, pleading for
me to take him back. But as the days went by it seemed like

that wouldn't happen, and the only way he'd come back was if Darlene was dead. So be it. I was that desperate to have him back. In spite of how he treated me, in spite of what had happened that night, I wanted him back. Every day, the second I woke up I thought of him, and it didn't stop all day.

I did a novena to St. Jude. Nine days I prayed, nine times a day, nine prayers each time. I checked the ads in the paper every day to see how to word mine, looked forward to the end of the nine days when St. Jude would grant my favour. Should I keep it simple — "Thanks to St. Jude for favours received, L. M."? Or maybe be a little more flowery, a little more effusive — "For granting my heart's true desire, dear blessed St. Jude, I offer my everlasting gratitude and deepest devotion, L.M."? But nothing happened.

Next I dug out Mami's Tzigane tarot deck from the old country, and tried to read them the way I saw her do it long ago. I knew I had to formulate my question for the cards carefully. That was easy enough, but the interpretation was tricky. Part way through I remembered that clouds in the pictures on some of the cards changed their apparent meaning, and could change the meaning of the cards around them, too. And then some of them meant one thing if they were close to the inquirer's card, but something else if they were far away. The Bear, for instance, meant happiness if far away, but signified caution if nearby. What if it was a moderate distance away? Cards like the Coffin had more than one meaning, depending on where they lay. But the Cross was always a bad omen — only the distance from the inquirer's card affected its degree of badness. And why did the cards seem to have a completely different meaning every time I laid them out? It was like trying to understand my dreams. Steve always insisted I needed to give them more thought after they happened, and then I'd understand what they were trying to tell me. But maybe they weren't trying to tell me anything. Maybe they didn't mean anything, just like the pictures printed on these paper cards, no matter how mysterious they looked.

These things didn't work but I had to keep trying, had to feel like I was doing something to get Bill back. Not having him made me crazy. I had insane dreams, when I could sleep. I'd lie awake for hours in the middle of the night. I felt restless, light-headed, not myself, and I had to do something about it. It became clear that I'd have to break it off with Jacob. If I really wanted my husband back, I'd have to have him alone in my heart. And really, I knew that had been true all along. Ending things with Jacob was the only fair thing to do.

Maybe it was fair, but it wasn't easy. I called Jacob late one bitterly cold night, asked if I could come over and talk. Though he offered to come and get me, I walked over. Small, hard snowflakes stung my face. I wanted to have time to go over in my mind once more what to say to him. Never mind that it would all evaporate the minute I walked in his door.

He sat me down by the fire, got me a drink.

"What's wrong?" he asked.

I had an impulse to say nothing was wrong, but I knew it was no good. "Jake, I've got to stop seeing you."

"Go on."

Damn him. Why'd he have to be so calm? And so sad-looking? "Oh, I hate to do it. You've been good for me, and I don't know what I would have done without you. But I still love Bill."

"I know that. I always knew that. It doesn't make any difference to me."

"Maybe it should. How can you stand to hold me when you know I still love him?"

"Because I know you'll get over him."

"That's where you're wrong. I've tried everything. But I just can't. And it's not fair to either of us to keep on like this. Especially not to you. You deserve someone who loves you completely."

"I'd hoped one day that someone might be you."

"Jake, don't say that. I think it would be better if I quit my job at the hotel."

"Don't you like your job?"

"It's not that. It would just be better that way."

"Listen, I don't think that's a very good idea. You keep your job, I won't make anything difficult for you. Things are just bad for you right now. I'm sure they'll improve soon."

Jake insisted on giving me a ride home. I crawled into bed feeling like an awful heel, but somehow better, lighter. More ready for the task of getting my husband back where he belonged.

ff

When the police came with the news the next morning, I was sure there'd been some mistake. I went to the morgue with them convinced that the man they'd found frozen in the alley wasn't Bill. Just before they pulled back the sheet, I thought what a big joke it would be when I told him about it.

I stood and blinked at him a moment, as if this could somehow change what I saw in front of me. His eyes were half-shut, dull, empty. His face was chalk, his lips purple. I touched his arm, somehow hadn't expected it to be cold, and pulled my hand back.

This wasn't supposed to happen, I kept thinking. When we retired, we were going to spend our summers in the Qu'Appelle Valley; we'd talked about moving to Fort Qu'Appelle, the verdant spot where Regina would have been if not for the treachery of the railroad. We'd play music, read, paint, swim, maybe play croquet. It had become a game between us. I knew exactly how Bill would look when he got old — his hair would recede to a certain point, then turn white. That would make his face look pink, like his mum's. He'd have bifocals, walk a little stooped. Instead, this is how he looked in the end: white, frozen, twenty-three years old. What'll I do, I wondered, with all those other images now?

They told me he'd been found in an alley early that morning. He'd been at a bar and got a cab home. The driver's trip sheet noted the time and the address. Then, they said, "You weren't there?"

"No."

"His keys were in his pocket."

"I wasn't home."

They said he'd started to walk, maybe headed back to the bar. He froze to death at the end of a dark alley.

I didn't cry or yell or scream there, nor in the squad car when one of the officers gave me a ride home. He took me into the house, asked if I had anyone I could call, and I said yes, I'd be fine. It was a lie. Who would I call? Darlene? Bill's mum? Actually, I would have to tell both of them. But not right then. I thought briefly about calling Jacob, but couldn't.

Bill had come home. I tried to comprehend it. He came home and couldn't get in. I'd had the locks changed, of course. After that night, Henry had changed them for me. Had Jake and I driven by him on the street? I wondered.

Before long I decided I did need to call someone. So I called Darlene. After all, why should dear Darlene enjoy herself when she could share in this horrendous grief?

"Darlene?"

"Lita, is that you?"

"Yes, it is."

"So, what's up?"

"He's dead."

"What do you mean? Who's dead?"

"Bill."

"Bill?"

"Yes. You know, our Bill."

"You can't be serious."

"Darlene, would I call you up to tell you my husband is dead for a joke?"

"What happened?"

"He froze to death last night."

She made a sound like an animal, something awful to listen to. Briefly, I thought about hanging up. I stayed on the line, though, and listened to her yowl for some time. Should I say something?

After a while, I did hang up after all.

ƒƒ

I tried numerous times after the policeman dropped me off to call Steve, but he wasn't around. He was the only person I could think of talking to right then, and I wasn't sure how much I could talk anyway, even with him. Then I decided I'd better call Ian, Bill's brother. I knew I should call my mother-in-law, too, but decided to let Ian deal with it. I could count on him, he was much more reliable than Bill was in many ways. After I told him the news he said he would go over and tell Mary and then come by to check on me. While I waited for him, I tried Steve again and then thought about calling Lena, letting my family know through my sister. But every time I thought about telling someone again, I didn't know if I could, didn't know if I had the strength to go over the story again when I could barely comprehend it myself.

Ian must have stayed with Mary for a time, but I had no idea how long. Time was strange that day. When he arrived, he looked tired. Neither of us said anything at first. He held me close for a minute and I rested my cheek against his grey wool coat, realized how good it felt to have someone to lean on.

"Do you mind if I turn a light on?" he asked. It struck me again how much Ian looked like Bill. His hair was blond and he was shorter than Bill, but they had the same long face, the same eyes. It hurt to look at him.

"No." I hadn't noticed it was dark. The day had passed in a blur. I could not tell when I had got back from the morgue, or what time I'd talked to Darlene or to him, but that was all I'd done since I got back except have some tea.

Ian sat on the couch and I sat on the chair across from him. We looked at each other, didn't know what to say, where to begin.

"Do you want a drink?" I asked. "I don't even know if I have anything."

"You sit. I'll find it."

"Bill might have some scotch in the cupboard beside the fridge."

He brought drinks, I didn't know what they were.

"How's your mum?" I asked.

He shook his head and sighed. "I'll go back over there later tonight, probably stay with her. She's not doing very well. How are you?"

"I don't know, Ian. I don't know."

"It's a hell of a thing. What was he doing?"

"I guess he tried to get in. I wasn't here, I had no idea he was coming. And by the time I got back he'd already wandered away."

"What was going on with you two? I mean, I know he'd moved out, but I couldn't understand it. He didn't ever say what the trouble was. He told me it was just temporary."

Temporary? "He never told me it was temporary. One day he just told me he was going to live with Darlene . . ."

"I'm sorry, Lita. I'm sorry. This isn't the time to talk about that."

Ian stayed for a while that long, strange night. He said he'd call me the next morning and help with the arrangements. Probably Mum would want to help with that, too, he said. After he left I tried Steve once more and still got no answer. I sat for a long time and looked at the drink Ian had poured on the little coffee table, the ice in it long melted. I thought a long time about that word *temporary* and what Bill might have meant when he said it. Over the next weeks and months I would think about it a lot. I never have come to a conclusion.

Eventually I switched off the lights. But before I did, I poured the contents of my glass down the sink. Right then, a drink was about the last thing in the world I wanted.

I went to bed but didn't sleep much. I wept, ranted some. Mostly I lay there and stared at the cracks in the yellowed ceiling. Sometimes I dozed off for a little while, got some blessed if brief respite from the thought that my husband was dead. But every time I woke up it was the first thing that came into my mind. It grabbed me by the throat and shook me.

Sometime about dawn I slept for a couple of hours. When I woke again the thought came to me but not as a slam in the head like it had all night. It was more that I felt the weight of it settled on my chest. I opened my eyes all the way. I got out of bed, made some coffee, lit a cigarette. There were only three cigarettes left in the package. I would have to buy some, soon. How, how could I go out of the house and talk to people after what had happened? Wouldn't they all know, wouldn't they all say, "There's the woman who locked out her husband and let him freeze to death"? I didn't know how I'd ever be able to face anything again. There it was again, that shame. Like the shame I felt after my father died.

I drank my coffee and smoked my remaining cigarettes, and then I had to go out and buy more. I washed my face and dressed, walked down to the corner store. It wasn't as bad as I thought it would be. The little old woman at the counter didn't say anything unusual, didn't look at me funny or anything. I wondered on the way back how the world could be so much the same, like nothing had even happened.

Once I got home I picked up the newspaper, shocked that it wasn't on the front page: "Singer Bill MacInnes Freezes to Death While Estranged Wife Visits Lover." I looked through the whole paper, but there was no mention of it anywhere. Then I got to the obituaries. An obituary would have to be written, it dawned on me. How could I do it? What would I say in it?

Some time after that Ian and his mother came over. Mary's face was swollen from crying, her eyes and nose were red. I hadn't seen her in months, not since Christmas.

She put her arms around me and I thought she wanted to comfort me, but then she pulled back.

"Why were you out that late at night?" she asked. "Were you working at that bar again?"

"I have to work. Bill left me."

"If he did leave you, I'm sure it was because you drove him away. And besides, that's what comes of your cheap behaviour. Do you think I don't know about how you lived in my house while I was in Toronto? Do you think my neighbours didn't keep an eye on you two? No wonder he lost interest if you just gave it away." She almost spat the words.

Ian took his mother by the upper arm. "Mum. Don't do this."

She looked at him a moment and then looked back at me. Her little round face had hardened into a knot, but I almost thought I saw the hint of a smile for a second. Perhaps she enjoyed the thought of hurting my feelings. Only this rant didn't hurt my feelings, it just disgusted me.

As it turned out I didn't have to do much when it came to the arrangements. Bill's mother took care of the funeral, and I asked Ian to write the obituary. I couldn't do any of it, could barely do anything at all those first few days, besides smoke. I might as well stick with something I'm good at, I figured.

ff

It took a long time, years, actually, before I stopped seeing Bill around. In the early days after he died it happened all the time. I'd see a man on the street and, for a split second, the look of the back of his neck or the way he wore his hat would make me think it was Bill, and I'd be ready to rush up to him when I'd realize it wasn't him. Sometimes I'd have to look for a minute, and it scared me. Not so much the idea that I might have seen a ghost, but the thought that I was losing my mind.

Because for a while I was sure I was losing it. For a time I lost my old self and became the Widow, the person overwhelmed by grief. I felt many things about Bill then, among them a deep anger. Not so much anger at his leaving me, but anger over his death. Anger over his death turning me into someone who could barely make it down to the corner store to buy a newspaper without weeping.

I had some black times in those early weeks after I lost him, make no mistake. One miserable day in April it poured with rain all day, which turned to snow after sunset. By 7 PM it started to look like a blizzard, started to remind me too much of the night Bill died. Alone in our house, surrounded by our things, I poured myself a glass of wine and switched on the radio to find something to distract me. I listened to *Amos 'n' Andy* for a while, then switched it to *Burns and Allen*. They did nothing for me, only made my mood worse. How could I have even found these shows funny before? I had another glass of wine and looked at my guitar case for a while. But I couldn't bear to bring the National out, to even think of playing it. As I watched the snow pile up on the windowsill, watched the odd car or streetcar go by on Dewdney Avenue, my mood grew blacker. So black I wondered what would become of me. What was the point in living anymore? I couldn't help but think of my father then.

That night I had a dream that I have never forgotten. I dreamt that I was outside in the storm — cold, lost, terrified. Snow swirled around me in every direction and I couldn't see where I was going, couldn't see anything. Then from out of nowhere a little boy appeared and stood in front of me. That is, I felt that it was a little boy. I couldn't tell for sure. He looked to be about three or four years old, all dressed in white. My fingers ached to reach out and touch his curly hair, which seemed to be glowing red, then gold, then brown, then even some pink tones. He said nothing, only smiled at me. I felt a deep calm looking at him, and my fear melted. Without saying a word, he made me feel everything would be all right, somehow.

The next morning I thought of the dream over and over. Was the child a ghost? An angel? A child I'd known at some point? I thought of my sister Hana. She'd died when I was too young to remember her, but I had a feeling this child was a boy, I was sure of that for some reason. I wondered if it might be a son I'd have one day. Or maybe it was just a silly dream. Maybe, but a voice inside me said it was important.

ff

My grief gradually eased. I thought it was great when I could go out and not burst into tears if I encountered a rude salesclerk or heard a sad piece of music. Music was terrible. There were certain songs, hearing them was like a punch in the stomach, like "What'll I Do?" And being able to talk about Bill to acquaintances without tears was a milestone. For many years things would still hit me, usually unexpectedly, and almost take me down. Once, only a couple of years ago, I turned on the heat for the first time after the summer, and the smell of dust burning in the furnace, strong, strange, immediately put me in mind of the dusty Quonset we used to practise in back in the 30s, and I had to sit and weep. I hadn't expected to feel that way more than sixty years later, but there you are.

Eventually I began to forget what he looked like. My memories of Bill became blurred. Such forgetting would have seemed ridiculous to me before he died, but all the same it happened. I'd take out his pictures to sharpen the details. Ah, yes, of course, this is what he looked like. What did his voice sound like? I puzzled over that. Of course I remembered the words he said to me, but what did his voice really sound like? Unfortunately, the only recordings the Syncopation Five made were the two where Darlene sang with him. I didn't want to hear them for a long time.

When I did eventually listen to the record many years later, it surprised me. I felt tense, a little angry, perhaps, during the intro of side one and until the singing started. But I melted when it struck me how young Bill sounded. When he died I was nineteen, and before long I reached twenty-four, an age he never attained. That was strange. Since he was older than me, I'd assumed he had wisdom, judgment, experience, but once I surpassed his final age it began to dawn on me that perhaps Bill didn't really possess these qualities I'd invented for him, or least not to the degree I'd imagined. And I couldn't bring myself to listen to the record until I was almost forty-two. It was made when Bill was twenty-two, and there I was over twenty years later, with this vast gulf of years I'd lived, and there he was crooning away with that silly bitch Darlene about love. Now they were both long dead, and I sat and listened to their long-ago voices on a record, and sucked on my thumb. So, obviously it upset me, but not in the way I expected it to. I'd expected to sob and carry on and all that. What I really felt was a keen awareness of the waste of it all. His death was a waste, what happened to our marriage was a waste. I didn't even notice what I sounded like on the record, I realized, after the needle had been popping in the groove at the end for some time. I thought about playing it again just to listen to myself, but it didn't seem worth it.

Seventeen

Lita
March 1937

MARCH OF 1937 WAS FRIGID, AND Regina got a lot of snow, maybe more than we got all the rest of that winter. The calendars from drugstores or insurance companies always amused me. *Litho'd in USA*, they said. No kidding. March would have a picture of an oriole singing on a branch of magnolia blossoms. Of course a picture of Regina in March would be bloody depressing, something an insurance company probably wouldn't want to distribute to its customers.

One thing helped to take my mind off Bill. I discovered a little after he died that I was going to have a baby. Almost lost to my grief, I found out I was carrying this new life, with no idea whether the father was Bill or Jake. Actually, when I thought about it a bit, Jake seemed likelier. After all, Bill and I were married a year, and not once was there ever a sign that I might be pregnant. Of course, by the end of that year, we weren't together that many times. But as it happened I'd been with both of them in December.

It wasn't so much that I'd wanted to have a baby with Bill, I was just surprised it hadn't happened. Other women I knew, like my sister Lena for instance, seemed to get pregnant as soon as they got married, or before, even. But I didn't really think about it that much. Bill and I were busy, and happy with the way things were, at first. I figured it would happen someday later, someday when we'd settled down a bit. I knew I wanted to have children sometime. But now it was happening I was afraid I wasn't ready for it.

The early days of my pregnancy were pretty awful sometimes. Something compelled me to sit and read the funeral programme over and over. *In Memoriam William James Cameron Stuart MacInnes.* Eventually I memorized it, could have recited it word for word. What I hoped to divine from staring at those words, I didn't know. I still struggled to accept the facts they represented. Then I'd remember the baby, remember it was time to eat or drink something, or go to bed. Many times, though, something made me think: this baby will save me. Maybe there really wasn't a better time for me to have a child. I thought often of the dream I'd had of the little boy. I must have known at some level that I was pregnant, and that little boy was the child I was bearing. It both pleased me and scared me a little to think that.

When I started to show, I told Jake I needed to quit working.

"You can stay as long as you want to, you know. I won't ask you to leave."

"I know that. And I appreciate it. But I think it's time I quit."

"What if I could find you something in the office? Maybe at the switchboard."

I smiled, shook my head. "I can't imagine being able to learn something new right now. My mind just seems to be somewhere else. And I'm tired all the time, too." I didn't tell him serving drinks was the worst part. I couldn't keep my mind off Bill when I was at work, wondering if the drink I was mixing would be the one that pushed the next guy off the edge and into the morgue. It got to me.

"Well, sure. I understand. If you ever need anything, just call."

Jake tried to give me some money, then, but I wouldn't take it. He did come by with my final pay envelope a week later, though, and after he left I discovered he'd tucked a fair deal of extra cash in with it. I didn't protest. My expenses were small, since I did have a paid-for roof over my head, but still, I had to eat.

When I was about six months along, Steve asked me if I wanted him to contact Bill on the other side. Steve had been wonderful, better than any sister could have been. He seemed to know how tired, how miserable, I was, and he'd often come by and cook dinner, keep me company in the evenings, tell me what he'd found out about Gypsies. He was apprenticing at an auto shop, and spent a lot of time at the library and at my place.

"Sure. I have a thing or two I'd like to tell him."

"All right. Well, I'll need a belonging of his. Do you have one of his shirts or shoes, something like that?"

"Steve. I thought it was a joke."

"No. I told you, I'm working on becoming a shaman. I'm kind of apprenticing with someone from the British Gypsy Lore Society. And it turns out Henry's got a cousin who's studying to be a shaman. I met him last summer, and he had a lot of good advice. I guess it's a family thing."

"I doubt Henry's cousin is a Gypsy."

"It doesn't matter. He's a shaman. Or a shaman-in-training. Another apprentice. Anyway, I think I'm ready to try and contact someone. It can be Bill, if you want."

"I don't know. What would you have to do?"

"I need something of his to hold and then I go into a trance. When I come out of it, I should be able to tell you what he said, if I can contact him."

I thought it sounded creepy. "I don't think so. I think it might upset me too much right now. You know."

"Yeah, sure. I understand. But you let me know if you change your mind."

ff

I was never actually sure if I had morning sickness. I did feel nauseated, off my food, unable to concentrate, but couldn't tell how much of it was actual morning sickness and how much was nerves. Morning sickness or mourning sickness? Most days I felt a rapidly fluctuating mixture of excitement, dread, nervousness, grief, and anger. Anger, mostly at Bill, because of so many things: for being a stupid ass and getting himself killed, for leaving me alone to bring up a baby. More than that, what should have been a happy time I now remember as a mostly dark, frightening place in my life. Even at the time it didn't seem fair, or right.

Eighteen

Lita
September 1937

Close to 5:30 on a cool September morning I checked into the Grey Nuns Hospital. When I gave the admitting clerk my name, she looked at me. "MacInnes, huh? Must be a black Scot." I just smiled. It reminded me of something Bill had said a couple of years before. As we waited for the rest of the band to show up for a rehearsal, he'd said, "You ought to drop the 'o' in your name."

"What?"

"You should drop the 'o'. Spell it K-u-d-e-l-k-a."

"Maybe I should just spell it K-n-i-g-h-t like my brother does. I mean, what's the difference if I spell it with an 'o' or without?"

"Hey, it's just a suggestion."

"Well, maybe you should drop the 'a' in your name. MacInnes, McInnes, what's the difference?"

"That's not the same at all."

I was in labour almost eighteen hours, then ended up having a Cesarean section. Failure to progress, they told me. It sounded like a diagnosis of my whole life, not just my obstetrical problems. The worst part wasn't the pain, although that was no picnic. The worst part was Bill. Was it pure agony, was it guilt, was it lack of sleep? It couldn't have been the drugs, because they didn't give me much until the very end, close to when they put me out for the operation. But Bill, I could have sworn, was there, not holding my hand, as you might expect a good husband to do nowadays, but there in my peripheral vision. Husbands now are expected to be there and do everything they possibly can for the wife. It's a nice idea, a nice gesture, but really — how much can they do for you, when it comes right down to it, except maybe chase down the doctor or nurse? Anyway, Bill was there at the edge of things, and when I'd turn to look at him, he'd be gone. I was tired, tired like I could never remember being before. I wanted to sleep, couldn't. A couple of times I did nod off between contractions and I'd hear Bill's voice. When I woke up and answered him, there'd be no one there, or maybe a nurse patting my hand. Once in that twilight between sleep and waking, I heard him say, "Whose baby is it, Lita? C'mon, you can tell me now. Whose is it?"

I jolted fully awake then, and screamed, the scream coinciding with a contraction. Sister Helen shook her head. "We'll get Dr. Schaumleffel in here to see you right away, poor thing. I think you've been at this long enough."

I nodded, thanked her weakly. Sister Helen didn't know the half of it.

$$ff$$

When I came to they brought me the baby. And much to my relief, I had no doubt from the second I laid eyes on her who Sarah Kali's father was. She was a MacInnes, all right: sandy hair, white eyelashes and, even as a tiny babe, her father's great grey eyes. If there was any Gypsy blood in my girl it wasn't apparent to the eye. Years earlier, I might have been happy about that, proud even. Now I wasn't so sure. I knew I wouldn't keep my daughter's background from her. All the same, I wept with joy, then with sorrow, when I saw her, the spit of her father. Even as this tiny thing, curled tightly still in the shape of my womb, she looked so much like him. She clutched my finger with that iron grip newborns have and I knew Bill would never leave me now. Whether that was good or bad, I wasn't sure. Now I can say it was good.

My baby was a girl, though, not a boy like in the dream I had. And her hair didn't look like his hair. Still, I thought, maybe that child was a son I'd have later.

ff

Darlene stood in the doorway of my hospital room and smiled shyly. She should be shy after what she did to me, I thought. She should die of shyness. I was gathering up my things, getting ready to leave the hospital. Steve would be there any minute to pick us up and take us home. I didn't want to talk to Darlene at all, but guessed I had to say something.

"I was just going home."

"I know. The nuns told me. Can I see the baby?"

"There she is." I nodded at the bassinet where Sarah lay curled in the warmth of the afternoon sun through the window. Angry as I was with Darlene, I didn't have the strength to turn her away, or to start a battle of any kind. In those days a C-section entitled you to a ten-day hospital stay. The nurses would wheel the babies in for feeding and wheel them back out to let you rest; not like the three or four days of what amounts to camping in a hospital room, baby beside you at all times, that C-section moms get now. Despite the rest I got, though, it was only for two to three hours at a stretch. A few days of that can start doing things to your brain. The path of least resistance was the only path I could follow at that moment.

"She's beautiful. She looks a lot like her daddy. What's her name?"

"Sarah. Sarah Kali MacInnes."

"Sarah Callie," she repeated. "Pretty. Must be Scots, huh?"

"No. Gypsy, actually. St. Sarah Kali is the patron saint of Gypsies."

"Oh." Then Steve came into the room. One look at Darlene, and he whipped off his hat, flashed her a wide smile. He'd never take off his hat for me, I knew that.

"How do you do?" he asked Darlene. Oh, God, not my brother, too. This is *her*, I wanted to say, the *gaji* who stole my husband. Don't flirt with her, for Christ's sake.

"Darlene, this is my brother, Steve. Steve, this is Darlene Klein. Steve's come to pick me up. But it was nice of you to come by, Darlene."

"Well, listen. I don't expect you to forgive me just yet. I don't blame you if you hate me, Lita, and maybe you never will forgive me. But you'll need help with that baby, and I think it's the least I can do to help you out as much as I can."

I didn't know what to say. I figured she had come to check out the baby, see if she looked like Bill or Jake. "You don't have to do that. We'll be fine."

Steve put in his two cents. "You've got to be kidding. This lady's kind enough to offer help. How could you say no to her?" *How could I say no to her?* If he had any clue. And here she is giving him the idea she's some kind of angel of mercy.

Darlene picked up her purse and gloves. "I'll leave you alone for now. But I'll drop by your place tomorrow and see how you are, okay?"

"Okay."

ff

Darlene arrived the next morning at 9:30, said she was ready to put in a full day's work. She washed and wrung and hung out the considerable pile of diapers Sarah had already gone through, kept me fed and watered, and let me sleep when Sarah wasn't demanding to be nursed, which was about every three hours. She stayed all day, every day for a full week, while Gus ran the hotel by himself. He was no doubt used to that. While Sarah and I napped, she cooked, baked, stocked the larder and icebox with things to eat. I'd never seen her work this hard at the hotel, had no idea she even had it in her.

Make no mistake, I was still murderously mad. But seeing her work like that, I had to respect her. She obviously felt bad about everything, I reflected while giving Sarah her four AM feeding, munching on some of the oatmeal cookies Darlene had baked that afternoon. And Bill knew what he was doing, too. He'd always been a terrible flirt. If it hadn't been Darlene, it would have been some other woman. Undoubtedly there *was* more than one other woman. And could I really hold Darlene responsible for Bill's death? He hadn't even been with her that night. Wasn't it just as likely he would have wandered home from the bar and frozen whether he'd left me or not? Wouldn't it be fairer to blame myself, since I'd changed the locks? If I hadn't, he'd be here right now, stroking his baby daughter's downy head as she suckled dreamily — for surely, once he found out I was with child, he would have come back to me, wouldn't he? In fact, he may well have been trying to do that very thing, the thing I'd been hoping and praying for, that night. And I'd been with Jake — but only to break it off with him. Why couldn't I have seen Jake another night? Why did Bill have that last drink?

The kitchen clock said almost five. Sarah slept. Tears of guilt and anguish streamed down my face, my state no doubt made worse by hormones, by lack of sleep. I didn't see how they could ever end. I took Sarah into bed with me, warm baby smell of her the best and only medicine I could think of for the ache I felt. After a time I slept, too.

$$ff$$

Darlene couldn't always come and work all day like she did in the beginning, but for a long time she came every couple of days to help out with the laundry and cleaning and do some cooking. Looking back, I have no idea how I would have functioned without her. I should have been grateful. Yet, as much as I wanted to forgive Darlene, I wanted to hang on to the hurt, hang onto it like a bone.

Sometimes I remember what it was like when Darlene and I were friends, before Bill, before things got all ugly. I liked her sense of humour, her smarts, her independence, her shrewdness. Funny I came to hate those same things about her. And then it seemed to me that she probably was the way she was in large part because of her father. I'd feel sorry for her, and then I'd feel guilty about her working so hard, but something inside would say Darlene owed me, owed me big. She destroyed my band, destroyed my husband, left my baby fatherless. I hated to feel beholden to my anger. I would rather forgive and forget. But I wasn't ready to forgive her yet, didn't know if I ever would be.

There were times when she suggested I take an hour off, go for a walk, go out and get a coffee or something. She and Sarah'd be fine, she always said. The way she clucked and cooed and fussed over the baby was, I thought, meant to demonstrate what a good caretaker she would be. But it only reminded me of the way she'd fussed and cooed and clucked over my husband. It took me a long time to understand that all her noise meant nothing. It made me feel like there was something wrong with me, that I couldn't be like that, too. But then I thought: the love I have inside me — I know it's there, I can feel it. Is it any less real if I don't make a big noise about it?

On a Saturday morning as Darlene hung out laundry I heard her talking to someone. I was nursing and didn't want to get up to see who it was. So I sat there with my mouth open when Ma walked in with a bunch of pink roses and a basket of food and presents for the baby. I grasped Sarah to my chest and started to get up, but Ma motioned me back down again. She came and put her arms around the two of us, Sarah completely oblivious at this stage to anything but food.

"She's beautiful," Ma whispered, and smiled. "And look, hair like her papa's. Sarah Kali. It's a pretty name, but you know it's just superstition."

How did she know about Bill's hair? She'd never met him. Of course, I realized, Steve would have told her about him. "I want her to know about her heritage. I think she should be proud of her background."

Ma shrugged. "I guess it's a good idea. Europe's a long time ago, now, though. She's a second generation Canadian.

You know, that's why we came over here, so we could forget about being Gypsies, which brought us nothing but trouble, and be something else. Be Canadian."

"I suppose you have a point." I couldn't imagine the other side of Sarah's family wanting to forget their roots. It didn't seem fair.

Sarah finished nursing, and I gave her to Ma. It was strange to see her again, but I was glad my daughter would get to know her, after all. "How are you?" Ma asked. "I wanted to come to Bill's funeral, but it seemed funny going when I'd never met him."

I guessed it was the pull of the grandchild that brought her back, although Lena had given Ma several grandchildren already. Still, from then on Ma was back in my life, acting like nothing had ever happened, like all those years hadn't gone by. I knew I could never mention the rift between us. And I came to accept that was just the way Ma was. She turned out to be a great help with Sarah, and I was very grateful.

Nineteen

Lita
March 1940

It wasn't long before Darlene's visits tapered off, then stopped altogether. But Sarah and I settled into a routine with Ma, who usually came by for a few hours midday to help out. And then, since she was around to look after Sarah, I was able to go back to work after a while, and found a job at the Temple Music Store downtown, selling all kinds of small instruments — guitars, banjos, ukuleles, harmonicas, wind instruments — and sheet music. It was a busy time of life, and although I was around instruments all day and played bits of music for customers, I didn't really *play* music. I would get up in the morning, feed Sarah, take her to Ma's, and then catch the bus to the store. After work I'd pick her up, we'd have dinner, have baths, listen to the radio for a while, read some stories, and we'd both be asleep before too long. The days went by in a blur.

But if I thought Darlene was no longer a part of my life, I soon found out that I was very wrong. Part of the reason was her being busy with Steve. Oh, God, how the idea sickened me, only slightly less than the idea of her being with Bill. How could my brother stand her? True, she was beautiful, but she had the personality of a viper. You'd think that telling Steve about my experience with her would have shown him what she was like. But men and Darlene were a lethal combination, as far as I could see. Lethal and inevitable.

After seeing her for a couple of years, Steve began to confide in me. Despite Darlene's assurances that she was true to him, he constantly saw her talking to other men, flirting with them. It reminded me of my old suspicions, the way they would build and build until I couldn't stand it any longer and confronted Bill, usually in an explosive manner. Bill would act shocked and hurt by my lack of faith in him, and he'd spend the next little while being super-sweet, apologizing for neglecting me, proving that he was indeed a faithful and wonderful husband. Then those attentions and gestures would taper off and soon I was back to my suspicions again. Every time we went through the cycle, it got shorter and shorter, until it all finally blew up in our faces. And now my brother, of all people, was caught up with Darlene. It was all too familiar.

No kidding, I wanted to ask him, you really think a girl like Darlene could be unfaithful? I didn't really know what to say, only that I didn't feel she was a girl to be trusted. As the months went by he became more and more upset. "How could she do this to me?" he asked one night, close to tears.

I had no answer, could only shake my head. How, indeed? I cursed my weakness, wished I could find the strength to overcome my own pain, in which Darlene had had such a large part, and help Steve. She was making a fool of my handsome brother. I hated to let him down but I didn't know what to do. If only I could have forgotten it was Darlene breaking his heart. I wanted to tell him to forget her, to stay away from her, but he was too far gone. Nothing I could say could make any difference.

He brought me books sent by his friend Jack Lee from the British Gypsy Lore Society. I skimmed through them a bit at a time while Sarah slept and got some ideas. I'd had enough of Darlene Klein. Not only had she ruined my marriage, I still blamed her for Bill's death, and now she was messing around with my poor brother. On the third anniversary of Bill's death, in March, I got a piece of fruit, an apple, like it said in *The Gipsy Magick*. I cut it in two with a silver knife and concentrated with all that was in me on Darlene and what she deserved.

The next day I felt oddly relieved by the little ritual. This was no doubt what it was meant to do. After that, when I thought of Darlene it was with a mild contempt, not a murderous hatred.

♪♪

Steve came by one bitterly cold night a week later, after Sarah was asleep. The next morning he was going to board a train for Newmarket, Ontario, for basic training before going overseas. He'd signed up for service, thinking at least that way he'd get to see a little bit of the world. He didn't say so, but I suspected he may have also felt an instinct to save himself from being destroyed by Darlene. He seemed excited about going to Europe, although he wasn't exactly excited about fighting. I wasn't sure which was worse, having him fight over there, or stay over here stewing about Darlene. He sat down at the kitchen table and asked if there was anything to drink in the house. I got him some wine, the only thing I had. I hoped he was perhaps nervous about the army, but I had a feeling that wasn't it at all.

"Are you all right?" I asked.

"I went to say goodbye to Ma this afternoon. Then I went to say goodbye to Darlene just now. I went into the hotel, and she was right there at the front desk, kissing a man. They were all over each other. And when she finally looked up and saw me, she didn't even act embarrassed or anything. She just smiled."

I could just picture her. "Steve, I'm so sorry. She really is heartless."

"I couldn't stop myself. When I saw them together like that, something snapped, and I went right over to them. I was going to knock him down. He ran out the front door. And she stood there. She said I didn't understand, that it wasn't the way it looked, the same stuff she always says. I lost my mind. I started to yell. She told me to leave, said I must be crazy. I said I wouldn't leave until I was done with her. All I meant was I wasn't done yelling at her, but I guess she thought I meant I'd hurt her. She ran into the office and yelled she'd call the police. So I left."

"Maybe it's better this way. Maybe it's better to find this out now than to be sent overseas not knowing the truth."

"But I might never see her again, Lita. I have to talk to her once more. I can't leave it like this."

Yes, you can, you *can*, dammit, I thought. "You could call her," I suggested.

"I can't talk about this over the phone. I have to see her."

"But she'll call the police if you go back."

"I know. That's why I thought if I could get that key to the hotel from you, I could get in the back way, catch her by surprise. I could explain myself, then, and maybe she

wouldn't be so mad. Maybe she's even cooled off by now."
He was starting to sound irrational.

"How do you know I have a key?"

"You had it when you and Bill moved your stuff out of the
hotel. Do you still have it?"

"Yes. But if I give it to you, what will you do once you get
there? You won't get yourself in trouble, will you?"

"Of course not. I won't hurt her."

"That's not what I'm worried about. I'm worried about
you."

"You're still angry with her, aren't you? You still haven't
forgiven her." He was enough in love with her that he
couldn't believe that I didn't at least like her. He just couldn't
understand it.

"No, Steve, I have not forgiven her. I try, but I have a long
way to go before I'm there. Put yourself in my shoes."

"I'm sorry. But I have to try and talk to her again before
I go. Please, will you give me the key? I promise I'll drop by
with it later. I have to see her."

I had to try to stop him. What good could going back
possibly do? "Really, you should think this over a little before
you run back there. Look how she's treated you."

"I might never see her again. I can't just leave things like
this."

"Please listen to me. This is crazy. Darlene will never
change."

"Lita. I know what I'm doing. Just let me have the key for
a little while, and I'll give it right back to you."

I gave in. Even as I fished for the key in my dresser
drawer, I had a feeling that it would only lead to trouble. But
I gave it to him. He thanked me, gave me a hug and went
back out into the darkness. This would have been around

nine o'clock. I realized as I watched my brother almost run down the street and back to Darlene that we hadn't even really said goodbye to each other. But when he brings the key back we'll do that, I thought.

Shortly after ten o'clock, I heard the sirens, wondered what was happening. Ma called. She said the Belleville, which she could see from her kitchen window, was on fire.

I was about to tell her that Steve had gone over there when I thought better of it. "Can you come over for a while and stay with Sarah, Ma? I have to go over and see if Darlene is all right."

As far as Ma knew, Darlene was just that pretty friend of mine who was such a help when Sarah was a newborn. She didn't know about Bill's involvement with her, or Steve's. In fact, Ma seemed to feel that since Darlene was so attractive, she must also be a nice person. "I like that Darlene," she'd said once. "She's so pretty." I couldn't even think what to say to that.

Ma arrived in about fifteen minutes. The snow creaked under my boots as I walked as fast as I could to the hotel. I wondered if I really wanted to do this, if I really wanted to confront this. My curiosity got the better of my dread, though. I told myself that it was likely a kitchen fire, and everyone was probably fine except maybe Gus, who would stew about the money it would cost him. But as I got closer to the hotel, the smoke and ash in the air and the glow on the undersides of the clouds in the direction of the hotel told me otherwise.

I stood among the gathering crowd, hand over my mouth, unable to believe or comprehend what I saw: flames tore into the night sky as the Belleville Hotel burned down. Policemen stood on the other side of a barricade, kept people away from the roaring orange wall of flame that engulfed the building and the rolling clouds of acrid black smoke and ashes. I wanted to ask the officers if they'd seen my brother, but I didn't dare. Fear froze me like the jets of water from the firemen's hoses froze when they hit the ground.

Was Darlene in there, or Gus? Was Steve? Then I caught myself. I didn't know for certain whether he'd even gone to the Belleville, even though that's where he said he was going. He could have stopped for another drink on his way there, or changed his mind. Even if he had gone, he might have left before this all started. He might not have started the fire. I should have tried harder to talk him out of going.

Even over the roar of the fire, the shouting, the sirens, the policemen talking on their radios, I heard the blood pound in my ears, felt the cold sweat on my palms. Did I know what was going on here? Perhaps. But for Steve's sake, I couldn't risk saying anything to anyone, because maybe I was wrong. Even worse, maybe I was right. And if I was right, all this wouldn't have happened if I'd been able to stop my brother. If I hadn't given him the key. *Oh, God, what has he done? I shouldn't have waited for Ma. I should have just brought the baby with me. I knew how upset he was. Then again, if I'd come earlier and brought Sarah, maybe we'd both be in there right now.*

Firemen carried two stretchers through the lobby and out the front doors, first one and then another a few minutes later. I couldn't see who was on them. They could have been Darlene, Gus, Steve, guests, anyone. I felt sick then, and couldn't stand to watch anymore, could no longer stand the smell of the smoke. I made my way through the crowd and walked home, weeping, mind reeling with a thousand questions I could ask no one. I could not turn to look back even once. And even now, I still dream about it sometimes.

The next day, the story was on the radio and in the paper. TWO DIE IN DOWNTOWN HOTEL INFERNO, *The Leader-Post* screamed. "Mr. August Klein, proprietor of the Belleville Hotel, and his daughter Miss Darlene Klein, both perished in Grey Nuns Hospital last night after a three-alarm blaze burnt their hotel to the ground." I read that sentence over and over, dazed.

Could Steve have done this? Had I somehow brought it about? I didn't know, but if the force of my feelings alone could have caused this, Darlene Klein would have burned to a crisp long before. I suddenly felt a great rush of sorrow for her. She was once a friend. I could hardly think of her as really dead. It wasn't her fault that she was the way she was. She shouldn't have died like that.

But what about Steve? Did he die, too, and they maybe hadn't found him yet? Was he on his way to Ontario? I didn't dare ask anyone, didn't dare even mention it to anyone.

ff

I'd just got Sarah off to bed one night when I heard a knock at the door. Alone with my little one, I was always a little nervous answering the door at night if I didn't expect anyone. To my relief and surprise, Jacob stood there. I hadn't seen him in almost three years.

"May I come in?"

"Of course, Jacob, please. It's good to see you."

"You look wonderful, Lita. How's Sarah? She looks just like Bill, Steve says."

"Steve? When did you see him?"

"I ran into him downtown a few weeks ago. Why?"

"Oh, just wondering. He's right, she does look just like Bill. I'm afraid there's no question there. I'd bring her out, but she's just gone to sleep."

"That's all right. Another time."

"Awful about the fire, eh?"

"Terrible. A real tragedy."

"I imagine Steve's pretty broken up about Darlene and all."

I wasn't sure what to say. "I think so. He's out in Ontario at training camp, left the morning after it happened."

"I understand they're still investigating the fire scene. There was almost nothing left."

"It was horrible."

We drank tea and talked. The whole time, I wondered what it was all about. It was good to see him again, so good. Jake and I could always talk easily. Finally, my curiosity won out.

"So, tell me, Jake, what brought you over here? Did you really just come to see if Sarah was yours?"

He smiled. "Of course not. I knew that if you'd thought so, you would have told me a long time ago. I've thought about coming to see you many times. I guess I wanted to tell you that I miss you."

"I've missed you, too. It's so good to see you again."

"Well, I'm glad you feel that way. Because I've also been thinking how hard it must be for you, a woman alone with a child. And we're both lonely. Maybe we ought to get married."

A million things went through my mind. First was that a proposal was the last thing I'd expected that evening. I wondered if he was asking because he felt sorry for me. I wondered if he knew what he was getting into. I didn't know myself what my feelings were about a lot of things right then.

"I've thought it over," he added. "I knew I wanted to be with you from the minute I met you. And I know things have been kind of crazy for you. You don't have to answer right away. Just think about it."

Amazing, I thought. All this time has gone by, so many things have happened. The way I ended things between us before was not exactly graceful. And yet, here he is. Still, so much had happened in such a short time. This wasn't a decision I wanted to make lightly.

"Let me think about it a little, Jake."

ff

Within a couple of weeks I got a letter from Steve.

> *Dear Lita:*
>
> *I'm just writing to let you know I'm all right. I'm here at training camp near Newmarket. It's pretty tough work, I'll tell you. I wanted to drop that key by your place like I said I would, but with the fire and all that night, things were kind of crazy. I'll get it back to you when I can though I guess there's no point now. My train left early in the morning, and I never did find out what happened in the fire. It's funny, I didn't really care. Was everyone okay?*
>
> *In the meantime, I'm hoping to get overseas and see some action soon. The Germans are rounding up Gypsies all over Europe, did you know that?*
>
> *I hope you and Sarah and Ma are well, and I'll write again soon.*
> *Love,*
> *Steve*

Though I was relieved to hear from him, glad to know for certain that he was alive, his letter brought up more questions than it answered. He didn't mention being at the hotel, but he knew about the fire. He seemed not to know about Darlene. I didn't know what to think. No matter what had happened, though, there was probably a limit to how much he would or could tell in a letter.

A few days later I wrote back, and told him the bad news. I didn't hear from him again for a long time. Then I received a brief, terse letter from overseas. Was he pressed for time, crushed by grief, or both? Or neither? I could not tell. I decided the only way I'd ever find out for certain what happened that night would be to talk to him in person, if he was ever granted a leave. Of course, he may not have known exactly what happened. But until I spoke to him, I wouldn't know.

ff

One of the first warm days we had that spring was a Sunday morning. I was hanging out laundry in the backyard while Sarah sloshed through puddles in a pair of red gumboots. I was surprised to see Jacob come through the gate from the front yard.

"Good morning. I tried the front door, but there was no answer."

"Hello, Jacob. This is a nice surprise."

"I was on the way back from the hotel and thought I'd swing by and see how you ladies are doing."

"We're fine. Happy to finally have some warm weather."

"It is a beautiful day."

"What were you doing at the hotel on a Sunday morning?"

"Sundays are so quiet. Most of the office staff isn't around. It's a good time to catch up on paperwork."

I wanted to tease him a little more. "You take your job pretty seriously."

"I guess so. It just seems natural to me. My family's been in the hotel business for a long time, even before we came to Canada. My father ran several hotels in Montreal before he joined the board of directors of CP Hotels."

"So how did you end up here?"

"After he passed away, CP offered me a job managing the Saskatchewan. And my mom decided we might as well all move west together. She didn't want to stay in Montreal after he died."

"That's understandable."

"So, uh, listen. Last time we saw each other I asked you a question. I wonder if you've had time to give it some thought."

"I have been thinking about it."

"And?"

I wanted to play with him a little more. But that kind of thing just didn't come naturally to me. "I'd love to marry you, Jacob."

ff

Before the wedding, I decided it was time to go through some of Bill's things. I hadn't got rid of anything yet, hadn't the heart to. And I knew I wouldn't be able to get rid of all of it. I wasn't sure I could part with any of it, but I had to try. Sarah and I were moving out of the little house on Dewdney Avenue to Jake's much larger place, not far from Bill's mum's. I knew there would be room there for whatever

I might want to keep, and I knew Jake wouldn't begrudge me anything of Bill's. But I had to try to unload some of it.

It took a long time. Poor Bill, at twenty-three, hadn't had much. I thought of older people whose spouses die after they've been together for forty or fifty years. Where would they even begin? His clothes and shoes, most of them, were easy enough to give to the Salvation Army. They were much too big for Steve, and Jake wouldn't want them. I kept his burgundy-and-black dressing gown, my only comfort some nights before Sarah was born. His few books, murder mysteries, I gave away. I kept all of his records, even the Russ Columbos, even the Bing Crosbys, yes, even the one Rudy Vallée I discovered tucked away in the back of the box. There was no question I'd keep all of the pictures. There weren't many: mostly publicity shots of the band, and the wedding pictures Mrs. MacInnes marched us over to have taken when she was ready to speak to us again after our elopement. Henry had sometimes brought his Brownie to practices and after Bill died he gave me a whole lot of his snapshots of them. Some of those really hurt to look at.

Little things, like his favourite coffee mug, I kept. Every once in a while I still have a drink out of that cup when I'm thinking of him. Another little thing I kept: tucked in under his socks, the big ill-fitting wool socks his mother knitted for him in bushels, was a little framed photograph I'd never seen before. A picture, carefully cut from a magazine, of Bing Crosby.

Twenty

Lita
September 1940

JAKE AND I WERE MARRIED AT City Hall on a bright September morning. Sarah and Ma and Jake's mother and his sister Rebecca were there. He looked handsome in the wide-lapelled brown pinstriped suit that brought out the brown in his hazel eyes. I wore a new light green travelling suit, a sleeveless cocktail dress, cropped jacket with shoulder pads, and a military-looking cap. I had that suit for years, got a lot of use out of it. After the ceremony we said our goodbyes to everyone — Sarah stayed with Jake's mom and sister — and walked the couple of blocks over to Union Station to catch the train to Montreal.

I loved riding the train almost as much as I loved seeing Montreal when we finally got there. I'd never travelled at all before, really. Bill and I had honeymooned in Minot, North Dakota, and we'd made a few southern Saskatchewan road trips with the band, all in Bill's Packard. But train travel was new to me. I loved watching the scenery roll by, seeing prairie gradually change to Canadian Shield. I loved going to the dining car, getting out and looking around the stations along the way. We were lucky that the weather was clear and mild almost the whole time. And I especially loved the sleeper berth we had, being lulled to sleep by the rhythm of the cars. The dreams I had on the train were particularly vivid and memorable. One night, as Jake slept beside me, I dreamt that I was lying in the arms of a man who wasn't Jake, or Bill. This man and I were in bed in this sleeper berth together, under the sheets, and it seemed like we had just made love. He was handsome, tall, had glowing red hair. After I woke up I thought about this. I had dreamt about the red-haired man before. What were these dreams trying to tell me? I fell asleep again, but in the next few weeks, I kept having a similar dream. Odd that I would dream of another man on my honeymoon. I almost felt guilty about it.

The fall colours in Eastern Canada really are as amazing as people always say. They have trees, like real maples with those flaming red leaves, that we just don't have on the prairies. We spent quite a bit of time walking the cobblestone streets of old Montreal, going to cafés, galleries, looking at the old buildings. We stayed at the Ritz-Carlton on Sherbrooke Street, in the Royal Suite, no less. It was more luxurious than I could ever have imagined, much bigger than the house Bill and I shared on Dewdney Avenue. There were three bathrooms, two huge, incredibly soft, king-sized beds in the bedroom, a study, a dining room. A huge fireplace in the living room, where we had a lovely view of Parc du Mont-Royal out the window. I had to laugh a little when I thought how only a few years before I'd been a chambermaid at the Belleville Hotel in Regina.

"I can't believe we're really staying here. It must be expensive," I said one night.

"It isn't cheap. And I would have preferred to stay at a CP Hotel, because we would have got a pretty nice discount. But they closed the Place Viger five years ago so we didn't have a choice. Still, this is our honeymoon and we're here to enjoy it."

"I can't wait to tell Sally at work about this place. She'll never believe it."

"You're not going back to work when we get home, are you?"

"I — well, I didn't think about it. I just assumed I would."

"You don't need to. You stay home and take care of Sarah now. I'll take care of the money."

ff

We were gone almost three weeks, all told, and had a lovely, relaxing holiday, though I missed Sarah terribly. We talked on the phone a few times and it sounded like she was enjoying being with her *bubbe* and Auntie Rebecca. I kept thinking all the way home how we really were starting new lives. The future looked so bright right then.

Among the stack of mail awaiting us when we arrived home, though, was a letter calling Jake up for army service. I was terrified. Not again, I thought. I'm only twenty-one. I can't lose a husband again. We'd just started to get used to each other, hadn't even had a chance to get settled as a family. He'd have to go, I knew. He was only twenty-five, though he seemed much older to me, so much more mature than twenty-five. The letter gave him an appointment time for a physical in three weeks, and after that he'd be shipped off to training camp.

Although I was worried about the war, and Steve, and about Jake going overseas, I couldn't help but be excited and amazed at the new life I now had. We had a beautiful home, and Jacob's mother and his sister Rebecca lived in town and were friendly enough, though not extremely so. They weren't sure at first about Jacob marrying a musician and adopting a child. But once they got to know us a little better, they were a great help. Sometimes I felt Jacob's mother might have been happier if I had agreed to convert, but I was reluctant to. Not, as I tried to explain, that I had any objections to Judaism in particular. It was the whole concept of organized religion that didn't sit well with me.

"You're an atheist?"

"No. Not at all. I just think God speaks to us in many ways. I don't think one way is better than any other."

Mrs. Stone blinked at me for a bit and then changed the subject. Hey, it could have been worse, I thought, imagining my first mother-in-law's reaction.

If opposition from his family bothered Jake, or the sudden adjustment from life as a bachelor to life as father to a young daughter, he never mentioned it to me. No doubt people talked, too, not that Jake would ever have mentioned that, either, but I was sure they did. And then the ghost of Bill MacInnes still loomed large, especially in my dreams. Jake knew that, seemed to understand it somehow.

Keeping track of my dreams helped me gradually come to grips with the memory of Bill. The dreams were sometimes horrible: he'd be alive again, but hiding from me, purposely avoiding me. Or living with Darlene and telling people what an idiot I was. I'd see him around town, always at a distance, but no matter how I'd try, he'd be too far away for me to talk to. Sometimes, I'd be out somewhere, and when I got home, there'd be his white, frozen body on the doorstep.

I'd dream about him every night for weeks, and then I might not again for months. But I wrote all the dreams down faithfully, remembered what Steve said, that dreams speak to you in ways that sometimes take a long time to understand. Writing them down helped me to see that over a period of years the Bill dreams abated, got less intense. After a while he would mostly be a background figure.

ff

Jake returned home the afternoon of his army physical looking grey-faced and grim, hung up his coat and hat without a word. I almost hated to ask him how it went. He looked pretty unhappy. Were they shipping him away even sooner than we had thought?

"So what happened?"

He dropped his gaze to the floor. "I'm not going anywhere."

"What? You're not? Why not?"

"They've classified me as unfit for service. I had a bad bout of rheumatic fever when I was a kid and they say it damaged my heart."

I let out a breath. "Oh. I'm so glad to hear that."

"Glad? About what?"

"That they're not taking you away from us. That you won't get killed over there. To me, that sounds wonderful."

"I'm not so excited about it."

He was hurt, I suddenly realized. It never occurred to me before this that Jake actually wanted to go. That he considered it his duty, part of his role as a man, to go and fight. I watched him creep into his study and close the door. I didn't see him again until dinnertime.

ff

There was a long stretch where the National sat in its case, in the basement, untouched. At first I blamed this on the baby. It was true for the first six months or so. I had no time then for anything else but Sarah: not for Ma, who was with us nearly all the time, not for myself some days. But once Jake and I were married, and Sarah was a little older, and I didn't have to work at the music store anymore, life got a lot easier. The idea of playing guitar again had been in the back of my mind, an insistent if not very loud voice, for a long time. So one day I got it out, thought it might please Sarah. She was playing with dolls on a blanket on the living room floor. I sat down beside her and started to strum.

But it made me too sad. Bringing it out of the case, the faint metallic tang of the strings, the heft of it in my hands, tuning it, the slight squeak now and then of my fingers on the strings — all those things were bad enough. Then I couldn't think of anything to play but songs the Syncopation Five did, songs I didn't want to think about. Sarah came over and touched the guitar. She asked me what it was, but seemed a little suspicious, maybe even afraid of it. I sat for a while with it in my lap, rested my cheek on the side, ran my fingers slowly up and down the strings. Then I put it away. What made me sadder, playing it and thinking of the old days, or not playing it, is hard to say. Right then, I was pretty sure playing it made me feel worse.

A few months later I brought it out again. Sarah insisted I let her try to play it, but soon grew frustrated when she realized she was too small to reach both the neck and the strings at once. Then she was content to play with her dolls while I played.

That was a great day for me. I played for the better part of an hour, and the fingertips of my left hand were sore and tender that night, my calluses having worn away in three years of domestic life. But I knew I was better that day. There was a lightening in my heart as I played the old songs, with some sadness still, to be sure. But there was the considerable joy of playing mixed with hearing the songs again. I could play and not cry, I could play the songs, period. That amazed me.

Soon I was playing again on a regular basis. Before long, I played every minute I could cram in. I'd plan my day around Sarah and playing. I didn't do it because of any anticipation of performing, any intention of seeking out other musicians. As far as I could see at that point, my life as a musician was over. Yet my creativity soared, possibly because of the freedom of not being in a working band, the absence of pressure. I wrote more of my own material than ever before, started to play other things as well as my own inventions, like some traditional Gypsy tunes I'd picked up records of. Steve would be glad to hear them, I knew, when he got back.

As it turned out, though, he never did hear my renditions of Gypsy songs. Ma got the notification that he'd been killed in December 1941 in the Battle of Hong Kong, which started just after the bombing of Pearl Harbour. It was rough on me. Steve had been the only member of the family I was always close to. He was there for me in those early days of Sarah's life when I was trying to deal with widowhood and motherhood all at once. He was there whenever I needed him, and I knew without question that he would do whatever he could to help me. He didn't leave much behind, and I decided that all his worldly possessions should be stored in our basement. Had Jake been a cynical man, he would have remarked that our basement was rapidly becoming a storehouse for the belongings of dead men. There wasn't much there: a wool coat, a suit, his books, some thick file folders full of research that he'd gathered for the Gypsy Lore Society.

After that I was grateful, even more than before, that Jake had been spared from going overseas. For him, though, it just seemed to get harder as the war went on.

One day he came home from work and told me about a woman he'd seen in one of the hotel's restaurants who made a not-quite-under-the-breath remark when she saw him.

"She said, 'I wonder if he's yellow.'"

I sighed. "I'm sorry to hear that. That was an ignorant thing to say. She doesn't even know you."

"That's what people think when they see an apparently healthy young man. Why isn't he overseas? Is he yellow? Is he a shirker?"

"Look, Jake. You can't let it bother you. You know it's not your fault that you can't be over there. And as far as I'm concerned, it doesn't matter what other people think. It's nobody else's business."

"I know you're right. But it's hard listening to little remarks and getting those looks."

"I know. I'm sorry."

I wished I could think of something else to say, something to make him feel better. But I just couldn't think of anything else.

Twenty-One

Elsa
Seattle, 1990

THE LATE 80S / EARLY 90S were the best of times for Curse Records. The Green Lanterns and Speed Queen were the first bands we signed, of course, and both bands put out several singles that sold fairly well. But soon we were swamped with bands giving us demo tapes to listen to, and before long we had fifteen other bands on the label. To my surprise, we paid back Dave and our other creditors pretty quickly. That was in the days when people were really starting to become aware of the Seattle scene. New indie labels had started to pop up all the time. Sub Pop was the best known of them. Not only did they record Nirvana, Soundgarden, and Mudhoney in their early careers, they were also amazingly good at getting publicity. They sent copies of Mudhoney's single "Touch Me I'm Sick" to the big British music magazines, *NME*, *Melody Maker*, and *Sounds*. Mark and I laughed when we heard that, thought it would just end up being a waste of postage. Incredibly, though, not only did they all review "Touch Me I'm Sick," they loved it. Not wasting any time, Mudhoney were then sent on a tour of England with Sonic Youth, which put "Touch Me I'm Sick" onto the British indie charts. Then Sub Pop offered to pay for a reporter from *Melody Maker* to come to Seattle and check out the scene. By this time, we'd stopped laughing at their publicity schemes and weren't really surprised when Mudhoney ended up on the cover of the March 1989 *Melody Maker*. Although the reporter called Seattle a "small, insignificant" city (I kept thinking he should see Regina), he said we had "the most vibrant, kicking scene, encompassed in one city."

Of course it didn't take long before someone came up with a label for this new music coming out of Seattle. We all knew punk was dead, and the term 'alternative' had been so overused it had ceased to mean anything. That June, Sub Pop held a big show at the Moore Theatre in the wake of all this press, featuring Nirvana, Mudhoney, and TAD, that drew over a thousand people, the biggest indie show held yet. And while the show got covered by the local mainstream media, it didn't exactly result in good press. Although I guess that old maxim about there being no such thing as bad publicity is true. For some reason *The Seattle Times* decided to send out a jazz critic to cover it. He wrote that "the whole point of this show seemed to be based on the perverse, reverse notion that grungy, foul-mouthed, self-despising meatheads who grind out undifferentiated noise and swing around their long hair are good — and 'honest' — by virtue of their not being rock stars . . . If this is the future of rock 'n' roll, I hope I die before I get much older." Well, well. Someone was having a bad day, weren't they? In any case, the "grunge" thing stuck. People do love labels.

So okay, maybe Curse Records didn't do anywhere near as well as Sub Pop. Few indie labels did. Sub Pop had chutzpah and luck and incredible savvy. And impeccable timing. But we did pretty well, too — we were happy with it for quite a while. Our bands played lots of shows, cut a single or two or three with us and then either broke up or got picked up by bigger labels — the usual thing. It kept us busy, and as Curse began to take up more and more of our time, The Green Lanterns and Speed Queen slowly but surely became defunct.

Part of it was Bill, of course. My focus had changed when he arrived, though I was slow to figure it out. I eventually realized I had to stay safe, so I would be around to take care of him. Some of those shows could be a little iffy, what with the out-of-control mosh pits, the druggies, the bikers. The late-night lifestyle itself wasn't really compatible with child raising, to say the least. So by this time, when Bill was almost eight, in the third grade, the band thing had sort of faded out of my life. Not that I didn't miss it, but it was what it was. Bill was my sweet, sandy-haired, freckled first priority. Mark still had a day job, still with his brother-in-law Dave's courier firm, although by now he was dispatch supervisor. Much as he would have loved to quit and do Curse Records full time, there just wasn't quite enough money in it, not for a man with a family. We both dedicated a lot of time to Curse, but both loved what we got out of it.

By the height of the grunge era we got to the point where we were renting a little office not far from our place in Fremont, on the second floor of an old stone flatiron building on Fremont Avenue. The office had a tall window that looked east onto the street, a couple of chairs on either side of the window, and a desk across from that. There was a backroom where we kept our stock, publicity materials, files, and a washroom almost big enough to turn around in. We didn't do any actual recording on site, of course; we'd rent time at one of the recording studios in town for that. The office was upstairs from a vintage clothes shop and always smelled a little of the sandalwood incense they used in the store to mask the old clothes smell. I liked to think it added a little counterculture feel to Curse's operations. I was really happy with the location because it was close to home, and close to Bill's school. Once he was in school full-time in Grade One, Curse became my day job. It pretty much cut out time for my own music, but since Speed Queen was no longer a going concern, having a job was more important. That's how it goes with bands most of the time, unless you have some compelling reason to stay together for seventy years, or whatever it is for The Rolling Stones. I guess all that money is a good enough reason to go on comeback tour after Depends-sponsored comeback tour. Anyway, I always told myself I'd ease back into my own music soon. As soon as we made enough money that we could hire someone to do all the Curse phone calls, correspondence, orders, shipping, filing, books. All that stuff that I did. Right.

Behind the desk, Mark had hung a framed quote from his hero Greg Shaw, who with his wife / ex-wife and business partner Suzy, ran the legendary indie label BOMP Records in Burbank, California, which is still around today. The quote read:

When you contemplate the monstrous weight under which rock & roll has struggled, the multi-billion dollar music industry dedicated to keeping it down, the superstar system and its complete negation of new talent, the stranglehold of radio, the closed doors of the record and concert industries, the obscene wealth concentrated in the mechanisms of disco, arena-rock, etc., and the self protective instincts of the Mafioso types who run it all — the fact is that all this is being swept aside by a few kids with nothing more going for them but an insane commitment to raw energy and a total contempt for everything.

I mean, how could a struggling record label not be inspired by those words? At the very least I hoped it would provide some validation to the band members who were forever showing up at the office demanding their royalties. Or stall them for a little bit while they read it, anyway. The worst was a band called Stupid Bloody Tuesday. I swear I saw Dennis, their gap-toothed bleached-blond guitarist, every few weeks or so.

"Elsa. Good afternoon," he said, flopping down in one of the chairs across from my desk. He looked like he'd just gotten out of bed. Grunge musician, indeed.

I sighed inwardly, knowing what was coming. "Thanks for stopping in, Dennis. How are you?"

"Not bad, thanks. So I'm here to see you about our royalties."

"Did you not get the cheque we mailed out in February?"

"Yes. But don't you send those out quarterly?"

"Dennis. We've been through this before. You know we send your royalties out once a year."

"Yeah, but that was it?"

"Ten percent of each record you sell. If your record's selling for four bucks, you get forty cents on each one."

"Okay. But man, I need some money now. Look, didn't you sell some records for us at that festival we played a few weeks ago?"

"Yeah."

"Okay. So can't you pay me out in cash for the royalties on those and deduct it from my next cheque?"

"Well, there's a couple of problems with that. First off, you guys sold thirty-seven records. So the royalties on that would be a little under fifteen bucks. Divided by the three of you, that's not quite five bucks. Besides, you know I can't just pay you out in cash, Dennis. I'm sorry."

He looked so dejected as he left. I felt sorry for him. And I wondered if we had to have this conversation over and over because he was that desperate, or because he really couldn't remember. Part of me wanted to shake him by the shoulders. Part of me wanted to tell him: listen, you want to make money? Get out of the music business. You could make more money picking bottles. And you'd get some fresh air and exercise, too.

Don't get me wrong, though. For the most part I loved meeting the musicians, listening to their demo tapes, seeing the thrill on their faces when we'd offer them a record contract. We were helping them make their dreams come true. Money doesn't seem like such a big deal when you get to do things like that. That's a pretty cool thing to be able to help people with.

Part Three

Twenty-Two

Lita
1961

I WAS NEVER SO TIRED AS I was after Sarah's wedding. Until then I had no idea what work weddings could be. Mine had both been simple affairs. An elopement with Bill; with Jake, another justice of the peace ceremony with Steve and Henry as witnesses. With Sarah, it was completely different. Ma had died of a heart attack the year before, and in the months leading up to the wedding I thought many times of how flabbergasted she would have been at the elaborateness of the thing.

I suppose a big part of the difference between our weddings was that Sarah's dad had money. Jake, that is. Jake adopted Sarah shortly after we married, and she became Sarah Stone instead of Sarah MacInnes. Which naturally scandalized Bill's mother, but by then I surely didn't give a damn what she thought. And Jake was a good father to Sarah. He was a good provider. In fact, as the years went by Jake became more and more preoccupied with money. Or with his hotel, anyway.

In the late 50s, the potash industry in Saskatchewan was in a boom phase. American companies started moving into southern Saskatchewan and mining for the mineral salts, mostly used for fertilizer and other industrial applications. When the Saskatchewan government started granting these companies subsidies to encourage growth in the industry, Jake saw it as a perfect time to open his own hotel. He bought the old Dinsmore Hotel downtown and it became The Hotel Regina. Although I had complete confidence in his ability to run his own hotel (he'd basically been running the Saskatchewan for more than twenty years), it worried me. Working for someone else was one thing; I was afraid that being a business owner would consume him entirely. But he was so excited about it, I said nothing to discourage him. Looking back, maybe I should have.

So when it came time for the wedding, he insisted Sarah have whatever she wanted. All I had to do was organize it. Oh, sure. Gowns, bridesmaids' dresses, dinner menus, rehearsals, musicians, receptions. Invitations, seating plans, receiving lines. Rob Taggart, her red-headed fiancé, was an Anglican, so they were married in St. Paul's on McIntyre Street. The reception was at our hotel. None of this was my kind of thing at all, and I felt I was in over my head.

After it was all over, I could have used a three-week vacation in Bermuda, but a day at Regina Beach had to do since Jake was too busy to get away. I don't know if it was the wedding or what, but I found afterwards I had a sudden longing for change. Watching Sarah and Rob embark on their lives together, all the newness and discovery that goes with it, I couldn't help but feel my own life was stagnant.

ff

Django Reinhardt, my hero, had died suddenly of a brain hemorrhage in 1953. He was only forty-three years old. I regretted more than ever that I hadn't been able to see him during the US tour he did with the Duke Ellington Orchestra in the late 40s. At the time, Sarah was little and I figured I could catch his show another time. His death shook me more than I thought it might and I think it was partly that he had died at the end of an era. The music I'd played in the 30s — traditional jazz, swing — had become passé, uncool, and Django's death kind of underscored that. When I heard Dizzy Gillespie and Charlie Parker shake things up with be-bop the late 40s, I already had the feeling that life was passing me by, that music was changing and I was being left way behind. At the time Django died, the cutting edge stuff was Miles Davis playing hard bop, cool jazz. And now, by the early 60s, with people like Ornette Coleman, Charles Mingus and John Coltrane playing free jazz, I felt like I didn't even know what jazz was anymore. And I think that I was not alone. A lot of people were alienated by the intellectualization of jazz music. So it was only natural to explore other forms.

A friend of Jacob's worked at CKCK TV and he remembered me from the Syncopation Five days. In 1957, when Sarah was twenty, I started to do a little piecework for them, played with the station's other studio musicians for commercials, local programs and so on. I really enjoyed working with other musicians again after so many years. The format suited me, too. While I loved my guitar and spending time with other musicians, I still disliked being onstage, unless it was my music. Working in the TV studio was perfect for me.

I hadn't been away from performing altogether. Earlier in the fifties I'd played a little at some of the better-attended Gypsy Lore Society functions. The maximum audience at these things was about fifteen, so it wasn't a really high-pressure performing situation or anything like that. And then, before long, Ochi Chornya started up. One night after I'd played at one of the Gypsy Lore meetings, a husky, dark-haired man with a moustache approached me as I was packing up my guitar.

He offered his hand. "Lita? I'm Bela Antonescu."

"Nice to meet you, Bela."

"I really enjoyed your playing tonight. You remind me of Django."

"Well, thank you very much."

"I play violin myself. And I heard about you from a friend who comes to these meetings, that's what brought me out here tonight. I wonder if you'd want to join me and some other musicians I've got together. Come and jam sometime."

"What kind of music do you play?"

"Traditional Gypsy music. There's me, a singer, a stand-up bass, and a drummer, but we need a guitarist. You'd be perfect."

I went to check them out at a practice they had in the back of Bela's grocery store and I loved them. And it wasn't long before I fell in love with playing in a group again. Ochi Chornya played at folk music events in and around Regina. Around that time folk music of all kinds was catching people's interest, and sometimes we found ourselves on the bill with acts very different from ours — vocal groups, Ukrainian folk acts, even groups who played Scottish folk music with pipes and violins. But the interest from young people of all backgrounds was good.

Mixing with people of different ages and backgrounds was good, too. By Sarah's wedding I had drifted away from the world of jazz and was gravitating towards the worlds of folk and blues music.

Folk music for me was the Gypsy material that Ochi Chornya performed, and my longstanding interest in blues, starting with Memphis Minnie in the 30s, suddenly deepened at that time. Listening to T-Bone Walker, Howlin' Wolf, Elmore James, and Willie Dixon gave my playing new textures and dimensions and I felt the stagnation start to lift. I felt excited about music again.

Jake and Sarah seemed to have different reactions to my actively becoming involved in the music scene again. Sarah was with fine with my playing as a studio musician, but thought my band Ochi Chornya was old fashioned and ridiculous.

"What's wrong with your mother playing in her group?" Jake wanted to know when Sarah made a remark about her mother the Gypsy musician at breakfast one morning. I'd played a late show with the band the night before and was a little slow getting started that day. I figured Sarah was in university, she could make her own breakfast. And she did, but complained bitterly about it.

"Don't you think at her age she should really forget about things like this?"

I cringed as I poured myself some of the coffee Jake had made. What is it with kids? They have the uncanny ability to zero in on your most vulnerable points and attack them. That was the one concern I'd been having then. "I'm forty," I'd said to Jacob. "Who I am trying to kid? That's far too old to be onstage." Jake had reassured me, pointed out that although our dark-eyed, dark-haired singer, Sofia Torok, was in her early thirties, Sergei Macek, the drummer, was close to my age, and Vlatko Dragomir, the bassist, and Bela were in their late fifties.

"What do *you* think she should do at her age?"

"I don't know. Something a little more dignified."

"Your mother is still a young woman. And there's no more dignified work than sharing what you've been given. Don't you forget that."

While Sarah never actually mentioned it to me again, her disapproval was always plain. I tried to tell myself that young people were bound to disapprove of their parents. Still, it hurt in a way Sarah could not know. Or worse, I thought, perhaps she did know.

The odd thing was that what Jake said to her made me think that he was behind me all the way. But one cold day, I got home a little later than usual from a session at CKCK. And I really don't know what he was put out about, exactly. Maybe the fact that I'd gotten a ride home with Frank, one of the musicians I'd worked with many times before. Or the fact that his dinner was a little late. Maybe it wasn't even anything that happened that day particularly, I don't know. Sarah was out with friends that evening. I warmed some lentil soup while I made sandwiches. He flipped through the *Leader-Post* at the kitchen table, said nothing. I brought the soup to the table.

"Something on your mind, Jake?"

"Well, yes. You don't really need to be out working, do you?"

I just looked at him for a minute. The session that afternoon had been long. I was tired. "What are you talking about? After all those things you told Sarah about sharing my gift and all that?"

"I don't mean you shouldn't play music at all. I just mean you don't need to do the studio work. We don't need the money."

"Well, no. We don't need the money. But I enjoy doing it."

He put his spoon down. "You have Ochi Chornya. And if you're out working, it makes people think we need the money."

"That's ridiculous. Nobody who knows us would think I'm doing this because we need the money."

"Maybe I would rather not have my wife out working. You never asked me, you just went ahead and took this job."

I rubbed my forehead, started to feel a pounding headache come on. "Asked you? Jake. I've been doing this more than two years and you've never said a word about it bothering you before. I had no idea."

"Well, I'm telling you now that it does. It's one thing playing music as a hobby. It's another thing having you working when I make perfectly good money."

We finished the rest of the meal in silence. I was seething inside but didn't have the energy to argue with him right then. I thought of when he'd said that he'd take care of the money, when we were on our honeymoon. Did he find the idea of me making money threatening in some way?

When we were done I cleared the dishes away and put the kettle on for some tea. Jake put his coat on at the front door.

"I'm going back to my office. There's some stuff I need to finish before tomorrow."

"All right."

"I might be late."

"That's okay."

"Think about what I said."

"Oh, I am," I said. I watched him get into his Lincoln and pull away. "Believe me, I am."

Twenty-Three

Lita
August 1965

I HAD BECOME GOOD FRIENDS WITH Sofia, Ochi Chornya's dark and statuesque singer. I often gave her a ride home, after our practices, in the aquamarine Buick sedan Jake got me for my fortieth birthday. It was a lovely gift. I'd never had my own car before. Only I would have rather spent a weekend with him. Or even a whole evening and have him pay attention to me, have a real conversation with me. As I had suspected when he first bought the Hotel Regina, he made a success of it almost right from the start, and by 1965 it was doing very well. But I also knew there would be a personal cost, for both of us. If he'd been a hard-working manager for CP Hotels, as a business owner he was obsessive. He worked seven days a week most weeks. It was very difficult to convince him to take any time off. And even in those rare times he did take off, he was talking about the hotel, thinking about it, almost all the time. And with Sarah gone, it became his sole focus.

Sadly, this was where we were by this point in our marriage. It had taken me a long time to realize that the very qualities about Jake that I'd admired so much in the early days — his stability, his seriousness, his strong work ethic — were the things that now antagonized me. As the years went by he became more and more conservative, more and more concerned with appearances and what people thought. And the older I got, the less any of that meant to me.

"This is such a nice car. I always mean to tell you that," Sofia said one night. "You're lucky to have studio work."

"Jake gave it to me. I never would have made enough to buy a car like this doing studio gigs. And anyway, he made me quit a few years ago."

She looked at me blankly. "Your husband wanted you to quit working? And you don't like that?"

"Yes. I mean, I know you think it's strange. But my working bothers him. He seems to take it as an affront to his masculinity or something."

"I wish I had that kind of problem to worry about." Sofia had left her husband shortly after I joined the band, when her daughter Charlotte was a toddler. She never said much about Manny, but I got the feeling he drank a lot.

"I know. It can't be easy for you to look after Charlie on your own. My life isn't so bad. But still — I just don't understand Jake."

Sofia shrugged. "Who can tell what men are thinking?"

I was never the type to have a lot of friends, and besides Sarah most of the people in my life were men, a result of working in the music business. I hadn't really had a close female friend since Darlene, and look how that turned out. But Sofia and I just hit it off. She and Charlie lived on Queen Street, not far from where Bill and I had lived. She had a job cleaning office buildings, mostly provincial government buildings downtown; some of the work was after hours, late at night sometimes, and I'd take care of Charlie. Charlie came to all our shows, and if Sofia had to work after a show, Charlie came home with me. We got along well, better than Sarah and I ever did, I hate to admit. She was dark like her mama, slight, had almond-shaped grey eyes. Her looks reminded me of my sister Maria as a child. She loved my guitar, loved to hear me play, and was getting me to show her how to play. Sarah, on the other hand, had always been uninterested in music, and was later embarrassed by me playing it.

I guess Charlie filled a kind of need for me. My granddaughter Elsa was two by that time, a blonde and bubbling little thing, but I only ended up seeing her a couple of times a month. The thing was, I didn't ever imagine I would end up having only one child, but that was just the way it worked out. I suppose it was possible that either Jake or I had a problem that we could have talked to our doctors about. Of course, since our relations had slowly, gradually, insidiously become almost nonexistent, it would have been pretty difficult for me to become pregnant no matter what else was going on. By the late 50s we had come to that state; by 1965 it had been years. It bothered me. Perhaps it bothered Jake, too, but he wouldn't talk about it, made me feel ashamed for even bringing it up. I didn't understand it, but I didn't know what to do about it, either. I thought about talking to my doctor, but I couldn't make myself. I was embarrassed, humiliated, felt it was somehow my fault. Had I become old and unattractive? Whatever the problem was, having Charlie around kept me occupied, and I was more than happy to step in and give Sofia a hand when she needed it.

One night in late August she phoned. "Lita, I hope it's not too late to call," she said.

"No, don't worry. It's only 10:00. What's up?"

"You know how I told you my sister's sick with cancer? Rose, the one who lives in Lumsden? She's really not doing too well."

"I'm sorry to hear that."

"I wonder if I could ask you a huge favour?"

"Of course."

"She needs someone to stay with her a while, take care of her. I think I can get some time off work. So I was wondering if I could leave Charlie with you for a few weeks?"

"I'd love to have her around. Anytime."

"Thank you, Lita. Thanks so much. I hate to impose on you, but I don't have anyone else to ask. And Charlie loves to spend time with you."

"And I love spending time with her. Don't worry about it. The place has seemed empty ever since Sarah left. We have a great time together."

I took Charlie to school in the mornings and picked her up. I hadn't been inside a school, except to vote, since Sarah went to Davin School on the corner of College Avenue and Retallack Street, just a couple of blocks from us. Charlie went to Sacred Heart School on Elphinstone Street, which was a little too far to walk, so I drove her there and picked her up in the Buick. Why not? I didn't have many other places to drive it.

ƒƒ

One Tuesday morning in October on the drive to school, Charlie asked, "Is it okay if we go to the library after school sometimes?"

I thought for a moment of Steve and how he'd loved the library, how much time he'd spent there. So much so that I wondered sometimes if he wasn't after a librarian. "Sure, we can do that."

"Can we go today?"

"Umm, I don't see why not. I could use a new book to read, come to think of it."

"How about Saturdays? Can we go to story hour on Saturday?"

I laughed. "Story hour? Sounds like fun. Let's go."

"Thanks, Lita. Now you can meet Mr. Lair."

I smiled. "That sounds good." Charlie talked about this Mr. Lair at the library all the time; how nice he was, how much fun he was. Of course, with no dad on the scene it was only natural that she'd become attached to some man in her life.

After school I picked Charlie up and we drove to the Central Library on 12th Avenue. She was amazed at how much faster it was to drive to the library than it was to take the bus. Almost as soon as we made it down the stairs to the Boys and Girls' Department, she grabbed me by the arm and started to drag me towards the desk.

"It's Mr. Lair," she said in a stage whisper.

She stopped when we got within a couple of feet of him. To this day I'm still not sure whether I gasped, "Oh, my God," under my breath or just in my mind when I first laid eyes on him. He was absolutely the most handsome man I had ever seen: tall and lean, deep-set eyes the colour of the sky on a warm day. His auburn hair was a little unruly, maybe a little long for a librarian. His smile was wide and open, and we both couldn't help laughing at Charlie's eagerness for us to meet.

"Hello. I'm John Lair," he said. He extended a hand, and I shook it.

"Hello, Mr. Lair. I'm Lita Stone. I take care of Charlie sometimes. We're good friends. She's told me a lot about you."

"Nice to meet you, Mrs. Stone."

"Call me Lita."

"Well, she's told me about you, too, Lita."

"Oh, really? Nothing bad, I hope."

"Oh, no. She tells me you're a guitarist."

"Um, yes. Yes, I am."

"That's really interesting. What kind of music do you play?"

"Well, a lot of kinds, I guess. I've been playing jazz for a long time, but I play some folk and blues these days."

"You're playing professionally?"

"I play traditional Gypsy music in a group with Charlie's mom. I used to play in a jazz combo in the 30s." I wondered how old he was when I was playing jazz. A little child, maybe.

"Really?"

"Uh-huh."

"Here in Regina?"

"Yeah. We were called the Syncopation Five."

"Amazing. I wonder if you'd want to bring your guitar into our story hour sometime?"

Just then I noticed the guitar case propped against the wall behind his desk. "Do you play, too?"

"I do. I'm not that good." *Ah, a musician. That explains the hair.*

"Well, I'd like to hear you."

"All right. You bring your guitar in one of these times and we'll compare notes."

A black-haired boy stood beside us at the desk. "Mr. Lair, can you help me find this book?"

I took Charlie's hand. "We'd better let you get back to work. But it was nice to meet you," I said.

"Yes. Nice meeting you, too."

I took off my coat and shoes when I got home, walked by the mirror hanging over the bench by the front door. For just a second, I saw Mami's lined, weathered face looking back at me. I blinked and looked again. It was me all right, but since when did my neck look so crepey? My skin looked dull and grey. I wondered how long I'd had those dark circles under my eyes — weeks, years? The phone rang and I snapped out of it. Just as well.

ff

Sofia came back to Regina after about three weeks. I picked her up at the Greyhound station late on a Tuesday afternoon and brought her home to have dinner with us. We had tea in the living room after, while Charlie did her homework in the kitchen.

"It's good to be back," Sofia said. "But I feel awful leaving Rose. She's so frail."

"What about bringing her back to Regina?" I suggested.

"We talked about that. There's a couple of problems with it. One — well, you've seen our apartment. I don't know where I'd put her, even. She came here for radiation treatments a few times, but I think they're pretty much done with that. She slept in Charlie's bed, and Charlie slept on the couch. I don't know if that would work for too long. And the other thing is, she doesn't want to leave Lumsden. She's lived there close to forty years now, since she and Pete got married. Pete passed away ten years ago, and pretty much everybody she knows in the world now, besides us, is in Lumsden. So she wants to stay there."

"That's too bad. It's a lot of worry for you, not to be with her."

"It is. The thing is, she's quite a bit older than me, looked after me a lot when we were kids. I kind of feel like it's my turn to look after her now. I was thinking on the bus that I might be able to work something out with my boss, Gabe, about working different hours for a while so I can be with her more. Gabe is Manny's brother and he feels bad about the way things worked out between Manny and me. So I think I can get him to give me a break, for a while, anyway."

"And if you need some help from me, you know you can just ask, Sofia."

"I probably will. Thank you, Lita."

The deal Sofia came up with was that she would do night shifts, Tuesday through Friday. She'd take the bus out to Lumsden Saturday night and get back Tuesday afternoon. She hoped it would only be temporary, mostly because it didn't leave much time for Charlie, but it was the best she could do.

ff

When Charlie and I arrived at the library for story hour that Saturday morning, Mr. Lair and a small group of children were just leaving the building.

"The weather is so gorgeous, I thought we'd have story hour in the park this morning. We might as well enjoy it while it lasts." He nodded in the direction of Victoria Park, down the block and across the street.

"Good idea."

"So when are you going to bring your guitar in?"

I laughed. "I didn't really think you were serious, Mr. Lair."

"Please, call me John. And of course I am. I'd love to hear you play. When would work for you?"

"I don't know. I'm pretty flexible."

"How about next Saturday?"

"I suppose so. Sure."

"That's great. Thank you."

"Oh. My pleasure."

John sat on the grass when we got to the park. "Boys and girls," he said. "Can we all sit in a circle on the grass right here? This morning we're going to read some books by Maurice Sendak."

I had been going to go back to the library during story hour and look for a novel, maybe *Up the Down Staircase* by Bel Kaufman. Instead, I stayed and listened to John read *One Was Johnny, Alligators All Around*, and *Where the Wild Things Are.*

After an animated discussion about monsters, we got up to go back to the library. I was just about to ask John what time I should arrive for next time when Charlie bounded up to us.

"Lita! Did Mr. Lair remind you about bringing your guitar?"

"Yes, Charlie. I'm bringing it next week."

She turned to him. "See? I told you she would."

"You were right, Charlie," he said, and we both laughed.

ff

The next Saturday was dull, overcast. I left Charlie to play hopscotch in the park with some of her friends from school while I took my guitar into the library. I felt a bit nervous as I descended the stairs, almost stopped and turned around. I didn't know what that was about. Stage fright? How silly. I took a deep breath, took another step and put my head in the doorway. John sat at the desk.

"Good morning," he said. He wore a soft grey sweater that brought out the grey flecks in his eyes. "How are you?"

"Pretty good, thanks. And you?"

"I'm well. I'm quite excited about having a musical guest this morning. We'll be in the story room over here. The only thing was, I wondered if you'd mind if we read a couple of stories before we get to the music part?"

"No. No, that would be all right."

"If you have something else you need to do, you can leave your guitar here and come back later. Sorry, I wasn't really thinking when we got talking about this last week."

No, I wasn't either. "That's all right. I can stay and give you a hand if you like."

"If you want to. That would be great. Listen," he said, opening up his briefcase, "I thought you might like to borrow these."

He brought out a handful of 45s. I picked them up and read the labels. " 'Another You' by The Seekers, 'Catch the Wind' by Donovan, 'I Knew I'd Want You' by The Byrds."

"You mentioned you were playing some folk and I thought you might want to listen to some folk-rock. It's kind of a new thing."

"It sounds very interesting. I would like to take them home and listen to them. Maybe when I bring them back you'd want to borrow some of my jazz 78s."

The kids began to file into the story room and I leaned against the counter under the windows in the back. John told them, "We have a guest in story hour today, everyone. This is Mrs. Stone. She's a friend of Charlie's, and she'll be playing some music for us a little later on."

Charlie beamed at me.

He continued. "Right now, though, we're going to read some stories with music in them." He started with *The Bremen Town Musicians*.

"Now, who knows this one?" he asked, holding up a copy of *Over in the Meadow* by John Langstaff.

"I do, I do!" said a couple of girls, putting up their hands.

"That's fine. You can help me sing, then," he said, opening the book. He began to sing the old folk song. "Over in the meadow, in the sand in the sun, lived an old mother turtle and her little turtle one . . ."

What a beautiful voice he had: low, clear, smooth. I didn't want him to stop. When he was done, he asked me whether I wanted to play.

"Sure." I brought the National out and started tuning it.

"Ooh, nice guitar," he said.

"Thanks. We've been together a long time."

The kids sat in a semi-circle on the rug in front of me while I played some Gypsy tunes, some jazz numbers. Then they started to pipe up.

"Mr. Lair, you should play, too."

"Oh, no. I'm not nearly as good as Mrs. Stone."

I smiled. "C'mon, Mr. Lair. We can do a duet."

"All right. Just one."

He had a nice mahogany-bodied Gibson LG-O. While he tuned it he asked me if I knew Duke Ellington's "Solitude".

"Sure do. You start and I'll jump in."

He played the melody and I played around him, echoed, harmonized. I was having a great time. When we finished, the kids' applause was pretty enthusiastic. I could tell from his flushed smile that he'd had as much fun as I had. And for a minute or so I couldn't tear my eyes from his. Soon enough, though, I had to. The kids loved our guitars. They rushed up and wanted to take turns playing. I showed a little blonde girl where to put her left-hand fingers on the National's fretboard, and I had a sudden flash back to Mami's long, leathery hands showing me the same thing so many years ago.

Story hour was done then. Charlie went to find some books, and after John saw the kids off he joined me at the back of the room, leaned against the counter beside me. He smelled faintly of coffee, and soap. "Jazz 78s? Really?"

We ended up talking quite a while, about music mostly, of course. Don't get me wrong, I enjoyed talking to him. Very much. But it did seem a little strange. After a while, I started packing up my guitar.

"That is a fantastic guitar," he said.

"Yes. It's far and away my favourite. I've had it since 1935. In fact, I won it in a poker game I was playing with some of the On-to-Ottawa trekkers when they were camped out here."

"Really? Okay, you have to tell me about this."

I told him how I'd won the guitar, and looked at my watch. It was almost noon.

"I should really go," I said, and picked up my guitar case.

He looked at his watch. "Ooh. You're right. Look at the time. I, uh, guess I should get back to work. But listen, thank you so much for coming. It was wonderful. You're an amazing guitarist."

"Thank you. You're pretty good yourself, you know."

"Thanks. It's great for the kids to be exposed to live music. If you'd ever consider doing this again, maybe once in a while . . . "

We started out the door. "Of course. I enjoyed it, too. We'll have to do it again."

"Let me know what you think of those records."

"I'm looking forward to listening to them. Well, goodbye, John."

"Goodbye, Lita."

I found Charlie sitting at a table, reading one of the huge pile of books she'd selected. We signed them out and started to leave. Up the stairs, out the door. As I opened the car door for Charlie and put my guitar in the backseat, I had the strangest feeling. I felt kind of lightheaded, had trouble focusing. Of course — I must be hungry, I thought. Or I need a cup of coffee. Or a cigarette — that must be it. I lit one before I started up the car, smoked it before we got home, but didn't feel any different. Inside, as I caught a glimpse of myself in the entryway mirror again, Charlie asked the name of the song I'd been singing all the way home.

Singing? "Oh, I guess that was 'Solitude.' Duke Ellington song."

"Uh-oh," I said to my reflection, under my breath.

Twenty-Four

Lita
Spring 1966

I ENDED UP COMING IN TO story hour as a musical guest fairly often, every other Saturday or so. I really did get a great deal of pleasure out of playing for the kids, but I'd be lying if I said I didn't have an ulterior motive. I loved spending time with John. He and I leaned on the counter in the back of the story room one afternoon as the children filed out. Charlie asked if she could play Chinese skipping with some friends for a while in the park before we went home. The sun through the window warmed our backs and it hit me all of a sudden that his auburn hair glowed in the light, seemed to be constantly changing colour — red, gold, brown, pink. He was just like the little boy in the dream I'd had so many years before.

"You were saying something," he said.

"Was I?" It took me a second to get back to what I'd been thinking before. "Oh, right. Well, I just don't understand. You say you want to play music, and you're good. There's nothing to stop you from doing it — "

"No, there's nothing to stop me," he'd said. "Nothing except what my family expects. What my wife expects."

"Are you going to live your whole life according to what other people tell you?"

"Music can wait. I don't have time right now. You know I have to work."

"You can't work and play music at the same time? Millions of people have jobs, and families. But they still make time to do what they love."

He turned his eyes from me, fussed with a loose thread on his sleeve. "You know what I mean. I'll take it up seriously later, when I have time."

"Listen. Maybe you'll be around another fifty years, or maybe you won't. My first husband died when he was twenty-three. How long are you going to wait to do what you really want to do?"

He shrugged. "It's easy for you to say, Lita. Listen, I'm sorry, but I've got to get going."

"I should, too."

He gave me a half-wave as he walked down the hall and out of sight. What a waste, I said to myself as I went up the stairs and outside to get Charlie. His voice was so beautiful it brought tears to my eyes. Like Bill's had been but richer, deeper, like rum or molasses. A gift. And he was going to squander it? Waste it, never use it? But then it was *his* voice. Who was I to tell him what to do with it?

Later that night I thought again about John and the child in that dream. Then I realized with a jolt that when I first had the dream he would have been three or four years old, just like the boy. And those men I'd dreamed about over the years — the man on the dock, the man in my arms on my and Jake's honeymoon — all had the same glowing hair with shifting colours. Had they all been John? The thought scared me a little. But in a weird way, it made perfect sense.

$$ff$$

Sofia convinced me to stay one night and have a cup of tea after I dropped Charlie off. It was late and Charlie was tired and went pretty much straight to bed. We sat at Sophia's tiny drop-leaf kitchen table.

"Lita. Listen, I'm worried about you," she said, and poured me a cup of strong black tea.

"I'm fine. Don't worry."

"I mean it. You look tired. Is taking care of Charlie too much for you? It's a lot to ask."

"No, it isn't. You know I love her, and I'd miss looking after her."

"So what is it, then? Something is bothering you, I can tell."

I hesitated for a moment. What was the point of lying to her, pretending everything was fine when it wasn't? Sofia was no fool. Besides I had to tell someone. I was going insane. "I guess I haven't been sleeping well the last few weeks. I — I've fallen in love with someone."

Sofia was silent for a moment and though I knew she would never reproach me, I wasn't sure what her reaction might be. Finally she asked, "Is it someone I know?"

"No. Charlie knows him, though. He works in the Boys and Girls' Department at the library."

Sofia just nodded. "Go on," she said.

"He's a very attractive man. And, well, we just seem to have so much in common. He's a musician, too. We've been trading records. And talking a lot. Talking quite a lot."

"He is interested in you?"

"Maybe he's just interested in antiques. He is a lot younger than me."

"Lita."

"You're right. I have to stop feeling sorry for myself."

"You're only human. You're lonely. I understand . . . and I don't blame you."

"Thank you, Sofia."

"It's easy to understand. Just be careful."

I sighed. "Sure. I will."

ff

The end of the school year and the end of story hour season drew near. I tried to steel myself: I would have to let go of him. I didn't know how, but I'd have to. This was crazy, and if he knew how I felt he'd probably think I was crazy. A line from a Bob Dylan record he'd lent me kept running through my head: *You are a walking antique.* It could never work. And yet there were little things that made me think it wasn't all me. Besides the long conversations we had leaning on the counter at the back of the story room.

The way he looked at me. Sometimes our eyes would lock, and I'd forget what we were even talking about. I'd catch him looking me over, and thought I must be imagining it. How could he find an old woman like me attractive? But it happened again and again. He'd touch me on the arm, on the shoulder, and it'd go through me like a jolt. He told me pretty intimate things about himself and his wife. Things were rocky between them.

"Lita, listen," he said in a hushed voice once, after the kids had all left. "My wife. She can't . . . well, she has a medical condition." He dropped his gaze, fidgeted with the pen in his hand.

My head started to spin a little. What he was getting at was obvious. What should I say? He looked at me again, and I nodded.

"Mr. Lair!" Kent, a freckle-faced loudmouth, peeled into the room at top speed, gasping for breath. "Marianne fell down the stairs! You have to come!" And before either of us could say another word, the two of them were gone. I've often wondered how the rest of that conversation would have panned out. I might have talked about Jacob and me.

One Saturday in the middle of May, we got talking again after story hour, about all kinds of things. Before I knew it, the clock said 12:30.

"I should go," I said. "I should let you eat your lunch."

"I guess so. Before you go, though, I brought those 78s back. The Charlie Christian ones."

He got his briefcase out from under his desk, opened it and looked for them. "Ah, sorry. I thought I put them in here last night."

"That's okay. Another time."

He got up from behind the desk and stood near me. "You know, I always enjoy talking to you. Here, it's difficult. We always get interrupted. We should go out for coffee sometime."

My face felt hot. I looked at my feet for a second, couldn't hide my smile when I looked back at him. My mouth felt a little dry.

"I'd like that. Very much."

He smiled, too. Just then another librarian put her head in the doorway. "John? I need to ask you about those intermediate readers . . ."

"I'll be there in a minute," he answered.

"I'll get out of your way," I said.

"I guess I'd better go," he said. "But I'll see you soon?"

"Yes. Goodbye."

It took all the strength I had not to burst out singing as we checked out Charlie's books and I carried the National down the hall, down the stairs, out the door, and across the street to the car. Charlie and I sang at the tops of our voices all the way home, and I kept singing the whole time I made lunch for the two of us.

ff

He's a very modern man, I thought many times. Maybe all these things, the words, the looks, the gestures that I interpret as flirting, are just friendliness. Maybe men and women relate in a different way these days. Or maybe it's just been so long I don't remember how it goes, can't tell the difference between flirting and friendliness. I told myself these things back then, but I think men and women are pretty unchanging. Attraction is universal, has been the same for all of human history.

This attraction, though, was certainly beyond reason or logic. I have language for it now. I didn't then. My body was crying out for him at a cellular level; I felt the endorphins rush every time I talked to him. They used to call women interested in sex nymphomaniacs, or hysterical. Especially women my age. They'd send us to doctors to have our sexual organs removed, so we'd be normal again. Maybe John thought I was after younger men all the time. I don't know. The truth was that the last time I'd been with a new man was with Jacob, in 1937. Nearly thirty years earlier.

But it was more than just attraction. I'd found a friend in John, an ally. Someone who understood me. Someone who knew how alone an artist can be. Who wasn't put off by the fact that I was different, seemed attracted by it, in fact. Always, I'd felt like an alien with other people, even before I understood why. I was a Gypsy. A woman working in a male-dominated field. For a long time I was poor. A musician, an artist. I was different from Bill's family, different from Jacob's. With John, I thought I'd finally found someone who'd accept me for who I was. I didn't realize it until I met him, but I was desperately lonely for someone who understood me, who was like me. Who maybe even wanted me.

Jake, when pressed, would say that he loved me. But he no longer acted like he loved me, hadn't for years. We didn't have conversations, beyond things we needed to talk about. He didn't want to go places with me, or spend time with me. I felt like another of his many possessions. I was his. His wife. I had been his wife for a long time, he had a right to me. All that was true in a strict sense. But was it love? Did he love me? I think our love had died a slow death a long time before this.

At times I felt selfish. How selfish of me to want to betray Jake. But then, was it any more selfish than Jake withholding affection from me? Maybe wanting John was wrong, but I had a hard time convincing myself of that. Funny, I never would have considered, when it came to Bill and Darlene, that his side of the story might deserve compassion, that maybe he really had loved her. Maybe he only did what he felt compelled to do. Maybe Bill never thought that what he felt was wrong, either. Because loving John never felt wrong to me. It wasn't so simple as right or wrong, black or white. Was loving him any more wrong than Jacob taking me for granted, treating me like a piece of furniture, ignoring my emotional needs? But it wasn't that I fell in love with him to spite Jacob. I know two wrongs don't make a right. I couldn't help feeling the way I did. It took me a while to start to understand all this, but it ended up giving me insight into why Bill did what he did, useless as it was to have empathy for him all those years after he was gone.

ƒƒ

All too soon the end of June came. John had gotten cold feet. After mentioning going for coffee, he backed off. I brought it up once and he said maybe we could go sometime in the summer when he wasn't so busy.

The last Saturday of June was warm and sunny. I wasn't even going to go in for the last story hour, but I decided I had to say goodbye to him. I didn't know what to think anymore. I guessed he was afraid. It made me very sad, and that morning I couldn't tear my eyes away from him, watched his every move. It was like I had to drink him in, keep him with me that way.

Charlie was distraught, too. She shook and wept and I tried to comfort her as best I could while the other kids left. John tried to talk to her, but she was too upset. She just could not say goodbye to him. I wasn't faring much better. Tears rolled down my face. I decided the best thing to do was take her home.

"Lita. I'm sure we'll be in touch over the summer." His eyes glistened, I swear.

"Goodbye." I put my sunglasses on, in hopes that no one would see the mascara streaking my face, put my arm around Charlie and guided her out. I looked back at him just before we went up the stairs. He stood in the doorway of the story room, white as a sheet, watching us go.

We went out the doors, across the street, got into the Buick and started driving. All I could hear was Charlie's sobbing, and the pounding in my ears.

"Charlie," I said as soon as I was able to talk again. "How about we go to the Milky Way and have ice cream sundaes for lunch?"

ƒƒ

The days went by, then the weeks. I thought he might call, maybe write a letter, or even drop by some afternoon. He'd said he and his wife were going to Toronto for a while, but they wouldn't be gone the whole summer. He was the first thing I thought of when I woke up and the last thing I thought of before falling asleep. It was like that for weeks. I dreamt of him almost nightly.

One stormy Friday evening at the end of July, I suggested to Jake that we go out to a movie. I thought it would help me get my mind off things.

"*Who's Afraid of Virginia Woolf* is playing at the Cap," I said.

"That's that one with Elizabeth Taylor and her husband, isn't it? I heard they argue all the way through it," Jake said, almost looking up from his paper.

"It's supposed to be good."

"Now, Elizabeth Taylor. There's a good looking woman."

"What is that supposed to mean?"

"Nothing. Can't a guy admire a beautiful woman?"

"So do you want to go admire her in this movie or what?"

"I don't know, Lita. I'm tired. Couldn't we stay in tonight?"

"We stay in every night, Jake."

"Look. How about if we go out tomorrow night? I had meetings all day. I am really beat."

"Fine." I thought about going by myself.

"Isn't there a movie on TV tonight? We could crack a bottle of wine. Nice night to stay in."

I picked up the *TV Guide*. "At 9:00, there's *Casablanca*."

"There. That's a good movie. It's lousy outside anyway."

I knew what would happen. So why did I let it bother me so much when he fell asleep after his first glass of wine? Shouldn't I have been used to it? In a few minutes his snores ripped through the air so loudly I couldn't even hear the TV. Was this what the rest of my life would be? Sitting in front of a TV listening to Jake snore? I couldn't stand the idea. I couldn't stand it. I poured myself another glass of wine, tried to watch the movie, but I couldn't hear it.

"Jake. Wake up."

"What? What happened?"

"I can't hear the TV over your snoring. Why don't you go to bed?"

"I wasn't sleeping."

"Jake, please. You were asleep. Why don't you go to bed?"

He stalked off, as if I had done something wrong. Now at least I could hear the movie. But I couldn't keep my mind on it at all. I kept thinking of John. Was that it? Was it over, before it had even begun? Would I ever see him again? Why, why, why had this all happened?

Then something occurred to me that hadn't before. Maybe he didn't know that I loved him. That could be. Hadn't Bill always talked about my icy exterior? Maybe I hadn't shown enough interest. Of course, that had to be it. Why hadn't I thought of it before?

I flipped the TV off, topped up my glass, and headed into the study. I found some nice cream-coloured heavy bond writing paper and envelopes and sat at the desk, listening to Jake's faint snoring from upstairs. The rain still pelted against the bay window that overlooked the lawn and the long driveway that led to Connaught Crescent. My heart was full. I had to think, had to word this carefully. I found some stamps in a drawer, looked up John's address in the Sask Tel directory. There was only one John Lair, on Retallack St. I addressed the envelope and then I started to write.

> *Dear John,*
>
> *The summer's been so long already. It seems like ages since I've seen you. It crossed my mind this evening that maybe you weren't aware of how fond I've grown of you over the last few months. But I have. And it's been very hard not to see you. I miss you so much.*
> *Fondest regards,*
> *Lita*

I read it over a couple of times, folded it, slid it into the envelope, and sealed it. I put on my raincoat, slipped out the front door, walked to the mailbox at the corner. I kissed the letter and dropped it in the mailbox. And I immediately felt better, lighter.

The rain fell even harder. What would Jake think if he saw me coming into the house after midnight, soaked to the skin and a little bit tipsy? As soon as I opened the door I heard the dull roar of his snoring. Just as if nothing had happened.

Twenty-Five

Lita
Winter 1966

"LITA, CAN I STAY UP AND watch the late show with you tonight?" Charlie asked me one rainy Saturday afternoon in late October. CKCK ran a late movie after the news, at 11:30. Sometimes the show didn't end until close to two. Kind of late for a ten-year-old.

"I don't know, Charlie. What's the movie?"

She pointed at the *TV Guide* entry. "*Anna Karenina.*"

"The one with Greta Garbo?"

"Uh-huh. It's supposed to be a good story."

I smiled. "Yes, it is. It's a very sad story, too. A love story." I remembered going to see it with Bill at the Cap. I'd sat beside him trying not to let him see me wipe my tears away. I don't know why I hadn't wanted him to see me cry at a movie. I guess it just seemed silly, weak. "Does that sound like the kind of movie you'd want to stay up late and watch?"

She nodded.

"Okay. Tell you what. We can watch it if you have a nap after supper."

I was glad to have someone to watch it with, actually. Jake was out of town again. Though, really, whether he was home or not made little difference by this time. Even if we did sit down to watch a movie together chances were very good that he'd fall asleep within the first half-hour. If he started snoring I'd send him to bed, but either way I'd end up watching the movie by myself. It would be nice to have some company for a change. Sofia's sister was now in Regina, at the hospital, so Charlie wasn't staying with us as much.

She went to bed at 7:30. While she slept, I steeled myself. I knew that watching this movie might be difficult, but this was a special occasion, the end of summer. I woke her up at 11:00 and she helped me make popcorn, got a bottle of Canada Dry out of the fridge while I poured myself a glass of wine. We settled down on the couch. Charlie talked and laughed. She was very excited to be staying up so late.

I'd made sure there was a box of Kleenex nearby, just in case. Turns out that was good thinking. If I'd been affected by this movie as a young girl, just married, in 1935, watching it at this time in my life was — not exactly a mistake, I knew what I was in for, but . . . I guess I'd forgotten the details of the story. I'd expected Charlie to fall asleep part way through, but she seemed mesmerized by the movie. It does cut out most of the intricate subplots of the novel and just sticks with the story of Anna and Vronsky, which is pretty compelling. The opening sequence with the soldiers playing a drinking game made me think of Bill, and of Steve. I'm afraid most of the rest of it made me think of the present, though. The train station in Moscow looked almost identical to the one in downtown Regina, although maybe it was just the snow. I wanted to cry out loud when Anna told Vronsky, "The days go by, life goes by without you." But I just couldn't upset Charlie. I brushed away my tears with the back of my hand as discreetly as I could. I don't think she noticed, though I couldn't say for sure.

She turned to me with dark circles under her eyes when the end credits started to roll and said, "Wow. I loved that movie. Thanks for letting me watch it, Lita."

I got up and switched off the TV. "You're welcome. I'm glad you enjoyed it."

"Did you enjoy it?"

"Yes, I did. More than when I saw it the first time, a long time ago. But it's twenty to two. Time for both of us to get to bed."

I put Charlie to bed. I didn't actually sleep for quite a while.

ƒƒ

I tried for a long time to make my guitar sound like coyotes at night. The sound is unearthly — kind of like a scream, like some hellish bird. Nothing else sounds like it. But I couldn't figure it out. How to make that noise with my guitar, I mean. I kept thinking, Where's Django when you need him? He'd find a way to do it.

Around Christmas, I saw John outside the library. I parked and went over to talk to him. It had been so long since I'd seen him. I felt silly about the letter. I'd felt silly about it the morning after I'd sent it. He never did get in touch over the summer like he'd said he would, and I kicked myself for sending it. I'd made a mess of things, but now I thought maybe I could explain.

He turned my way as I approached him, looked at me for a moment and then turned his back and went inside. I stood there feeling a little dizzy, a little sick. Had that really just happened?

But if I rationalized what had happened that morning — he hadn't seen me, he was nervous, or late for something — over the next few weeks he made it abundantly clear that he didn't want to talk to me. He walked away every time I tried to come near him, avoided making eye contact. Needless to say, I was crushed. If things happen for a reason, I had a hard time seeing the reason for this. To break my heart? To kill me? To teach me a lesson — that being what?

There are a couple of questions I've learned not to ask. One is, "What next?" Often you don't want to know the answer. Another is, "Why?" Like Bob Dylan said, "Don't Think Twice It's All Right." Amen to that.

At any time a voice in my head, one that sounded like Ma's, would start up. *You should be happy. Don't you have everything, and more? You're spoiled, that's what you are.* All that was true. But deep in my heart, I knew it wasn't. Maybe I had all the material things I could ever want: a beautiful home, car, money to buy whatever I wanted. But I was lonelier than I ever imagined it possible to be, and I wanted John more than I could remember ever wanting anything or anyone before.

The weeks went by. I tried to forget him, but it was no use. Finally, one day in January I decided I had to talk to him, clear the air. I went to the library one Saturday morning and waited outside the story room. The kids ran out the door and up the stairs and in a moment he came out, too, carrying books and a coffee cup.

"Hello," he said. He didn't stop, though, just kept walking and went up the stairs. It all happened so fast. I thought about calling his name, get him to come back and talk to me, but I felt sick. I went home and wept like a schoolgirl.

The next day the phone rang.

"Mrs. Stone? This is Marian MacKay. I'm head of the Boys and Girls' Department at the Central Library."

"Yes, Mrs. MacKay?"

"Mrs. Stone, I . . . I'm calling concerning John Lair."

"John Lair?"

"I understand you helped out in his story hours last year. He tells me that you wrote him a personal letter last summer. Is that right?"

"Yes."

I sat down on the chair that seemed to be spinning around the room.

"And then you showed up at his story hour on Saturday. He said you were waiting for him."

"Well, yes. I was . . . "

"He said that you looked angry."

"Angry? No, I . . . not at all. I just wanted to talk to him."

"He says that all this — the letter, waiting for him — is making him very uncomfortable. He asked me to tell you that."

"I don't know what to say." I felt my voice growing quieter and quieter. I wanted to disappear.

"Mrs. Stone, I'm sorry to have to tell you all this. I really thought that he should have called you himself, but he insisted I do it."

I felt like I had to get off the phone before I started crying. "I'm sorry you had to get involved. Tell Mr. Lair not to worry. I won't bother him again. Thank you for calling, Mrs. MacKay."

I put the phone down and lit a cigarette. For some reason I didn't feel like crying right away. But when I did start a little while later, it was really hard to stop.

Why would he hurt me like that? I didn't understand. Did he hate me, and I just couldn't see it? Was he afraid I'd get violent or make a scene? What about my side of the story? He'd asked me out, hadn't he? I suppose this was easier for him. But it hurt me so much to hear it from someone else. Rejection is one thing. Cruelty is another. He was a coward.

$$ff$$

After that the wind was knocked out of me. I was finished. I don't remember ever feeling that way, feeling that bad, before or since. It wasn't just disappointment or losing face, though there was definitely some of that going on. This was a deep sense of loss and melancholy, worse than I'd ever thought possible. Worse than when Bill died, strange as that sounds. I couldn't help sometimes thinking of Pop, wondering if this was how he felt at the end. I know none of us knew for sure what was going through his head that day. But that winter, suffering the twisted rejection from John, I thought I had a pretty good idea.

One bitterly cold, dark afternoon at the end of February I looked out the frost-framed kitchen window and saw nothing but swirling white, heard the wind whistle and pitch and howl. It sounded remarkably like the coyotes whose voices I still failed to mimic on my guitar. My heart sank. More of this weather. I didn't know if I'd be able to stand the madness of another prairie winter. Not so much the madness of being inside, alone, isolated much of the time, or the madness of my heart feeling emptier than it had ever felt before, but the whole idea of being in Saskatchewan in winter at all seemed mad. What lies the Canadian government told the poor and desperate of Europe about this paradise on the other side of the ocean — verdant, fertile, welcoming. They didn't mention how much the prairies resembled Siberia, especially in winter.

It was my day to pick Charlie up. I drove over to the school as usual. The ice-covered streets reflected the low indigo clouds; skiffs of snow blew across the road.

"Lita, can we drop into the library for a minute? I need to look something up in the encyclopedia."

"Of course, Charlie."

I parked the Buick across the street from the library and carefully took Charlie across the street. But I just couldn't stomach the thought of going in.

"Do you mind if I wait for you in the car? I'm feeling kind of tired today."

"Sure. I won't be long."

When she was safely inside I started back to my car. I couldn't help but glance up at the second floor window that I knew to be the staff room (we'd gone up there together to get coffee once), and there he was. It was hard to tell from that distance, but he seemed to look at me for a moment before he turned and disappeared. I kept walking. As I neared the curb and turned to watch the yellow headlights of passing cars, it crossed my mind how easy it would be to do an Anna Karenina, or a Joseph Koudelka, right then. How simple to step out into the blowing snow on the icy road in front of a car, and have this pain and longing and loneliness over. And no one would ever know it wasn't an accident.

But of course there were Elsa and Sarah to think about. Jake would be upset, though I was pretty sure he would get over it. Last but not least there was Charlie. I remember how

I felt after Pop died and I knew I could never do that to Charlie, who really had only Sofia and me in the world.

I'll tell you what was almost worse than anything else about all of this. Charlie loved him almost as much as I did. I knew that. And John knew it, too. Once story hour was done that spring, she was miserable for a long time. That tore my heart out, watching her cry over the summer, and I tried to do what I could to help her feel better, though God knows I felt pretty horrible myself.

After a while Charlie's crying stopped, but it wasn't long before she started sleepwalking. The first time, I didn't know what was happening. She came into the living room one night just after midnight, where I was watching the late show, *Brief Encounter* with Trevor Howard and Celia Johnson.

"Charlie, it's very late. Maybe we can watch the late show together when you're here on the weekend sometime."

She didn't answer, and stopped in front of the window.

"What's the matter? Did you hear something outside?"

I went to the window, but saw nothing. I looked at her. Her eyes darted around the room for a few seconds and then she started to cry. I put my arms around her narrow shoulders and guided her over to the couch.

"What's the matter? Did you have a bad dream?"

She said something I didn't understand. At first I thought she might be speaking Romanian, though I knew Sofia was careful to always speak English to her.

"Charlie. Look at me."

Words tumbled out of her mouth, but made no sense. It scared me, but in a few moments she snapped out of it. I gave her some water and took her back to her bedroom and she fell asleep immediately.

"John," I whispered on the way back downstairs, fighting back my own tears now. "Look what you've done to us."

When I told Sofia about it, she said Charlie had never done anything like that before. But over the next few months she sleepwalked at home and at my house several times. It gradually stopped. And after that she never mentioned Mr. Lair again.

ƒƒ

I wished forgetting John could have been as easy for me. As the days passed, I began to see Mami's face again when I looked in the mirror. What was wrong with me, anyway? I must have been insane, absolutely insane. A man like John attracted to me? Once again, I felt a deep shame. Shame that I could be so stupid, that I could let myself get so carried away. The truth is I couldn't help it. I was lost to him as soon as I saw him, maybe even years before I saw him, crazy as that sounds. But I was so ashamed of my loneliness, my desperation.

One day I took the National off the stand where it usually sat. I hadn't played in a while. Instead of picking the guitar up, though, I sat down in the chair I usually played in and just looked at it. I looked at it for a long time. The sunshine from the window it sat near glinted on the metal.

You don't have to actually play it. You could just clean the fingerprints and dust off it.

Dust. I hadn't noticed until then that it was dusty, had sat there so long untouched that it was covered in dust. That spooked me. I could not make myself walk the three feet from my chair to the guitar stand to pick it up. I could not move. A heavy weight in the middle of my chest pinned me to the chair, and the more I thought about picking up the guitar, the more impossible it seemed. We'd played Duke Ellington's "Solitude" together, John and I. That day seemed so long ago, like a dream. Did it really happen, did any of that really happen? I wasn't sure how long I sat there, but the phone rang and broke the spell and I got up to answer it, something I normally didn't do when I was playing. But of course, I wasn't playing.

Day after day it went like that. I did pick it up and dust it off once in a while, set it back on the stand. But actually play it? No. I could not. I had no drive to make music at all. I felt guilty and sad about it, but ultimately powerless, like this beautiful thing I had, this ability to make music, was gone and there was no way to get it back. I felt like that after Bill died, when Sarah was little.

After a while of this I decided to take it off its stand and put it back in its case. To keep the dust off, I told myself, but that wasn't really why. I didn't want to have to look at it. Having it locked up in its case made me feel even worse, though. I thought about selling it, playing one of my other guitars, though the National had always been my favourite, and for a long time my only guitar. It crossed my mind that I ought to sell them all, get rid of them. What was an old woman doing playing guitar, anyway? I should sell them, get them out of my house, spend my time gardening and taking care of my granddaughter, like other women my age did. I knew I could never really go through with selling them, but found some twisted solace in concocting this backup plan. A plan to chicken out, completely, if things got bad enough.

It occurred to me then that I wasn't even fifty and that I might simply be blocked. After all, if writers could be blocked, maybe musicians and other artists could be, too. When I was away from playing after Bill died, I'd used

Sarah as an excuse, and maybe that was true for the first six months or so, but I'd left off playing for three years. Three years, after which I kicked myself for leaving it so long. Three years of my life that I could have been playing. It's easy to say that to yourself when you're on the other side of it. It's another thing when you're blocked, another thing entirely.

Many times over the years I'd thought about what had happened to Darlene, and couldn't help thinking that it had been my fault, at least partly. No matter how many times I told myself my little ritual and the fire were coincidence, a nagging voice in the back of my mind whispered that my evil intent caused it. And now that same voice was telling me that it was my turn now. That what had happened between John and me was payback, that I deserved all the pain, and more. I had brought it all on myself.

The thing I really didn't get was this: how could you miss something so intensely that you never knew you needed before?

Twenty-Six

Lita
August 1967

THE SUN BEAT DOWN ON JAKE and I as we lay on our backs on a blanket on the sand of Regina Beach. It was midweek, so there weren't as many people around as on the weekends. Still, it was a hot day, so there was a fair crowd. We were near the grass, a little ways down from the concession.

It had taken some work to convince Jake to take a day off midweek. When I suggested we spend a day at the beach, he'd laughed, said he was too busy. He had a hotel to run, he insisted. And yes, the hotel was thriving, doing better than ever. But I kept after him and finally, he'd agreed.

He'd been working way too hard, I thought, for a very long time. Lately he'd seemed tired, distracted, irritable. I'd even been wondering for a while if I might broach the subject of retirement with him. He was a relatively young man, not yet sixty. He'd worked hard for many years, dedicated himself to the Hotel Saskatchewan, then to his own hotel. We had all we needed or wanted, the house had been paid off long ago. There was no reason for him to continue to work the way he did. What did he want to prove, I wondered? Then again, maybe I was the one who wanted a change. That was definitely part of it.

I could tell, even at breakfast, that getting away from work was already doing him good. We hit the road at about eleven, stopped at the Blue Bird Café in the town of Regina Beach for lunch, and then hit the sand. We opened our blue-and-white striped beach umbrella and lay and read, took dips in the lake and listened to our new portable transistor radio. Jake always kept it tuned to CBC, because he was fond of classical music.

By about 4:30, I was half dozing, no longer reading the book propped up in the sand. Getting away was good. I'd hardly thought of John since we'd left that morning. Well. Hardly. I had wondered a little if he and his wife ever came to the beach. I supposed they must. Everyone did. I nodded a bit as I thought about the little place in the Qu'Appelle Valley I'd always dreamed of having. Had John ever been to the Qu'Appelle Valley? It was one of the most beautiful places on earth. As far as I was concerned. The sun was too warm on my skin.

But then a piece of piano music caught my attention, woke me from my doze. I reached over and turned the radio up a little and Jake, back from the water, rejoined me on the blanket.

"What is this music?" I asked. "It's Beethoven, I know, but what's it called?"

He listened for a few seconds. "It's the *Pathetique Sonata* . . . I think this part is the *adagio*. It's beautiful, isn't it?"

"It is. Beautiful." We listened in silence. I was thankful Jake could have no idea of my associations with this piece of music. My mind stretched back to an afternoon over thirty years earlier, when Bill MacInnes had made love to me in the cool of a stand of trembling aspen, and some anonymous pianist had provided us with this background music. The day he'd asked me to marry him. I'd been to Regina Beach many times since that day, and sometimes thought vaguely of that afternoon. But the music brought it into the sharpest focus. I felt the cool of the shade on my flesh, smelled the damp earth and the trees, felt Bill nuzzle my neck. I could almost feel that damned tree root digging into the small of my back.

The piece ended. I wasn't sad, exactly, not really. It would have been easy to lie there and think of all the unrealized dreams, all the promise Bill and I had had right then, and how soon it had ended. I didn't let myself think of that. I thought of the aspens, Bill's young, hungry mouth on my young, hungry body, the cool shade, and how pleasant it could be to drag out an old memory. Especially nice because John still festered inside me, all the hurt and regret, what had happened between us.

Then out of the blue a thought came: forgiveness. I had to forgive John if I ever wanted to feel better. I still thought of him every day, first thing when I opened my eyes and last thing before I slept. I'd told myself that I'd forgiven him, but I hadn't really. I was still hurt and angry. I watched a lone seagull circle high overhead, become a black speck in the blue before it disappeared. The more I held onto the Beethoven sonata, the more it seemed there were a lot of people besides John who I thought I'd forgiven but hadn't at all, not any of them. Pop. Ma. Gus, Darlene, Bill. John. Jake.

"Jake?"

He'd fallen asleep again. I thought I'd let him snooze while I swam one last time, and then we should probably think about packing up. I swam out a long ways, thinking again of Bill and the dumb things he did, like swimming out past the buoys. But I had to forgive Bill for those dumb things. I had to forgive all those people who'd hurt me. Holding onto my hurt and anger was making it worse for me. I had to let go. And maybe some of those people were angry at me, or felt hurt by me. Maybe if you want to be forgiven, you have to forgive yourself. In pardoning we are pardoned, or something like that.

When I reached the buoys I turned around, headed back to shore. Maybe we might stay in a hotel overnight and spend another day at the beach. Jake looked more relaxed than I'd seen him in months, and I knew I was more relaxed. I'd give it a try.

I sat down on the blanket and towelled off, lit a cigarette. He was still asleep.

"Jake? Wake up, I want to talk to you."

I shook him. He didn't move. I shook him again, called his name. The water on the lake was still, the sounds of the other people on the beach became muffled. What had seemed peaceful just moments ago now seemed empty and terrifying. Everything moved in slow motion. A lifeguard came over, and after a minute he called an ambulance. I knew Jake was gone. Maybe he even died during the *Pathetique Sonata*. But I hoped it was when I was swimming and thinking about how relaxed he looked.

Turns out I never did retire in the Qu'Appelle Valley, not with Bill or with Jake. Or anyone else.

f

Part Four

Twenty-Seven

Lita
September 1982

On a warm Sunday afternoon I was out on the verandah with the National when a blonde girl with a knapsack on her back and a guitar case in one hand opened the front gate and started up the walk. As she got closer, I could see she was very pregnant.

"Elsa?"

"Yes, it's me. Surprise, Grandma."

She smiled and put her guitar down like it weighed a ton. I made her sit down and have a glass of water before I started asking questions.

"I thought your band was touring."

"We were. I mean, they still are. But for obvious reasons, it's just not working out for me anymore. I'm tired all the time. I have a bladder the size of a peanut. I've only got six more weeks to go. It's time to take a rest."

"I should say so. Does your mother know about this?"

"She does. She's none too happy about it. So I wondered if you'd mind if I stayed with you a while. I could crash with some of my friends, but . . ."

"Don't even think about it. You need some rest. You can stay with me as long as you like."

Elsa fell asleep before it was properly dark, almost before I pulled down the faded green blinds in the front room. I remember when I was heavily pregnant with Sarah in the summer of 1937, I tossed and turned and never got a decent sleep. The huge belly always got in the way. I'd lie with a pillow between my knees because of my strange new widened hips and hormone-loose joints, had to get up what seemed like every few minutes to pee. I stupidly looked forward to the good night's sleep I'd get once the baby was born. But Elsa slept like a babe, a gently snoring babe, on my old couch. I wondered if she'd be in any shape to celebrate her twentieth birthday, less than a week away. I thought about throwing a surprise party and then wondered if she was a little fed up with surprises right then.

I forget where it was she decided to drop out of the tour. I think the band was somewhere in BC, maybe Kelowna. A long way from Regina, anyway, poor girl. A first pregnancy can throw you like that, you can go along and think you're fine, think you'll be able to carry on the way you are until the last minute, then a couple of hours of pushing and voila. Somewhere along the line, you find you're not quite in control the way you thought you were. It can be more than a little unsettling. Come to think of it, though, you don't even have to be pregnant for that to happen.

I knew I would have to clear out the back bedroom for her. I'd also have to call Sarah and let her know that Elsa was here. And we'd have to make a little shopping trip, get some food appropriate for an expectant mother. But all that could wait. If there is one thing I've learned, it's what can wait and what can't. Right then, I meant to enjoy the weather and sit and play some of the old songs on my National steel guitar, my first and truest love.

An hour or so later I called Sarah.

"I hope you don't mind her staying with you, Mom," she said. "If you do, just let me know. I can't believe that girl. I would have thought she'd know better. I mean, imagine, in this day and age . . . "

"Imagine what? That young people fall in love? I have no doubt they still do that."

"Love. Yes, well I don't know how much that came into the picture. But with birth control these days, I would have thought this couldn't happen."

"If I recall correctly, you weren't much older when you were pregnant with her."

"I was twenty-four. There's a huge difference between nineteen and twenty-four. And I was married."

There was no point in pursuing the matter. I could hear the exasperation in Sarah's voice. Oh, if anyone had told me when my precious Sarah Kali was a little child that she'd turn out to be so judgmental, so rigid, I never would have believed them. But it was true. She was a throwback to Bill's dear old Mum in some ways, though she was never racist, or mean. She just had a very circumscribed way of looking at the world. It disappointed me, puzzled me. Bill's mum had died when Sarah was only four. I didn't think she'd had time to influence the girl that much. Maybe it was genes.

From a very early age, Sarah was nothing like me. Other than her looks, she wasn't much like Bill, either. Bill had been easy-going, relaxed, at least in the early days of our relationship. Sarah was conscious of what people thought even as a small child. She was very concerned with appearances. Maybe she learned that from Jake. I don't know. But where Bill and I were creative types, a bit on the wild or carefree side, Sarah wasn't interested in creative things at all. She excelled at mathematics, and became a math teacher. She married Rob, a young bank manager, at age twenty-three and Elsa came along a year later, followed by Jacob two years after that.

We didn't ever get along the way I dreamed we would when Sarah was a little smidgen cuddled in my arms. When she got older, it was apparent that she was at least puzzled by me playing guitar while other mothers ironed sheets. By the time she was a teenager it was obvious that I embarrassed her. She hated it whenever I mentioned my band, called it "that Gypsy stuff." It turned out that she wasn't an eternal reminder of Bill for me. If anything, she was a reminder of Bill's mother. Oh, joy.

Elsa and Jacob, on the other hand, I could relate to. My grandchildren were both musically inclined, and neither, I was relieved to discover, wanted to play the bagpipes. Jacob was also academically inclined and went to Queen's on an engineering scholarship. Elsa was smart, too, smart as a whip, but school just wasn't the place for her. She barely made it out of high school before her band hit the road. And now, here she was, less than a year later, on my doorstep.

Things had changed since I was Elsa's age, mostly for the better. Well, I knew I'd changed. Who knew I would become so crotchety, so opinionated? When did that happen to me? But really, things were better in many ways, especially for women and people outside the WASP mainstream. Which my dear first mother-in-law would be mortified to hear. Back in the 30s, even though I was the most talented member of the Syncopation Five, I had little say in what they did. I was a woman. A girl. It wasn't my place to make decisions about the material we played, the bookings we'd take. Now, Elsa's band, Speed Queen, really was Elsa's band. She wrote the songs, sang them, and played lead guitar. She decided what they played, where they played, and if someone in the band displeased her, she gave them their walking papers. In the 30s that kind of thing was unheard of. Good for her, I thought. I just wished it could have been like that when I was a young thing.

But in those days, racism and sexism were simply part of the fabric of everyday life. You never heard of homophobia because you never heard of homosexuals, or most people hadn't, anyway. Certainly not in Regina. I get tired of listening to my contemporaries (fortunately they are fewer each year) complain about the way the world is going, what the world is coming to. We didn't have all this divorce, child molestation, abortions in our day, blah blah blah. Well, there should have been more divorces in the old days. What's the sense of people who despise each other showing their children how to make the entire family miserable by putting each other down for thirty years, and then saying, "We stayed together for the children"? If you think child molestation and abortions haven't been going on since the dawn of our species, you truly are naïve. Every horrible thing that you can think of we've been doing to ourselves and one another all along. And does anyone need reminding that the 1930s gave the world the Holocaust? Please. Sometimes it makes my head swim.

ff

It took a few days before I got around to the topic of the baby's father. I wanted to tread carefully, didn't want to harp, didn't want to meddle. I did want to know how she felt, what kind of ground the relationship stood on. Luckily, it wasn't much of a problem. We got on so well.

"What about the baby's father?"

"Do you mean does he know? Oh, yeah, he knows. When I first told him, he suggested getting married right away. I don't know about that. His name is Mark. Mark Jelinski. He's a musician, too, a bassist. They're just playing around town right now. He doesn't know I'm here, yet. I guess I should probably call him."

It sounded like the relationship with Mark was like many human relationships: a work in progress, and not easy to define with much precision. That, I could understand.

Only I wanted to say something like, "gather ye rosebuds while ye may." Get what happiness you can out of the relationship while you can. But I didn't know what that might mean. I didn't know then if she loved Mark, whether it was one-sided, or a one-night thing or what. The way she spoke about him, it was hard to tell. She sounded cool.

Then I recalled that when I'd fallen in love with Bill, I couldn't say much about it either. Maybe because I figured if I talked about him much, people would know without a doubt that I was in love. That would leave me vulnerable, and from the day I left home I was determined not to let myself be in a position like that again. It was too dangerous. Eventually, though, Darlene figured it out. Darlene represented the epitome of all I did not want to be. She came across as a frothy, bubbly, giggly thing, and when she fell in love (which seemed to be every couple of weeks or so) she absolutely could not contain herself. She would sing horrible, sappy love songs to herself. She'd doodle elaborate hearts in the ledger at the front desk with the initials D.K.

+ whoever. If it got serious (in the second week), the hearts would contain variants of her own name, now married: Mrs. Jurgen Klatzel, Mr. and Mrs. Jurgen Klatzel, Mrs. Darlene Klatzel.

I, on the other hand, saw no reason to reveal myself just because I happened to be in love. In fact, I felt I must contain myself at all costs. And yet Darlene sussed me out within a couple of weeks. I wonder if she thought I wasn't in love with Bill as much as I should have been. Eventually Bill thought the same thing, I guess, that I didn't love him as much as Darlene did, because I didn't sing, giggle, whisper about him all the time. Sometimes I wonder, if I had it all to do again, would I be more demonstrative? And would it make a difference, would he have stayed? I don't know. I know that I have woken up thinking of the men I loved and gone to sleep thinking of them for many years after the fact. And still not a day goes by that I don't think of them. Bill. Jake. And John. The three of them.

If Elsa felt that way about Mark, I would tell her to make her feelings known, if they weren't known already.

ƒƒ

Elsa developed a real interest in her roots in those few weeks before the baby was born. At first I thought it was politeness, asking about family because she was staying with me. But she asked about all kinds of things, particularly about Bill and the band. We listened to the Syncopation Five 78 over and over.

"I can't get over how great you and Granddad sounded together."

I was confused. For a minute, I thought she'd mistaken Darlene's reedy whining for me singing. "How do you mean?"

"Well, he had a great voice, didn't he? And, you, we've always known you were the virtuoso. But the way you play around the melody he's singing, fill in during the bridges, echo him. It's so well done. It's just too bad about the whiny chick on backup vocals, eh?"

That's my girl, I thought.

"Listening to this music makes me think about your grandfather," I said. "All the regrets."

"I'm sorry, Grandma. I should have known it would make you feel bad."

"Oh, it's a long time ago, now. All I mean is I haven't thought about any of this in a long time. Some of the things I should have said to Bill. Don't have regrets in your relationship with Mark, Elsa. I mean things you can do something about. Because you just never know . . . you might not have a chance to make it right again."

"I do love him. But he's talking about quitting his band. I don't want him to feel like because I'm having a baby his whole life has to come to an end."

"Does he feel that way?"

"I don't know. I guess I should find out, eh?"

I shrugged. "I would."

"I haven't exactly been on great terms with Mom the last few years."

"Sarah's worried about you," I said.

"Yeah. She wants me to go to university, get a career, stop wasting time."

I recalled Sarah calling me one night, worried, using almost those exact words about Elsa.

"You have to let her live her life," I said.

Sarah sounded exasperated. "That's what I want her to do. I don't want her to waste it. She's got so much potential."

"Of course she does. But she's living her life right now, whether you like it or not."

"I just don't want her to make a mistake."

"We all make mistakes. Anyway, what's so bad about being a musician? She has talent, you know."

"Maybe. But she's got to eat."

"She'll be fine."

"I guess I'd just hate to see her fail."

"She can't fail unless she stops trying, Sarah."

It was easy enough for me to say. I didn't worry about Elsa at all. I knew my granddaughter had the brains and the ability to go far. But I knew Sarah would worry, no matter what anyone said.

ff

"I'm not sure I'm ready for it," Elsa said one day. "I mean, a baby's enough of a change. I think Mark's freaking out. I don't know if we can pull off the house in the suburbs and the day job and all that all at once."

"Ease into it gradually. You don't know anything yet. Take it one day at a time," I advised.

"That's a good idea. I mean, Mark's talented. Maybe he'd be okay working some 9 — 5 job for a while. But I'm sure he'll get to resent it, maybe even resent us, eventually. I don't want that to happen."

"You're right to be concerned. I guess he just wants to make sure that Bill is provided for. But what about you? You're talented, too."

"Well. I've thought about that."

"After all, look what happened to me."

"You did go a long time without playing, didn't you?"

"I did. And I don't want you to have to go through that. Maybe you two can work something out where he works part-time, and you both play a little. Or something."

"That's a good idea, Gram. Thanks. I think we should try to do something like that."

Why is it that I find it so easy to give Elsa advice, while Sarah usually leaves me at a loss? Why is that?

Twenty-Eight

Elsa
Seattle, Washington
March 2006

IF SOMEONE HAD TOLD ME YEARS ago what a cliché my life would become when I hit middle age, I never would have believed them. Not on your life. Me, discontent, wondering what it's all about, wondering just what it is that I've managed to accomplish in my forty-plus years on this planet? Never. But I'm afraid it was all true. Sad but true.

Bill was well into work on his master's degree by this time. He lived at home while he was doing his bachelor's but moved out when he started his master's. His thesis supervisor got him work as a teaching assistant, and his apartment in the U District on 10th Avenue was a short walk from campus. He was almost twenty-three, a good six years older than I was when I left home. Fair enough. Still, I wasn't prepared to miss him as much as I did, though he was home to do laundry and eat dinner with us every Sunday. I have to say the little house in Fremont did seem empty when he left.

And there Mark and I were, still running Curse Records. "Record label" was almost a misnomer by this time, since most of the recordings we were making were released on CD, although more and more bands were asking to have their music available in both CD and vinyl formats. I hated to think the vinyl thing was retro — it made me feel old — but that was part of it, audiophile preferences aside. Anyway. The house seemed so empty. Mark and I seldom seemed to be there at the same time. I took care of the web stuff for Curse at home, most of it, while he was at work, but of course orders had to be filled at the office since we had all the stock there, so one of us (mostly me) was there evenings when the other was home. We'd talked about giving up the office, trying to run everything out of the house. But our house wasn't even a thousand square feet, we never would have had room for all the stock and files and office equipment. Not only that, but it was important, I thought, for us to have one physical place that was work and one that was home. I had wanted to keep the lines between the two from blurring quite so much. The problem was that by this time Mark happily worked all day every day, either at his company or occasionally doing Curse stuff at the office.

I had started to wonder by this time what we had in common anymore. Well, besides our son, and Curse Records. Mark had bought out the courier firm from his brother-in-law, Dave, in the mid-90s. It was great because it meant an increase in our income, which meant we could afford to float our not-for-profit record label for longer. It also meant that Mark's involvement in Curse, by necessity, became pretty minimal. At first that was all right by me, because as Bill got more independent, I had more time to devote to Curse. Still, what had started as Mark's idea, and had become something we worked on together, had now grown into something I was essentially doing on my own. We seemed to be living in two different worlds much of the time.

One night I was working late at the office. The vintage store downstairs was closed and there wasn't anyone else in any of the other offices. The main building door downstairs was locked. I heard footsteps in the hall and panicked for a second. Then the door opened. I didn't recognize him for a second. And it hit me all of a sudden that Mark looked older. His features were softer now, his hair had receded, he'd let his ear piercings grow closed long ago. And I was still getting used to the beard.

"What are you doing?".

"Just got a few orders I want to ship out tonight," I said.

He sat on the desk. "You need a hand?"

"Nah. Thanks. I'm almost done."

"Do you want to get something to eat, maybe a drink, when you're done?"

I blinked, resisted the urge to ask him who he was and what he'd done with my husband. "Yeah, sure. Where do you want to go?"

"I don't know. I kinda feel like seafood. Do you want to walk over to the Dock?"

"Sounds like fun. As long as you help me carry these packages to the post office at the 7-Eleven before we go."

We sat at our usual table in the Fremont Dock, beside a window, looking out at the water. How many times had we been to the Dock? Thousands, maybe. It was an unassuming pub / sports bar / family restaurant. Good prices, good pub grub, near home, and they were always willing to play our records. We came when Bill was just a baby, brought him here all through his life. This was where he wanted to eat on his thirteenth birthday, I remembered, and the amount he ate that night frightened me. "Shapes of Things to Come," as The Yardbirds said.

Mark ordered halibut and chips and I ordered mussels and we sipped pints of Diamond Knot IPA while we waited for our food. This was so unusual nowadays, this going out together thing, that I wondered if something was up, if he had an agenda. To the extent that I felt a little nervous. But as the evening wore on it became obvious that he just wanted to have dinner and a beer with me. More likely he just wanted to have dinner and a beer, and figured he might as well take me along for company. Maybe there wasn't anything much to eat at home. That was entirely possible.

The waitress came by when we'd finished eating and took our plates and we ordered another beer. What the hell? It was Friday night, and we were out — past 9:30, even. Living dangerously.

"I've been wanting to talk to you about this idea I've had for a while, Mark."

"Yeah?"

"Yeah. What would you think if I hired someone to come in and help out in the office part-time?"

He stroked his beard a minute. He was thinking over what it would cost. He didn't say anything, so I continued.

"That way, you won't have to do much anymore. Unless you want to, of course. And it would free up some of my time so that I can get back to what I really want to be doing."

He gave me a blank look. "What do you want to be doing?"

He couldn't really have to ask, I told myself. Could he? No, impossible. I wouldn't have married a man who could be so uninterested in who I was. And yet, lately, this was the kind of man he increasingly seemed to be. It frustrated me. And no matter how I tried not to, it was impossible not to take his lack of interest in me personally. I tried to convince myself I was blowing it out of proportion in my mind, that he was just too busy. But at times I could only conclude that he'd lost interest in me. How could you live with someone for twenty-five years and not know what they wanted to be doing?

"You're not serious, are you?" I asked.

His jaw set a little before he spoke. I heard an edge of exasperation in his voice. "I am serious. What do you want to be doing?"

"Music. Mark, how could you not know I want to have time to play music?"

"Well, you do play music."

"Sure, for a few minutes here and there if I have the time. I mean I want to get back to being in a band, maybe even record again."

"Still? Really?"

"Yeah. I mean, that's what I've always wanted, from when I was a kid. And Curse has been good, you know. But it kind of mushroomed into taking up all my time, especially once Bill got into school. And now I want to do my own music again. Don't you ever want to?"

He shook his head. "No. I can't imagine going back into that world. The late nights, the long hours. Never making any money. It was great when we were young, but I just have no interest in it anymore."

I sighed. "Look, I don't mean going on a world tour or putting out a series of concept albums. I just mean finding some people to jam with, maybe record a few songs. I need to do this, Mark."

"Well, sure. I guess you're about due for a mid-life crisis."

Lucky for Mark I was enjoying my IPA far too much to consider pitching it right into his face. Had it been a lesser beer, I would have done so without hesitation.

"Mid-life crisis? What are you talking about? Because I want to get back to playing music I'm having a mid-life crisis?"

"I haven't heard you say anything about wanting to play music. Until now."

"You haven't heard me say anything about anything recently. We never see each other. And when we do, one of us is either on the way out the door or already asleep. I thought hiring someone might help with that, too."

"All right. Don't get excited about it. I think we can go ahead and hire someone."

Hang on tight to that beer, Elsa. "I'm not excited about anything. I just don't appreciate your attitude sometimes."

"I'm sorry. I didn't mean anything."

I looked him in the eye. *Sure, you didn't.* "All right, then. So I was thinking maybe we'd look at hiring someone for fifteen or twenty hours a week to start with, see how it goes."

"Sure. Are you going to advertise?"

"Not right away. I know a couple of people who might be interested. I'll ask around."

ff

Kirk Davis played crazy kamikaze high-speed guitar, a bit like Yngwie Malmsteen but rougher, not so frilly, in a band called Monkey's Uncle that we'd recorded a single with a few years earlier. The record didn't go anywhere, nor did the band, and they broke up. The old story, you know. But Kirk hung around the scene, I saw him at shows. Not that

I went out to shows recreationally much by this time. Even though I no longer had a child at home to think about, I found the late nights just took too much out of me, and the people coming out seemed younger and younger all the time. But I would usually go and sell records if one of our acts was playing in town. I'd show up and check things out, set up at a table near the doors, hang around for a while. If things were going too late or if I was getting bored I'd pass on the sales to a trustworthy band member, or simply pack up and go home. The Saturday night after Mark and I went to the Dock for dinner I was packing up during the set break of a Knuckledragger show at the University when Kirk appeared.

"Elsa! How are you?" He was a lean, loose-limbed guy with waves of dark blond hair framing his face. His faded black Howlin' Wolf T-shirt had a couple of small holes in it. Holy shirt.

"Hey, Kirk. I'm good. How are you?"

"Good. Hey, you're not going already, are you?"

"Well, yes. I am." I couldn't help smiling. "These late night shows are too much for an old lady like me."

"Old lady nothing. Why is it that every time I see you somewhere, you're just leaving?

"Am I?"

"You are. I'm starting to think it's something personal."

"I just can't handle late nights anymore."

"You like Howlin' Wolf?" he asked with a grin. I realized my eyes had wandered again to the holes in his shirt.

"Of course. Nice shirt." I cleared my throat. "Listen, how'd you like to do me a favour?"

"Anytime."

"Would you be interested in selling some of The Knuckledraggers' CDs for me?"

"You trust me, do you?"

"Sure. And I've only got about ten left, so it's not like I stand to lose that much money if I turn out to be wrong."

"No worries. For you, anything."

"That's perfect. So they're fifteen bucks each. If you could drop by the office with any money you get and any CDs you don't sell, I'd be eternally grateful."

"Grateful enough to buy me lunch?"

"Of course."

"It's a deal, then."

"Thanks, Kirk. I really appreciate it. We'll see you soon."

As I drove back to Fremont, I wondered if I'd see any money, or the CDs. But I'd always liked Kirk. He was easy to talk to, funny. Quite nice looking. Nice looking enough that my judgment was a little clouded, I wondered? Maybe. Yes, maybe.

So I was completely pleased when he showed up at the Curse office at noon that Monday. He walked in without a word, smiling, reached into the inside pocket of his brown corduroy coat and put a wad of money down in front of me.

"Good morning," I said. "Oh my God. Did you sell them all?"

"Good afternoon. I sold them all. And there's your $150."

"Wow. Thank you so much. You're a salesman. I have to say, I wasn't expecting to see you so soon."

"No?"

"In fact, I wasn't sure that I'd see you again at all."

He pouted. "I'm hurt."

"Well, I apologize. I misjudged you."

"I accept your apology. So what about that lunch?"

"Today?"

"Sure. Why not?"

Why not, indeed? We did not go to the Fremont Dock for lunch. Instead we went to Costas Opa and had Greek. I'd been there lots of times before, although never with Mark. When it came to food, Mark was not adventurous at all. The older we got, the less adventurous he seemed to become. Kirk and I ordered calamari, horatiki and a half carafe of retsina. Well, we started with a half carafe, that is. When I came back from the washroom at one point, the empty half carafe was gone and there was another in its place.

"I hope you don't mind," he said. "We were just having such a cool time talking and all . . ."

I smiled and wondered whether he would have ordered another if he'd been the one buying lunch. "That's all right. You're right, it'd be a shame to break up the nice chat we've been having. And besides, the boss said I could I have the afternoon off."

"Did she?"

"She did."

"Well, isn't that interesting?"

We seemed to be able to talk so easily. Of course, we had band stories to swap, we could talk music. I could have talked anything with him, it wouldn't have mattered. He really was handsomer than I had noticed, in a scruffy way. I've always liked the scruffy ones. His leg kept brushing mine under the table, then he rested his knee up against my thigh. Wow. Long time since that kind of thing had happened, no kidding. After lunch we stumbled out of the restaurant. Well, maybe he didn't, but I did. It didn't take much for me anymore.

"Holy shit, it's bright out here," he said, squinting as he checked his pockets. "And I left my sunglasses at home."

"You musicians ought to get out in the daylight a little more. The Vitamin D would do you wonders."

"Seriously, I need my sunglasses. Do you want to come up to my apartment with me while I get them?"

I couldn't help laughing. "That's the best you can come up with?"

"What?"

"You can't think of a better line than that?"

"Okay, how about this: Hey, Elsa. You want to come up to my apartment and have some fun?"

Fun. That sounded like . . . fun. I took a deep breath and let it out again. "Oh, boy. It's tempting."

"What's stopping you?"

"Bunch of stuff. It's kinda complicated. Can we go for a coffee instead?"

He put his arm around me and gave me a little squeeze. "Sure."

ff

So Tuesday I called him first thing after I got into the office. He didn't answer, so I left a message for him to call me.

I picked up the phone on the second ring. "Good morning, Curse Records."

"Hey, Elsa. It's Kirk." His voice sounded a little husky.

"Oh, you weren't sleeping, were you?"

"Well, I was when you called. I let it ring through, 'cause I'm not much of a conversationalist first thing."

"Sorry."

"That's okay. I had kind of a late night after a long lunch yesterday. So, uh, did you change your mind?"

"Change my mind? I — no. Well, this isn't about that."

He laughed. His laugh was deep and rich and round and I could feel it through the phone, almost. "Isn't about what?"

"Listen, you. This is about business. How'd you like a job?"

"A job? Doing what?"

"I need someone to help me out in the office here."

"Really? That sounds interesting."

"Do you want to come in and talk about it?"

"Sure. Over lunch?"

Musicians. "Tell you what. You come in the office and we'll get this sorted out and then maybe we'll see."

"How about this? I'll have a shower and see you in about an hour. We'll talk and then I'll take you out for lunch this time."

"You're on."

ff

Kirk's apartment was nicer than I expected it to be, not the stereotypically messy bachelor pad I was picturing. And had been picturing all through lunch. The guitars were all on stands. The concert posters were mostly framed. Empties and pizza boxes did not litter the floor. I even saw a few plants — houseplants, that is.

He was eager to work for Curse. And we figured we'd see how fifteen hours a week would go at first — three afternoons. After all, we wouldn't want him to have to get up too early. After we got that worked out, we went for Italian food, had a little red wine — only a single half carafe this time.

And then we ended up at his place. That's not to say that I didn't have misgivings, didn't feel guilty. I did. And yet, I had developed a huge crush on Kirk. Sure, he was attractive, and funny, and sweet, all of that was great. But the thing was, we could talk, really talk. And he was actually interested in me. There was a part of me that was not going to let an opportunity like this go by. Absolutely not. Life is too short. Besides, my body was telling me it was way too late to change my mind now. Way too late.

Twenty-Nine

Elsa
Seattle, Washington
October 2006

I liked the recording technician we used for sessions at Ballard Studios. He was really good. Good ear, good instincts. His name was John Lair, an older guy. He made me think a little of George Martin, the Beatles' longtime producer: tall, soft-spoken. Must have been quite handsome when he was younger. Then it turned out he was from Regina, too. He and I were listening one night to takes of a jazz group we were doing an EP for and he mentioned that the guitarist was using a National steel guitar.

"I thought so," I said. "Sounds just like my grandmother's guitar."

He gave me a sidelong glance. "Your grandmother's guitar?"

"Yeah. She has a beautiful National steel guitar. Resonator type, late 20s model, I think. I learned how to play on it when I was just a small fry."

He had an odd look on his face, like I'd just said something really weird.

I couldn't help laughing. "What's the matter? You look like kind of shocked. Is it so odd that my grandmother taught me to play?"

"No. It's not that at all. I just used to know someone — a woman in Regina who played a National guitar."

"Yeah?"

He blinked. "Your grandmother's name wasn't Lita, was it?"

"Yeah! Still is. Lita Koudelka. Lita Stone."

He stroked his jaw. "Played in a jazz group in the 30s, right?"

"The Syncopation Five. Oh, my God. How do you know her? You're not that old."

"I met her when I was working at Regina Public Library in the 60s. She was looking after the daughter of someone she was in a group with. A Gypsy group, I think."

"Oh, that's crazy. Ochi Chornya."

"That's right. She brought her guitar in for story hour a few times. She was good. Really good."

"And did you know she won that guitar in a poker game?"

"I know. She told me all about it one day."

"No kidding. That's so insane that you knew her."

"It is. So how's she keeping these days?"

"She's all right. In pretty good health as far as I know. My grandfather passed away quite a long time ago, also in the 60s, and she never remarried."

"Is that right? Does she still play?"

"She does. She's been at it a lot the last few years."

"That's excellent."

He was quiet for a long while after that. John was that way — either talk, talk, talk or very quiet.

It's so weird. What a small world it is.

Later that night, at home, I couldn't stop thinking about Grandma Lita and how I missed her. She and I could talk in a way that Mom and I never could. A personality thing, partly, I suppose — we're a lot alike. I wished I could talk to her then, about all the stuff going on. Kirk and Mark mostly. And I knew that if I picked up the phone right then and started telling her, she would listen. She would let me cry on her shoulder. But I didn't know that even Lita would get this thing between me and Kirk. She was an extremely cool person, especially for her generation. She was also good, in a way that I never have been. I mean, she was married to Grandpa Bill and after he died she married Grandpa Jake, and she was married to him for close to thirty years. She never remarried after that. Mom would just call me trashy if I told her about Kirk. I know that. Lita, I think I could go there with her, maybe. But I wasn't sure. And I was kind of ashamed. Although I was pretty sure she'd be cool with it, I hated to think of her thinking less of me. I just couldn't take that chance.

ff

Things got serious between me and Kirk pretty quickly and went on underground. I felt awful about Mark. But I couldn't help but think this wouldn't have happened if our relationship hadn't deteriorated quite as much as it had. Kirk and I spent a lot of time together — of course, being co-workers was part of it, but we were together a lot of time outside work, too. Mark didn't really seem to notice or care. He worked long hours, and at night seemed only to want to sit in front of the TV watching sports, which just added fuel to the fire as far as my feelings for Kirk went. Finally, one night after about six months I decided to tell him what was going on. He was watching football. I sat down on the arm of the couch beside him. He didn't look at me, didn't say anything.

"Mark. We need to talk."

As soon as I said that, I realized I should have worded it differently. Those words are guaranteed to get people's backs up. He sighed, looked at me. "What's up?"

"Can we talk with the TV off? This is kind of important."

He switched the TV off, waited for me to begin.

I cleared my throat. " I'm thinking about moving out."

"Moving out? Why?"

"A lot of reasons. I know it seems sudden, but I've been thinking about it for a long time. For one thing, it seems like things just aren't working between us. We don't talk anymore, not really. You don't seem interested in me. And sex. Well, you know that hasn't been happening for a long time."

"There's someone else."

"Well. Yes. There is."

"It's Kirk, isn't it?"

"Yes."

"I knew it. I knew it as soon as you hired him. The way you talk about him, how good he is at his job, the funny things he says."

"Well, he talks to me. At least he's interested in what I have to say."

Mark was hunched on the edge of the couch now, took a long swill of his beer. Red crept into his face. I hadn't seen him this animated in months. "So that's what you're up to all the time. You're out with him."

"Yes, I am. I love him."

For just a second, I was afraid of him, and I never had been before. The muscles in his cheeks rippled, his nostrils flared, and I thought he might hit me. Then he seemed to calm down a little, sat back into the couch.

"Mark, it's not that I love him and don't love you. You know I love you and I always will. But our love has changed. Our lives have changed. I feel like you don't care about me anymore, like you're not interested in me anymore."

"That's not true, Elsa. I've never stopped loving you."

"But then why do you ignore me so much of the time? Why do you fall asleep in front of the TV night after night instead of talking to me?"

"I work all day, dammit. I'm tired. And then you want to sit here and talk. I just want to relax. I watch TV so I can relax."

"You never used to be like that. Back in the band days you loved to talk, loved to go out. You had so much energy, so many ideas. When you had the idea for Curse, it was like nothing could ever stop you."

"Yeah. Well, that was like twenty years ago. Life changes. I'm not the same person I was twenty years ago. Are you?"

"No. Of course not. But I still love music and I'm not prepared to spend the rest of my days watching TV. When Bill moved out, I hoped maybe we would recapture the old life a little bit. We have the freedom again. But you just don't seem interested."

He went to the kitchen and got another beer. He cracked it open and took a long draw on it before he answered. "So I figure I deserve some rest after working all day. And because of that, you have an affair."

"Mark. Please listen — "

"No, Elsa. You listen. I think you've made up your mind. You're moving in with him?"

"Well, I wanted to talk it over with you before I decided for sure."

"As far as I'm concerned, you're free to go. Anytime."

"That's it? After all these years, that's all you have to say?"

"Maybe you should of thought of that before you started fucking Kirk. Maybe you should have mentioned it earlier. You are my wife, after all these years. "

Before I could say anything else, he continued. "I think you should go now. I don't want you here anymore."

"Mark, I was really hoping we could have a reasonable discussion about this."

"Not tonight. Go stay with him. I'll call you in a few days."

I went upstairs and called Kirk to tell him I was coming. I cried silently as I folded clothes and supplies into a backpack. I couldn't really blame Mark. I probably would have done the same thing if it'd been me. But I couldn't help the way I felt about Kirk, the way I felt about our marriage. And somehow I hadn't thought this part of it would hurt so much.

I went to the bathroom, blew my nose and cleaned up a little. Then I got my purse and my backpack and went back to the living room.

"Mark. I'm going now. But I'll talk to you soon, okay."

He wouldn't even turn from the TV. "Goodbye."

I closed the front door behind me, got into my car, and started for Kirk's. While I couldn't actually say that at that moment I felt much better, it wasn't long before I did. I had put something really hard behind me. It was done.

Thirty

Lita
Regina, Saskatchewan
June 2008

SOME DAYS I LOOK IN THE mirror and can only shake my head. I can't be ninety years old, I tell myself. Of course, I did the same thing when I was forty, more than half a lifetime earlier. I thought I was old then. And when I was half again as old as that, a girl of twenty, I was a widow. Amazing. So that means I'm now more than four times as old as I was when Bill died seventy years ago. It doesn't seem possible.

I live in one of these assisted living residences. I have my own apartment, and can choose whether I want to do my own cooking or have them do it for me (they do it for me). I have regular visitors: Sarah, of course. Sofia from Ochi Chornya (Bela and Vlatko are gone now, and Sergei is in and out of hospital). Charlie is a doctor now, lives somewhere in Ontario. Jake's sister's girl, Miriam, comes to see me every once in a while. I've been here almost three years now. I like it. But I didn't always like it.

I slipped on some ice outside my house one day when I was clearing the walk, and broke my hip. Sarah gave me hell for it. I didn't blame her. It was stupid of me to clear the walks at eighty-seven, I knew that. But there wasn't much snow, it wasn't that cold out. Jason, the neighbour boy who usually did it for me, was sick with the flu that day. Anyway, I spent some time in the hospital, got a hip replacement. It should have been easier for me to get around after that. But it wasn't. Maybe it's all in my mind, maybe I'm just afraid I'll fall again. For whatever reason, walking has been painful since then.

Sarah never said in so many words that I should think about moving into one of these places, I'll give her that. She didn't want to tell me what to do. But she did worry. She phoned once a day, without fail, to check up on me, and bought groceries for me. She or Jason looked after the yard. Except for the perennials out front, that was the end of my gardening days. I started to feel guilty, useless, and decided to make inquiries about these residences.

Then there was the whole process of selling the house and paring its contents down to an amount I could keep in a one-bedroom apartment. I'd never been a great collector of things, but over the course of a lifetime as long as mine it's difficult not to build up a sizeable collection of junk. Nothing like the tiny amount of personal effects Bill MacInnes left after his twenty-three years on the planet. Sarah was a huge help with all of that. And most of the stuff that was actually worth keeping, furniture and so on, I gave her. Only on the condition, I insisted, that she really wanted it, that she wasn't just keeping it out of a sense of obligation. But then, Sarah's always been fond of antiques, so for the most part she was very happy to take the stuff off my hands.

Moving from my house to the assisted living complex was strange. It sounds so cold, so clinical, doesn't it — assisted living complex? But calling it an apartment doesn't really describe it. The strangest part at first was how much it reminded me of living in the little house on Dewdney Avenue — I don't know why, exactly. Something about the way the light came in the front window, that was part of it. And the fact that it was mine alone. I always thought of the house I shared with Jacob as his house. The house on Dewdney Avenue wasn't mine alone, but I did spend a lot of time there alone. And those days, even though I was there less than five years, were eventful.

After I moved in here I had a long string of dreams with Bill in them, as real and as close as if he stood next to me. Often, when I thought of him during waking hours, I'd get a two-dimensional, generalized image of him: tall, sandy hair, grey eyes — but no real detail. I'd have to get out a picture to remember details (the exact shape of his ears, the tiny scar on his chin from a barroom fight). But in my dreams the detail was all there, from the morning light glowing on his hair, to the warm scent at the nape of his neck, and the lay of faint freckles on his shoulders. Why should this be so, I wondered? Even more interesting, the Bill of my dreams, who'd existed almost four times longer than the real Bill, was a maddening figure. Sometimes he'd be nice, charming, and I'd wake up missing him dearly. But more often he'd flit in and out of the background, and almost as soon as I realized it was him, he'd be gone. Or he'd cuddle up to me and then dash off to talk to someone else. Often he'd ignore me. Sometimes I didn't even realize I'd had one of these dreams, but I'd be walking around all morning with this vague feeling of frustration, of anger. Then some slant of light or a word in the newspaper would remind me, and the whole dream would rush back.

Was all this my brain telling me that Bill was a jerk? It's not as if I didn't know that. I have been painfully aware of it since that day in 1935 when I figured out I was in love with him. What seemed more likely was that part of my brain could recreate him — maybe that tiny little part of me *was* him, and when I slept it got a chance to express itself. A strange idea, perhaps, but then a tiny part of Bill did once implant itself in my body, the result being Sarah. Anyway, those dreams have subsided now.

So I found myself living in an apartment. I'd never lived in one before. The closest thing would have been the Belleville. For the first while, I found it depressing being stuck with all these old people, sleeping in a little apartment, nothing like the beautiful house Jacob and I shared on Connaught Crescent, incapable of taking care of myself, locked away and waiting to die. Until I started to relax a little, make a few friends.

One of my best new friends was Roger Schmidt, a big man, gruff on the outside, on the inside not so much. He remembered me from the 30s, incredibly enough.

"Lita Stone. Why does your name ring a bell, tell me? Were you ever on TV?"

"No. Well, not really. I was a studio musician for CKCK years ago, but I was never actually on TV."

"No, no. Couldn't know you from there. Were you a singer?"

Still always that same stupid assumption. "No. I played guitar. Still do, actually."

"Lita, plays guitar . . . " He squinted with the effort of reaching back in his mind. "Your maiden name wasn't MacIntosh?"

I laughed. "No, my maiden name wasn't anything like that. But my first married name was Lita MacInnes."

"MacInnes! Lita MacInnes. You're the little gal who used to play guitar in that jazz group."

"The Syncopation Five."

"Right! Of course. My brother and I used to come out to see you weekends when you played the Hotel Saskatchewan."

"That was about the best gig we ever had."

"Really? I always wondered what happened to you. Figured you must have gone off to Toronto, or New York."

"Ha."

Eventually I told him the whole story, and we've been pals ever since. Roger introduced me to all of his friends and, of course, he had to tell them all about the band. Though I was a little embarrassed at first, it was a good ice-breaker. I started to feel more comfortable here, and wasn't shy to sit in the lounge or outside and play. Soon I was playing a lot, and my energy levels were way up. I can always tell what my energy levels are like by how much I play.

Life's been good. I didn't used to think that. I've had some dark times, no question. But then, who hasn't? A lot of people living in the complex don't feel good, don't have the luxury of enjoying their lives so much. But most days I feel pretty good, pretty content. Roger, too, he's okay most of the time. He has his days, so do I. Everyone does. But I've come to accept that, and life mostly isn't so bad. The socialization part is important, I know. Otherwise I'd go for days without talking to anybody at all. Maybe I would have become one of these little old ladies you read about in the paper, the ones who have a million cats and the city has to come in with a bulldozer every so often and clean up. I know how easy it is to be caught in the sinkhole of your own mind, your own isolation.

ff

For many years I thought things like, "You're only as old as you think you are. You're only as old as you feel." I used to think that if people my age seemed old, it was because they let themselves be inactive, useless, and were waiting to die. But I figured I wasn't old. I kept myself busy. I had important things to do. I still think there is truth in these ideas, but now I *am* old, no two ways about it. And I accept it. My jet-black hair has been snow white for many years. Arthritis has slowed my fingers down, so I can't play the lightning fast stuff the way I did in the 30s. Of course, there's a lot of things I can't do the way I used to in the 30s.

But I can still play. I don't have stage fright at all anymore. I play "Ochi Chornya" and Django's "Ultrafox" still, just not at breakneck speed. And I play the old Syncopation Five stuff, too. It doesn't hurt anymore. Well, just the fingers a bit. I even play "What'll I Do?" The ladies still love that one. Sometimes when it's warm I sit outside and play in the sun and think how lucky I am. It makes me happy to think of my family, Sarah, and Elsa and Jacob and young Bill. I think of Jake. I think of Steve. I think of my Bill, of course, and I think of John Lair. In my mind, he's still young and handsome. I suppose he's not so young anymore, either. And I think of myself, able to sit in the sunshine and play my National steel guitar. There was a time I thought seriously about giving the National to Elsa. After all, she's a damn good guitarist, too. I know she'd love it and take care of it the way I did. But then I thought — hell, no. She can wait until I'm done with it. She can wait till after I'm gone.

Something I never expected to happen after I moved in here was writing songs. Even after I started playing again, back in the mid-seventies, I didn't have the urge to write anything. And now this song has come. It is so strange.

I dreamt I was back at the public library, sitting on a chair across from John. I was showing him how to play something. I clearly saw my fingers slide up and down the fretboard, just two fingers, like Django. And the guitar made a noise I've never heard any guitar make before — like a scream. When I woke up, I got my guitar out, and did what I saw myself doing in the dream, and it worked. I couldn't believe it. And before long it became a new song, "Coyote Rag."

Many times I've wondered why John came into my life, what was the purpose of all that pain? Maybe this was it, this song. Maybe he's my muse, now. That's what I tell myself, anyway. I have to think there was a reason for all that. Otherwise, it's just too sad.

ff

It's a warm summer afternoon, and I sit in the courtyard playing around a new song. Roger is calling for me.

"Come into the dining room, Lita. There's something on the TV I think you'll like."

He knows I rarely watch TV.

"What is it?"

"It's a short with The Harmonicats. They're doing 'Smoke, Smoke, Smoke That Cigarette.'"

I sigh, put my guitar into its case and start into the dining room with him. I'll go and see, even though I never could stand The Harmonicats, because Roger is a good friend. I even trust him enough to let him carry my guitar. He holds the door to the dining room open for me.

A big crowd is gathered around a table. I turn back to see Roger's grin. I should have known something was up. The dining hall is all decorated. A big banner wishes me a happy ninetieth birthday. That feels funny, ninety, like a coat that doesn't fit. But I'm sure I'll grow into it soon, won't even notice it after a while. Amazing the things you can get used to if you hang around long enough. I feel a hand on my shoulder, think it must be Alice from the suite next door, but when I turn around to look, it's Elsa. Still blonde, still beautiful. I'm so happy I almost cry.

"Surprise, Grandma! Happy birthday!"

Sarah emerges, hugs me, too. "Happy birthday, Mom!"

I want to talk to my daughter, and to my granddaughter, here all the way from Seattle, but of course, all my friends and neighbours are singing "Happy Birthday." They bring in a big cake on a wheeled cart, and presents. And I tell myself to relax, enjoy the party. Sarah and Elsa aren't going anywhere, I hope.

After an hour, I plead tiredness and the party breaks up. I get my daughter to carry my guitar, and my granddaughter to bring the pitcher of iced tea from the table, and we sit out in the courtyard on this gorgeous afternoon.

"Elsa. It's so good to see you."

"It's good to see you, too, Grandma. It's been too long."

"It has. But that's all right. You're here now. I haven't seen you since the divorce. So how are you doing with all that?"

"For now, it's good. It really hurt. Things didn't work out after all with Kirk and me, but you know what? I've never lived by myself before and I really like the freedom. I do get lonely sometimes. But freedom is so good."

"I'm glad. Good for you, Elsa. Sarah tells me you sold Curse Records."

"Yes. And not only did we sell it, we sold it to a massive corporate interest. A faceless, soulless, media giant. But they came around with an offer, more money than I ever imagined Curse could possibly be worth. We did have to think about it for a while, but they said the Curse Records name would live on."

"That's excellent," I say.

"Yeah. They said we were a brand in Northwest rock, and they didn't want to lose that 'indie cachet.' I thought that was pretty silly, too. But, Indie Cachet — awesome band name. And the money's given me the freedom to get back to my own music, finally."

I pick up my guitar, start strumming mindlessly. "Elsa. That's us. We need to be playing."

"I know. In the end it's the only real thing."

"It's not profound, but it's true."

"It absolutely is. And now I have enough money to make my own music for the first time in a long time. And you know what? I'm good with that."

"That's wonderful," I say. I strum a little more, and look over at Sarah. Oh my God, does she look like Bill just now. But you know what? She's smiling. Smiling in the midst of all this music talk, which used to drive her crazy. That's lovely to see.

"Oh, Grandma. Holy! What are you playing?"

"It's a song I wrote a few months ago."

"What's it called?"

"Coyote Rag."

"It's incredible!"

"Thank you. You're a sweet granddaughter."

"I'm not kidding. It's fantastic. How'd you like to record it?"

I laugh. "You are kidding."

"I am not. How'd you like to come to Seattle and do a record with my new band?"

"I haven't recorded any of my own stuff since the 30s. And you know how that turned out."

"I promise you this will be a better experience. I have a surprise for you. This amazing recording technician from Regina."

"From Regina?"

"His name is John Lair."

I stop playing. *John.* I can't think what to say at all. My face feels hot.

"Grandma. Really, I'm serious. We want to get some jazz guitar going, and you're still the best. Come and stay with me for a while. Give me some guitar lessons."

I look up. Sarah's expression is still surprisingly benign, though it may be that she's just not listening. That's entirely possible.

"Elsa, you know, I just might do it. Well, me and the National."

Descended from a long line of music lovers, Lori Hahnel is the author of two previous fiction titles: *Nothing Sacred* (Thistledown, 2009), which was shortlisted for the Alberta Literary Award for fiction, and *Love Minus Zero* (Oberon, 2008). Her writing has been published across North America and in the UK including CBC Radio, *The Fiddlehead*, *Prairie Fire*, and *Room*.

During the early days of Calgary's punk scene, Hahnel was a founding member of The Virgins, a power-pop punk group that carved its place in Calgary rock history as the city's first all-female band. Hahnel lives in Calgary where she teaches creative writing.